Praise for *A Stra*

"Buckell's writing always satisf   *'el*
brings it: tense, explosive oh-my-god-what-will-they-do-now
action; appealing characters you *care* about, even when you de-
plore what they do; rich, surprising worldbuilding; a fascinating
story of words and the people who guard them."
—Nalo Hopkinson, author of *Falling in Love with Hominids*

"With *A Stranger in the Citadel*, Tobias Buckell writes to the
moment we live in, with a clarity and urgency that only fable
can provide. Read it."
—John Scalzi, author of *The Kaiju Preservation Society*

★ "Buckell's latest (after *The Tangled Lands*, 2018, with Paolo
Bacigalupi) begins by deceiving readers, presenting a postapocalyptic setting as fantasy, gradually dropping clues to the reader
relating to our current world. Protagonist and narrator Lilith,
the youngest musketress of Ninetha, privileged with guardian-
ship of the mystical Cornucopia which provides for all of the
city's needs, is equally unaware of her world's history, largely
because books and reading were banned in exchange for the
Cornucopias. When a librarian, Ishmael, stumbles into Ninetha
as the first visitor in a generation, Lilith's actions to defend him
ripple into the destruction of her home and family by her own
mentor, Kira, who was offended by the family's heresy of secretly
owning a single book and hoarding the provisions from the Cornucopia. When Lilith flees Ninetha with Ishmael, she discovers
how sheltered her worldview was as he shares tales of his travels
and his love of learning. Inspired by *Fahrenheit 451*, Buckell
masterfully crafts this coming-of-age story for a strong, com-
passionate heroine who needed a bit of reality thrust upon her."
—*Booklist*, starred review

"Tobias Buckell packs a trilogy's worth of action and invention into this riotously paced novel, which builds to a moving conclusion. It's an exciting and surprising book, a thriller which also happens to be a thoughtful meditation on power, knowledge and loyalty."
—Alastair Reynolds, author of the *Revelation Space* series

"VERDICT: In World Fantasy Award winner Buckell's (*The Trove*) latest, Lilith undergoes a journey from innocence to terrible experience. Recommended for readers who enjoy stories that reveal in layers and any who liked the postapocalyptic, flawed reconstruction of knowledge in *The Starless Crown* by James Rollins."
—*Library Journal*

"*A Stranger in the Citadel* is a powerful story that explores the strength of the written word and those who fear it. Tobias Buckell has crafted a disturbing and page-turning tale of banned books, outlaw librarians, killer angels, and world-changing secrets—set in a far-flung dystopian future that chillingly resonates with our present."
—P. Djèlí Clark, author of *Ring Shout*

"The message about the importance of literacy could not be more timely, and Buckell's sure-handed plotting keep the pages flying. Readers will be hooked."
—*Publishers Weekly*

"*A Stranger in the Citadel* is a smartly written book, full of deep, layered worldbuilding and complex relationships, all built around a thoughtful exploration of the power of story."
—Jim C. Hines, author of *Libriomancer*

Praise for *Hurricane Fever*

★ "Buckell has written a smart and well-constructed tale that's filled with excitement and the flavor of the Caribbean isles."
—*Kirkus*, starred review

"The scenes of sailing and spying action move quickly, and the climax, set on a supersized satellite-launching cannon, is one white cat shy of a Bond movie."
—*Publishers Weekly*

"*Hurricane Fever* pays homage to (and puts interesting twists on) the classic spy novels of Ian Fleming, Robert Ludlum, and John le Carré."
—*Fantasy Literature*

Praise for the Xenowealth novels

"Violent, poetic and compulsively readable."
—*Maclean's*

"Fulfills all the expectations of an ambitious space epic, but also works as a clever allegory about resistance to oppression."
—*Caribbean Beat Magazine*

"A writer to shelve there with C. J. Cherryh, Alastair Reynolds, Dan Simmons and those few other writers who have managed to adopt the advantages of mainstream literature without giving up the skilled storytelling and sense of wonder of old-style SF."
—*Critical Mass*

Also by Tobias S. Buckell

The Xenowealth Books
Crystal Rain (2006)
Ragamuffin (2007)
Sly Mongoose (2008)
The Apocalypse Ocean (2012)

Novels
Arctic Rising (2012)
Hurricane Fever (2014)
The Trove (2017)
The Tangled Lands (with Paolo Bacigalupi, 2018)

Halo
Halo: The Cold Protocol (2008)
Halo: Envoy (2017)

A STRANGER IN THE CITADEL
TOBIAS S. BUCKELL

Interior and cover design by Elizabeth Story
Author photo copyright © Scott Edelman

Tachyon Publications LLC
1459 18th Street #139
San Francisco, CA 94107
415.285.5615
www.tachyonpublications.com
tachyon@tachyonpublications.com

Series editor: Jacob Weisman
Editor: Jaymee Goh

Print ISBN: 978-1-61696-398-9
Digital ISBN: 978-1-61696-399-6

Printed in the United States by Versa Press, Inc.

First Edition: 2023
9 8 7 6 5 4 3 2 1

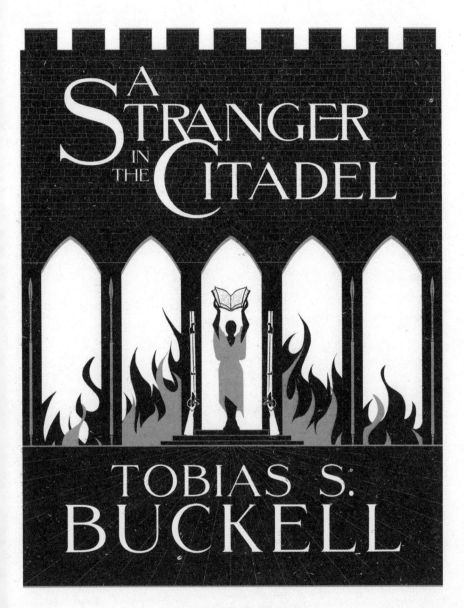

A STRANGER IN THE CITADEL

TOBIAS S. BUCKELL

TACHYON
SAN FRANCISCO

ONE

THE
CITADEL

The gods say, "You shall not suffer a librarian to live."

I knew those holy words well, even as far from the center of the world as Ninetha was. But I truly didn't understand the weight of them until I saw the man in the jagged brown-and-red-patterned cloak brought by his bound hands across the sandy mud under the Afriq Gate's arches, where the lions carved from the stone glared at the boundary between the wastelands and the city. The seven herders around the stranger yanked at the ropes they usually yoked their goats with as they pulled him into the city.

"Stop that!" I shouted.

The captured man's hair looked like a ragged bush; clearly, he'd walked the wastelands for far too long. It bobbed in the air as he stumbled, as the herders ignored me and forced him along.

"He's a traveler!" I yelled. Travelers deserved hospitality. They deserved to be treated like treasured family members. So few of them ever came over the far horizon of sand that stretched all around Ninetha. We didn't want them to return to their own lands with stories about Ninetha's barbarity.

As one of the daughters of the Lord Musketeer of Ninetha, I had to make sure our actions represented the honor of our city, and my father. My duty here was plain.

"Leave him be!"

"This is no traveler," one of the herdsmen spat.

The stranger pulled back against them and tried to stand. Some of the herders yanked back on the two ropes around his neck to choke him, until his eyes streamed with tears. Another jumped in between the ropes and hit the man in the chest with a heavy wooden crook. I heard the thud from a full street's width away as I walked toward the small crowd.

"I said, stop that!" I imitated my father's cold, hard voice. I tried to act as if the fact that my order would be followed was a foregone conclusion, just as he would.

But the small mob didn't respond.

"She said, stop it," said Kira, who was standing to my right. She stepped forward and swept her hands free of her bright-green robes to point at the other two bodyguards following me.

The herders paused to look over at us with a bit more attention, and their faces twisted with fear as they recognized Kira.

"Guardian, we found him out by the eastern grazes," one of the herders said, raising his arms and backing away from the beaten captive.

Another herdsman dropped to his knees in front of me and held a bundle of fabric up to us. "He tried to capture one of our goats. He carried this with him."

Kira sliced the twine wrapped around the bundle with one of her long daggers, then slid the dagger softly back into its leather sheath.

"It's—" one of the herders started.

"A book," Kira said, loathing clear in her voice.

She dropped it to the ground, as if it had burned her hands. We all stepped back away from the paper that flapped in the wind as the pages rustled about. I stared at the book. It felt so wrong to be in the middle of the street near something so forbidden.

"Burn it," Kira ordered one of the guardians.

"No!" The bound man lurched forward, dragging herders with him as he struggled to grab the book. Kira kicked him, a leather boot to the side of his desert-scoured face, and knocked him clean out.

One of the guardians knelt beside the book and snapped a flint until sparks showered the pages. The thin, symbol-marked paper flared up into flames in the middle of the street, and black smoke curled up into the air around us all.

Everyone moved back away from it, scared to breathe the ink-stained smoke.

Kira looked relieved. "Stay here. Keep it burning until you see only ashes on the street," she ordered the guardian with the flint.

"But Commander Kira." The guardian stood up from the burning book and looked at me. "Two guardians must remain with her at all times."

"I'll be the second," Kira said. "It is my decision. I am the Lady of the Watch."

Kira commanded the One Hundred Guardians, but every single one of them knew who ruled Ninetha. And my father had ordered that two guardians walk with me. Always.

I watched conflict struggle across the guardian's face, until she surrendered to Kira's will. "Yes, Commander."

"I can spare a guardian," I whispered to her.

"No. Your father is right. There are desperate people here. Hungry, starving folk who would see you as an easy meal."

"One day, I'll ask my father whether it's he or you who truly rules Ninetha," I said from the corner of my mouth.

Kira paused. She bit her lip for a second, and then leaned close to me. "That is not a joke, Lilith. Never repeat it around the guardians, and never, for my sake, please, ever say it around your father."

I looked at Kira's normally pleasant, angular face and cheeks. And in her dark eyes, just a shade lighter than the brown skin on her arms, I saw no humor or patience. Instead, she looked scared, and maybe a little haunted.

I had thought of her as steady, unshakeable, and a ruler of the world—like my father.

In fact, I thought of Kira as a mother.

But this was all a small reminder for me of how Ninetha really worked. Kira had pledged her life, her authority, and her all to my father.

"Well, you are more a ruler than I am," I said to her. "Those herders didn't stop beating that man when I said to."

"You'll learn to hold your authority in your voice yet," Kira promised me. She cupped my chin with her hand and kissed my forehead. The glazed, clay beads woven through her tightly curled hair clacked as she came so close, and the smell of sweat, sand, and oil filled the air between us. "Besides, the man they captured is a bookist, a librarian, a profaner of the commandments. They were right not to listen to you. There are higher laws than just our city's. There are the godly laws, and every one of us is bound to follow those no matter where we live, or who we are. And that law says we must put him to death."

"Of course," I agreed, and wondered if Kira, who had

carried me on her side before I could walk, could hear the lie in my tremor of a voice.

It just didn't feel right to harm a defenseless man. I loved Kira, like the sun and the moon, but the way she so easily talked about killing another person blew a confusing flurry of feelings through me—worry, fear, and a small stab of revulsion that then made me feel shame, as Kira was one of the most trusted people in the citadel, and she was my teacher. Who was I to doubt her?

Kira gently grabbed my shoulder. "You are a good person, Lilith. But you have to let go of your feelings about this. Society requires us to punish criminals. You can't let your dog root around in the trash barrel, or soon your house will be that barrel. I know this won't be easy, but it is important."

She'd said the same thing before a flogging once. She'd made me watch the woman's bare back bleed as the price for her thievery.

"We will strangle him right here, on the street. The herders can take the body back out into the wastes," Kira announced as she stepped away from me.

I didn't have Kira's presence. I could not make pronouncements, or calmly tell people what they were going to do in such a way that they felt compelled to do it. But I had some skills in turning people to my will. My mind raced furiously to find a way out.

"Kira, you're right. The stranger is perhaps a librarian, certainly a book lover. There is a higher justice he has to face. Death. But this is Ninetha, not the wastelands out beyond the Five Gates. And the one who decides how a man dies should be my father. Not us."

Kira stopped in place, then turned back to me. She spread

her arms, acknowledging the point. But I could see her jaw clench for a second. "You are correct, Musketress."

She always used my formal title when I annoyed her, but she couldn't disagree out loud with what I'd said.

"We'll take him into the citadel," I said. "And let the Musketeer of Ninetha himself judge the stranger's death. That is the right thing."

I tried to keep the nervousness from my voice. As a child, when I challenged Kira, she would pay me back by throwing me into the dust when we trained later. The bruises would turn a slow purple over the next days, a reminder to me of the cost I paid for my obstinance.

Kira would find other ways to torment me as well. Night duty on the walls, cleaning details. Always an unexpected consequence when I angered her that I couldn't really complain about to my father. I knew Kira wouldn't let this go easily.

But what a shame it would be if the man died before he told us where he came from and what he was doing crossing the wastelands, when it had been almost a full generation since Ninetha had seen a visitor. And why he was risking holy wrath by protecting a book.

I couldn't help my curiosity, as always.

Kira finally nodded. She was bound to my father, and Kira, more than anyone else, respected the rules. The godly rules and the hierarchy of Ninetha. "That is the right thing. Of course, Musketress. You all! Pull him to his feet and bring him with us."

I let out a deep breath.

Kira shoved past me and muttered, "All you're doing is delaying the inevitable. You're making it much harder on yourself."

She was right. I stood against the will of the gods by trying to delay the stranger's death. A dangerous thing to do. But surely the gods could look into my heart and see that I didn't want blood on my hands. If I stood by and watched a man be killed, what was I?

But there was something else.

I knew something that Kira did not.

There was a room deep in the citadel, hidden from even Kira. Every moment of the day, my twelve siblings—the only people of Ninetha other than my father who were allowed to be called musketeers and musketresses—guarded that room. I knew about it from following them to see where they disappeared to when they left our rooms with their muskets at the ready. I'd just been curious.

Hidden away in a nook in a tunnel dug out of the hard rock that Ninetha sat on, I'd peered through the open door of the room they guarded as one of my brothers looked inside to make sure everything was in order.

There, chained behind a heavy metal door and sealed with a lock the size of my fist, my father had hidden a book.

Dust whirled through the Hawk's Gate and over the city walls, down into the five common streets. It choked us and left the back of my throat bitter with dirt, even when I pulled my dayscarf up over my mouth.

The main boulevards that led past the bountiful houses—the large multistory buildings between the common areas and the citadel's walls—had calm, clean air. The hard stone under my sandals didn't leave much for the wind to grasp and fling our way, and there were few, if any, cook fires in this part of Ninetha.

I always relaxed when I passed the pillars and the soft, bubbling fountains in the courtyards of the bountiful houses. The fresh smell of cypress, ever so faint, came from the sentry-like trees standing in orderly rows down the inner streets leading to the citadel.

Olive trees peeked over the mud-brick walls of Ninetha's most powerful homes. On my left, I passed the house of Aykris, which had joined its walls and conical temple complex to several smaller houses via targeted marriages over the years. The bright lapis lazuli that rimmed the doorways twinkled as we marched by.

Children perched on the garden walls saw us on the move, and they began shouting. Word spread quickly among the small, twisty private roads of the bountiful homes, and eventually their parents and grandparents drifted out to see what was happening.

"It'll be an execution," one of the herders announced, and that sent a ripple of nervous excitement around the observers as they all craned their necks to make sure the man didn't belong to any of their allied families.

But, of course, no one recognized him. And that by itself generated a second round of interest as everyone realized a stranger had come through one of the gates.

Ninetha was our oasis in the wastelands. But now, fifteen thousand souls huddled around the citadel and tightly packed up against the roads that radiated out to the five gates. It required order, and a steady hand, my father said. I knew he was right, and although I didn't like it, I'd seen thieves whipped or branded to mark them as criminals. But I hadn't seen an execution yet.

An execution felt like blood curdling the water of something pure.

We halted before the citadel as guardians in polished chest plates stepped forward from the cylindrical sentry huts. They held their spears out, not sure what the sudden crowd meant.

"Spears up," Kira commanded. The guardians smartly snapped the points upward to the clouds with a quick crack as we plunged into the cool shade of the citadel—the heart of Ninetha, and my home.

Kira led us on through the lime-washed bright kitchens and tribute rooms, then down into the circular subfloor of the cornucopium, the room the ancestors had built up around the cornucopia itself. A pair of guardians in simple robes, with long, curved daggers at their sides, pushed the cedar doors aside for us.

I smiled at my father, who sat on a simple wooden chair to the side of the chamber. The sign of power, two muskets longer than he was tall and dipped in gold, hung crossed on the wall above him. Above us all, the cone of the roof rose on dark wooden beams.

The sun circle at the top used to open to the sky above so that smoke could leave the room, but now it had been covered by delicate glass. A single shaft of light, a pillar at the center of the round room, struck the cornucopia at its center.

The herders threw the stranger to the ground before the cornucopia and my father, who stood up with a frown on his face. The elder and younger advisors at the petitioning tables also stood, and the communalists ringed around the cornucopia turned away from the midnight-black, matte engines and snouts to look at the sudden disruption. It could be hard to see the god-machine that was the cornucopia, when the walls pressed so close, but I'd walked the gallery enough to discern the double clover-shaped structure and deformed baobab tree shape in our midst. The god-black pipes that crisscrossed the drooping limbs pulsed like veins as the cornucopia drew sustenance from roots deep under our feet.

"Kira?"

So much could be conveyed in my father's raised eyebrow. A question, surely, but also irritation.

"Lord Musketeer, I'm sorry to bring this to you without warning." Kira bowed to him. "The herders found a librarian outside Ninetha."

Father's light-brown skin looked nearly black in the dim light of the room's edge as he stepped forward to look at what had collapsed on the clay floor before him. "A librarian?"

He pulled the man's clothes off him, gently, as if undressing a child before a bath. The brown-and-red-patterned cloak was thick in his hands, some sort of leather. "He looks near dead."

My father's compassion and tenderness relaxed me. I knew this version of him, the one who checked on me when my fever burned. Who had worried about me when I went on my first desert run with Kira and my very own musket.

One of the guardians stepped forward as my father beckoned him over. "Continue."

The guardian put down his weapons and started tugging at the stranger's underclothes. He wasn't gentle like my father; I heard thread rip.

"He tried to steal one of their goats," I interrupted, as the herders looked at their feet and kept quiet. "He looks like he's starving."

I wanted to head off Kira's calm demands for an execution

by painting a picture of a desperate traveling stranger who needed our help.

My father held up a finger to quiet me. "I don't see a book or any writing on him."

"We burned it immediately," Kira said.

"Yes," the herders agreed.

"Lord, look closely at his skin," one of the communalists said.

I felt pity for the stranger, who could barely open his eyes. The guardian had stripped him to his loincloth, his skin bare for us all to stare at.

His skin.

Swirls of patterns crossed his chest. Loops and squiggles. They connected scars across his chest and arms, old burns that may have ritualistic librarian markings. But they looked to me almost like the scratches the grumpy old kitchen cat, Alsa, had given me when I was barely able to walk and kept bugging her. Only these marks were bigger, and deeper. Much deeper.

"Words," one of my father's advisors hissed, getting up from the stout brick table.

"They're patterns," I shouted. "We don't know their meaning!"

"Even if this *were* writing, no one in this room would know how to decipher it," my father said, and rubbed his forehead in annoyance.

Our eyes met for a second, and I wondered if he realized that I knew about the book deep in the basement of the citadel. Could *he* read it? I'd often wondered about that, but I'd never been brave enough to ask him, or even my brothers and sisters.

To ask that would be to admit that I knew about the book. I felt like it officially made me a participant in some great sin.

And why did my siblings keep the truth from me? Would they reveal all to me when my father decided I was ready to join them in guarding our family secret? Was that when I would *really* become a musketress?

"Execute him now, while he's in his stupor," Kira pressed. Her voice remained level, but I could sense how tautly she was drawn. A rope about to snap.

My father crossed his arms behind his back. "Wake him, and let's see what he has to say."

Kira bowed her head toward the ground, but I could see no humility in the movement. She pressed her hands together and took a deep breath. "Lord—"

"I want to know where he came from, and if there are any others outside our city. I want to know what they are planning. Wake him, Kira. Do it now."

Kira walked to the well at the corner of the cornucopia, her face calmly expressionless. She filled a bucket with water and threw it at the stranger. He spluttered, groaned, thrashed, and then curled back up.

"We'll get nothing from him," she said. "He is on the threshold of meeting the gods. Let's not stand in their way."

"He was starving. He tried to capture a live goat," I said. "Maybe he doesn't have the strength to talk."

"So, now you want us to feed and revive him, so that we can put him to death later?" Kira asked. "You're being cruel. Leave him to die in peace."

"The cornucopia will have something. Some medicine." I looked from my father to the communalists. The four men and four women, all of them in burnt-umber dresses and flat white scarves tied around their necks, watched the entire exchange. "Right?"

They listened to me, but said nothing. As one, they turned to regard my father.

He brushed his simple white robe, pinned in place with a not-so-simple golden pin at his shoulder, and nodded to them.

One of the communalists cleared her throat. "We can ask the cornucopia for medicine. If you wish, Lord."

My father cocked his head to look down at the stranger. "Commune for it," he ordered.

Kira dropped the bucket to the ground, the disgust clear on her face. "This is a waste of everyone's time. We all know what our duty to the gods is here."

"We do. But I have a duty to this city, and to make sure it is safe." My father sat down on his wooden chair, and propped one of his feet up on the petitioner's table. He scratched at the inside of his leg, shoving his ringed fingers down the edge of a leather boot, and casually continued. "Kira, the gods demand we execute a librarian. They don't say anything about how much time it should take. Are we to kill a librarian the moment we see them? Or do the gods allow us some time? Would you like to tell us more about what the gods demand that I do, and when?"

Kira could see the trap, and she realized that she'd stepped over her authority with her comment. She said, in a carefully controlled voice, "Lord, his life is clearly in your hands."

"As is everyone's in Ninetha." My father's voice trickled, as cold as the water from the well under our feet, and I shivered.

The communalist turned to the insect-black tubes and pipes of the cornucopia's bulbous trunks. The tangled nest of god-machinery hummed in the absence of human voices.

Each pipe, shaped like a flower that sprouted from the

base of each trunk, touched an infinitely black table that stuck out from the machine like a tongue at human height. This would be where the horns-of-plenty would deposit their gifts, if the communalists could communicate their need to the machine properly.

Even now, the cornucopia chugged away to create large piles of vittle, the brown, nugget-shaped food that was the basis for almost all of our cuisine. Other tables held vats of curries and spiced rice, delicate pastries, or fresh bread for the citadel. Scurrying servants tiptoed around us in shifts to take the bounty to the kitchens and storage rooms.

The communalist moved to one of the god-machine's eight niches and leaned into it, her palms out to touch the machine's surface.

"May my wish be made real," she said, as the niche surrounded her with a soft, red light.

"We hew to the pact made with the infinite gods, that our needs may be met," the other communalists muttered.

I shivered as I watched the communion. This holy act kept our entire city alive, delivered us food, and gave us the medicines we needed. Without it, we would starve and fade away, and the desert would reclaim this land.

It felt voyeuristic to stand here and watch.

An egg slid out from the petals of the infinitely black flower nearest the communalist. She picked it up and dried it with the sleeve of her robe. When she turned away from the niche, she looked out at us all with glassy, unfocused eyes.

"Who will feed this to him?"

Everyone glanced around, hoping someone else would step forward. I grabbed the egg. "I'll do it."

I cracked it in front of the stranger's face. I expected the yolk to fall out, but instead, some kind of fluffy bread inside filled the cornucopium with a pleasant lavender scent.

The man stirred at the smell, so I broke the pieces up and fed them to him.

I could feel eyes locked onto me. But I ignored them. And my father said nothing, so nothing happened.

The prisoner grabbed the rest of the bread from me. He ate like there was nothing else in the world for him but that fist-shaped chunk of bread I'd pulled out of the egg's shell.

I watched in awe as his vitality flickered back. His eyes firmed, his trembling stopped, and his movements became sure.

"How do you feel?" I asked.

He swallowed the last of the bread and looked around, realizing he had an audience. He jerked back from the herders. "They attacked me."

I moved between him and the raggedy-looking folk who'd followed us into the citadel. "You tried to kill a goat they were sworn to protect."

Kira stepped between us, breaking the trusting eye contact I tried to project to the stranger. Before I could ask the questions burning up inside of me—where he'd come from, what places he'd seen out beyond the wastelands—she pointed at the man. "You have writing on your skin."

The man looked down. "They're my tribe's sigils. They mark my allegiances and commemorate the scars."

"You're a librarian," Kira growled. "Confess your sins."

"You have a curious way of treating strangers."

"No one asked you to come here." Kira looked at my father. "I burned the book he carried. Now, we should burn him."

My father acted bored, but I could see that he paid attention to every word as he slowly cut an apple into portions and ate the pieces off a kitchen knife.

Kira turned to me, frustrated, but still pressing. "Ask Lilith if she saw the book."

My father set the knife down and stood. "Leave my daughter out of this."

"Lord—"

"Quiet, Kira." I watched him take control simply by walking between Kira and the accused. "The book. What was it about?"

The man shook his head.

My father squatted in front of him. "I am the Lord of all Ninetha. My forefathers willed this city into being. They built the walls of the citadel all around you. I can protect you from anything. Tell me what you read in that book, and I will listen to you."

Kira looked horrified.

The man bit his lip. He looked down at his knees and pulled them closer to his strangely scarred chest. "I have nothing to say."

My father sighed. "I suppose that would have been too easy."

"We saw the book, Lord Musketeer," one of the herders said, voice cracking slightly.

"We took it from him, and then Commander Kira burned it right there in the street," another said.

My father looked over at me as he stood with a grunt, not seeking confirmation, but just curious about my reaction. I bit my lip, but I know my face confirmed what I had seen.

"That is enough evidence, I guess," he said in a soft voice. "Take him, Kira, from here to each temple in the bountiful homes. At each, stop and whip him with a wolf strap."

I felt sick to my stomach as I heard the words. I pictured

the cutting flails of the wolf strap and the small stone shards that dangled from its five ends. I met Kira's eyes. She did not look triumphant. Rather, she looked tired, as she shook her head sadly at me. The man would suffer far more than if I had left all this alone.

My father continued, "Don't stop until he confesses to the crime of literacy."

I thought about the book that my father protected, hidden away under the citadel.

How could he do this so calmly?

My father left the cornucopium and walked me back toward the musketeers' rooms in the east wing of the citadel, up on the second floor. It was as tall as the old structure could reach, unlike the bountiful houses that could stand four stories, or the commons, which were sometimes even higher. My father let his hand trail along the white plaster walls as his sandals slapped the red tile floors. I used to focus on the echo that came a split second after each of his heavy steps, but today a cloud hung over me.

"There is nothing you can do for him," my father said.

"I know I shouldn't want him to live," I said. "I know what he did was a terrible sin."

"The greatest sin," my father said.

I looked closely at my father's time-lined face and his newly gray stubble. But his brown eyes showed not a single hint of regret. He had a book! I knew he had a book. Yet he was so outwardly pious.

I wanted to ask about the book.

I wanted to ask him: why?

But I didn't have the courage to do it right there in the corridor. I didn't want to just come out and ask him if he was committing one of the nine sins.

When I had found out about the book, I'd imagined that he kept it there to keep us safe from it, chained away and guarded by my brothers and sisters. But as I got older, I started to suspect a darker secret. None of my siblings had ever spoken about it, and I knew that meant I couldn't either.

I danced around the forbidden topic. "Why would anyone want to read? I don't understand. The other sins, I can see how people fall to them."

"Oh?" A raised eyebrow, and I felt like a little child again, tagging along beside him, yammering about anything and everything as he gently answered me.

I blushed. "I can see wanting to kill someone."

"Is there someone in particular you want to murder?" my father asked with mock alarm.

"No!"

He laughed and slapped his hands together. "How do you see it, then? What would drive you to murder?"

"If someone were to kill a person I love," I said quickly.

"Vengeance." My father bit his lip and nodded. "But what would that do to *you?* A murderer gets barred from the godmachines and is thrown out into the land, to wander without grace."

"I could live out in the land," I said. "Kira trained me to fight. She trained me to run over the sands, to find the water. I ate insects and honey from the comb!"

"That's exciting for a few days. But the rest of your life?"

"I didn't say I wanted to do this; I just said that I could understand what would lead a person to it," I said.

"And what about the other sins?"

He was leading me away from what I really wanted to talk

about. A gentle path. I had to turn back to it. I sighed. "I understand those sins. But reading is the one that confuses me. What do you get from it? Really?"

My father put a hand on my shoulder, turning me slightly toward him.

"Lilith, I think there are some things we shouldn't dig too hard at. Some things, they will eat us up."

"I don't want forbidden knowledge," I said quickly. "I don't want to transgress. But surely it can't be dangerous to understand why people do things, so that I can prepare myself. I am a musketress. I am your daughter. I am the last line of defense in the citadel. I carry our family's future on my back."

Kira had told me that when the cold metal barrel of a musket rested against my palms for the first time, and she then continued etching it into me every chance she had.

"You are a child of the citadel, and its last guardian," Kira would say. "That is why only you wield this weapon. It is a sign of your status, and a tool."

My father stopped in front of the arches that led to our rooms. Two guardians uncrossed their spears to let us through and pressed their left fists to their foreheads.

"Curiosity has always chewed at you," he said. "When you were a child, you would drive your nurses insane with questions: How far away is the edge of the world? How does the cornucopia work? Where do babies come from?"

I looked over at the guardians, as embarrassment pricked at me. "And I never got good answers."

"I think some turn to literacy because there's a hollowness, something missing in them, and they seek to fill it," my father said.

"And what is that?" I asked. "What is that missing thing?"

"Well, if I knew that," he laughed, "we could stop anyone from turning to books. And then we wouldn't have to pass judgment on these poor sinners. If it were an easy riddle, it would have been solved a long time ago."

"I guess that's true," I muttered. "Even the gods haven't figured out how to take the desire to sin with the written word out of us."

"Exactly." My father pulled me into a hug. "Go get some sleep. It's been a long day. And Lilith?"

"Yes?"

"Don't ever leave the citadel without your musket again."

"I was hoping you hadn't noticed," I said into his shoulder. His robes smelled like jasmine, curry, and the stale-rice smell of vittle.

"How could I miss that?" My father let go of me. He looked serious, as if he were about to pronounce a ruling. "You know why you should never leave without your weapon."

"The desperate ones lurk in the common streets," I said. "And even the bountiful might think about doing something dangerous. Be aware, be ready, and always keep my powder dry and at hand."

"My daughter." He chuckled and left me. I walked under the black granite keystone of the arch into the family quarters.

Anwago caught me by the lion fountain. The statue's wide, sculpted eyes glared out at the hallway as water shot from behind its snarl. "I heard something happened in the cornucopium. How are you?"

He stared off at our father, who walked away, tapping the walls as he went, to music no one else could hear.

"There was a traveler who had a book on him. Kira wanted to kill him, right there in the street!"

"But no one harmed you?"

I rolled my eyes.

"You're well?" Anwago prodded again.

I was the youngest of the twelve. Almost every conversation and action with my brothers and sisters reminded me of it. At least Kira, pious and hard while training me, didn't treat me like a delicate vase.

No wonder I preferred her company to my siblings.

"I'm well," I told him. "But they're going to kill the first stranger to come to Ninetha in years."

Anwago turned back from the arches. "You're well; that is all I wanted to know."

He ambled off, back to his room.

A babble of noise and motion filled the hall as Yusi and Endu swept in past the guardians. Yusi threw a long, wooden bow on the tile behind a couch. It clattered and bounced until it hit a wall.

"That's a beautifully crafted weapon!" Endu shouted, but I could hear the mocking in his voice. He took very little seriously. He was always the brother who waited by a door outside a toilet to grab your arm while wearing a dog mask to try to scare you. "You'll destroy it."

"It was dogshit," she said. "I missed five shots."

"Nothing wrong with this fine piece." Endu picked up the bow. "Just the archer."

"I've spent more time in the weapons room than anyone here," Yusi snapped.

"And yet you still have the grace of a monkey trying to eat at a fine table."

Yusi scowled. "You goat. See how much grace I give you the next time we spar."

"Promises! Nothing but empty promises with you." Endu gave the bow back to Yusi, presenting it as if it were a valuable gift. "You should treat this with the respect it deserves. Like a lover. Caress your weapon. Sleep with it. Get to know it."

I got the joke. He was channeling Kira.

"Kiss your weapon, take it to dinner with you!" I shouted.

Endu smiled at me. "Maybe take that bow back to your room," he said to Yusi. "Like you snuck in that boy from the kitchen. Really get to know—"

"Was that Anwago sulking off back into his room?" Yusi asked quickly, changing the subject.

"Yes. Still not talking to either of you," I said. "Not since the ice bucket."

"Ah, the ice bucket." Endu looked proud of himself.

"Your hair is a mess," Yusi smiled and kissed my cheek. "Let me braid it for you."

Endu handed me an apple. "Eat, little sparrow. Eat."

I sat on a stool and fiddled with the apple as Yusi started to tug at my hair. Kira preferred my hair in tightly braided rows.

Siblings wandered in and out, exchanging delicacies pilfered from the kitchen and, in one case, a blue fruit pie lifted right from the cornucopium. Conversation spun around me like a small whirlwind. I couldn't pay attention to it any more than I could grasp the air.

"Why aren't you eating?" Yusi asked.

"I can't stop thinking about the stranger." I folded my arms. "To risk the wastelands, starve, and finally reach a city where they kill you. What if that were any of us? I did everything I could, Yusi. They say we should not suffer a librarian to live, but it was just a single book. We don't really know what he was doing with it."

Yusi wrapped her arms around my neck and whispered, "It's a dangerous thing to look like you condone reading."

I grabbed her hands. "I know. I know it's dangerous."

"You have to be careful," Yusi said softly. "We are the citadel's musketeers. But we're not invulnerable. You played with fire, and you were lucky you didn't get burned."

I groaned. "I know."

"The citadel is your home, Lil. But that doesn't mean the world can't strike you, even within these walls."

"A crime is a crime, even for us," I said.

"Kira's right," Yusi said, recognizing the words. "Listen to her wisdom."

They had dragged the stranger into Ninetha in front of me. I felt like his blood stained my hands. Sin or not, I couldn't wash that away. Even if he was a criminal.

"You're right," I lied.

Yusi tugged at my hair. She started talking about the most inane things. The boy who fell out of the fig tree while trying to impress her. The new paint pattern the artist Andia painted on the back of the Sun family's temple.

I leaned back against her and whispered, "What about the book that you guard every day for Father?"

Yusi froze.

All day long I had felt strength solidifying inside of me, like a mud brick hardening in the sun. I didn't want to bend so easily to everyone anymore.

"How do you know about that?" Yusi asked after the longest pause. She started pulling at my hair again, trying to tame the kinky spirals that exploded free when she unloosed my braids.

"I'm not a child anymore," I complained.

"We know. We've all watched you grow so confident. So well trained by Kira."

"I can stand guard at the door, just like you," I said to her. I wanted to take on whatever responsibility they all carried. But more than that, I wanted to understand it.

"No," Yusi said, the edge in her voice so sharp that I winced. "That is not something you will be doing yet."

"But what is this book *for?*" I asked. "Can you read?"

When I listened to the griots down in the amphitheater off the Swan Gate as they told tales of heroes long since lost to time and the mists of legend, I would think that maybe my family had been chosen by the gods to protect something dangerous. It sounded epic. It made me feel good. It made me feel better when my brothers and sisters whispered things in the corners of their rooms when they thought I wasn't paying attention.

"Of course I can't read," Yusi hissed.

"Then what are we all hiding?"

"Sometimes we must protect things, and sometimes the rules aren't as simple as you think. Lil, you have to keep this a secret."

"I know."

"If anyone finds out, it will be dangerous for us. Very dangerous."

I pulled my shoulders back. "I've known for months, but never said a word. I'm not stupid."

"But you're thinking about how they're going to execute that man, aren't you? And then you think about the book."

"It just seems wrong," I said.

"Ikari, the head of the house of Azil-Ha, told me that when she was a child, she saw a librarian executed here in Ninetha."

Ikari could barely walk, and when she came to visit the cornucopium, I would have to lean in close to hear her trembling voice. My brother Kame once said that Ikari was older than the city walls.

Yusi continued: "She said he came on a donkey with a crate on its back, filled with rolled papers, ink bottles, pens. He walked through one of the gates to be a martyr. They stoned him to death in the middle of the spice market, and she had nightmares for weeks and weeks."

"Is that supposed to make me feel better about this?" I shifted to look across at Yusi.

She shrugged. "Apparently the guardians burned the donkey and the papers at the same time. The poor thing ran off into the desert, screaming, paper flying every which way into the air. And then, Ikari told me, it rained black ink for the next week as the spells in the librarian's books reached the clouds."

I slumped against her. "There'll be nothing I can do for him."

Yusi finished a braid. "No more than you can stand against a dust zephyr. The gods see into your mind and know the concern you have for another soul, no matter what sin they have committed. It's good to pray for him."

"To which god?"

"Ors," Yusi pulled another row tight, her fingertips scraping at my scalp. "The rain god knows compassion. And if burning paper puts ink in the air that then rains down on us, maybe it's good to ask for some mercy for all of us."

I thought maybe I would burn an extra length of incense at the hearth's prayer table. The gentle Ors, who spoke only with the whisper of light rain hitting a roof, had never tilted the odds in my favor before. But it couldn't hurt to pray.

"Don't beg Father for mercy either, Lil. He will do what has to be done. He will do it his way. Stay away from Father, do you understand?"

"Yes, Sister."

"And stay far away from that man of books. Promise me?"

"I promise," I lied, looking directly into my sister's eyes as she turned me around to look at my braids in a hand mirror.

"And don't," Yusi said, her face stony and hard, "tell anyone else about the kitchen boy."

Kira came to my room several hours later as the sun kissed Ninetha's walls in red. The north winds swirled an intense cloud of rusty orange haze up over the temples of the city, and cornucopia globes set into walls and ceilings all over the city started glowing as they sensed daylight fading. A dog howled somewhere in the distant common streets.

Kira slipped past my door to the balcony. She turned into a silhouette against the artificial light.

"Come out here. I want you to listen to something."

Kira gripped the lip of the stone rail and looked toward the Wazu temple complex, where green smoke rose into the air. I wrapped my nightsilks tight against the cold evening, slipped on fur slippers, and walked out to join her.

Thousands of baubles lit up the windows and alleys in Ninetha's bountiful quarters, like the glint in dried sand. The light faded near the city's commons, where baubles were few and far between, and darkness settled like a heavy old blanket.

I often slept out here, where I could look out over the hints of the city's buildings in the night air and enjoy a cool wind.

"Do you hear it?" Kira asked.

I listened. And then I realized it wasn't a dog howling, but a man screaming from inside the Wazu temple. A man broken so hard he sounded like an animal.

"I can see you hear it for what it is, now," Kira said. She walked back in to sit on the edge of my bed and peeled an orange. The bright scent of citrus hung between us as she cut the skin with one of her long fingernails. "They'll beat him until he cries bloody tears and says anything we tell him to. We don't need his confession. You and I know that he had a book on him. But right now, to get it to stop, he would tell us he's secretly a duck. It's unfair, Lilith."

I sat heavily next to her. "I didn't want this. I tried—"

"If there's one thing I've worked to show you, Lilith, it's that there are always consequences to our choices. I've tried to help you learn how to identify the right paths, because you are heir to great power here in the citadel. All of you are. I've tried so hard to prepare you for that."

I grabbed her hand. "I know, Kira."

She handed me the peeled orange. "Do you?"

I knew what she wanted to hear. "If you had strangled him there, while he couldn't feel a thing, I wouldn't have to hear him scream now."

She patted my knee. "This place, it might feel safe to you, but there are threats. Reading is one of them. Remember when the commons got sick last year?"

The coughing had spread through the packed, unlit warrens of the desperate folk. Bodies were spilled into the streets, left by people who couldn't find the energy or will to take care of them. The communalists had to investigate, then return to the cornucopia with those images burned in their minds to make medicine for us all to take so it didn't spread.

We quarantined so many houses.

"Literature is like an infectious disease," Kira said softly, "spreading ideas through a city. You may feel pity for the disease carrier, but you cannot let them through your door."

"I understand."

Kira turned my head to look at the rows of braids. "Who did those?"

"Yusi."

"She has deft fingers," Kira said. "It's a shame they can never hold a weapon right. She's more interested in her lovers than her duties."

"She practices hard," I said.

"Only because the guardians she spars against take off their shirts to grapple," Kira said.

I smiled. "And they oil themselves. Don't forget that. So very nice and slippery."

Kira pretended to look slightly scandalized. "You grow up too fast."

"Everyone keeps telling me that," I said. "You can't control every little aspect of my life forever, Kira."

I stood up to close the balcony's thick cedar doors, but Kira stopped me.

"Leave them open," she said, her voice cold again.

I let go of them. I crawled into my bed and put the peeled orange on the stand next to the pitcher of lemon water that a servant had left for me.

"How will they end it?" I asked Kira, as she crossed my room.

She paused, hand on the door. "Locked in one of the cells

and starved. Only water to drink. Do you remember from our training outside the walls how long I told you it took a person to starve?"

The door shut.

I did not sleep at all as I listened to the distant screams.

Thirty days. A person could survive as long as thirty days without food.

The librarian still lived. He had thirty days more of life. A life of imprisonment and starvation.

In the days that followed, it rolled around my mind as I lay in bed. It sat heavy in my stomach at family dinners, as the petitioners fawned over us while we delicately nibbled at ice cream, still hard-frozen from the cornucopia. And it clouded my responses in the gym when I trained.

"Head up!" Kira shouted.

A smack from a wooden spear pierced the sandy haze of my mind.

I could parry, but I could not attack.

Kira knocked me in the face, swept my feet out from under me, punched the air from my lungs, and made me pay for my lack of concentration.

Dammit, I was a musketress, not a guardian. I would never use a spear. My sword was decorative. The bow was a joke.

I was a god of fire and brimstone.

In the firing room, I aimed at the painted targets. Fired. The air around me exploded, and the sharp smell of powder filled my lungs.

"Reload!"

I grabbed a paper cartridge, ripped the end off with my teeth, and spat. I pulled the trigger back to half cock, poured a smidge of powder into the pan, and shut it in by pushing the frizzen back. Automatic motions, drilled into me by Kira. Musket to my left, ball and paper down the gullet, ramrod out, shove it all down.

For faster loads, drop the ball in, and smack the stock against the ground to seat it. But when it rattled around in there, accuracy dropped.

Paper and ball jammed in, I returned the musket to my shoulder.

"Fire!"

Another target obliterated. The paper punched clean through, the bullet embedded in the mud wall behind it. I could make five shots per minute, but I would be drenched in sweat and gritty with black powder.

But that's what Kira wanted today. Speed.

"You think you're fast," she growled. "My archers can fire ten, twelve arrows in the time it takes you to fire once. And there are even a few archers I can push to higher rates."

True, but it didn't look like hell itself had ripped the air open. And although my musket, Alice, came almost up to my shoulders—making it hard to load the gun quickly—that long barrel could hit a target at nearly two hundred paces.

Only *some* of her archers could, just barely, hit a target at half that.

I would choose Alice any day over those bows and arrows. I had named my musket after the hero of my favorite griot's tale, *Alice in the Underland*. I saw myself as brave enough to go exploring the strange realms of the afterlife, where cats floated and queens tortured sinners by chopping off their heads.

Today, the sweat dripping onto the sizzling barrel meant that for a moment, I didn't have to think about the man starving somewhere on the other side of the citadel.

"Reload! Your great-grandfather protected the cornucopium with weapons just like this, before he built the citadel around it." Kira looked at the targets with a raised eyebrow. "One day, you might have to do the same. You must be fast and true."

I grabbed another cartridge.

My father wanted strong children. Skilled musketeers and musketresses.

One of us would carry the title of Lord someday.

I suspected some of my siblings didn't want the title. They wanted to chase girls or boys. Or they wanted to eat everything they could imagine the cornucopia could deliver. And Vikkor would collect every jewel in the city if he could. Not to wear, just to decorate his room.

Many of us who carried the heavy, long weapons around took the responsibility seriously, though.

Someone would have to rule Ninetha after our father was gone.

We were raised to it. Trained for it. Prepared for it almost every day of our lives. It wouldn't be me. Not the youngest. Not the most curious, the most troublesome to Kira.

But it would be my responsibility to protect that chosen sibling. It would be my responsibility to understand threats to the citadel and act to stop them. By learning everything I could about the world, I could protect my family.

That was my role in the citadel, and what I trained for.

So, one week later, when it was safe, I slipped in through the door of the cell where the man of words sat on a bench, staring at the wall. He stared at the piece of paper that I held up in my left hand and slowly shifted to look at me.

"Tell me what these markings mean," I whispered, and I held up an orange with my right hand. "And why they are so dangerous to us all. I need to know."

The starving man snatched at the orange, and I pulled it back from him. I hated myself for doing that; a lump of bile arose that I had to force back down.

I thought about my father's words: *"Someday, they'll try to break the citadel. They always do."*

I would ask, "Who?" and he would shrug fatalistically: *"Those who think that vittle isn't enough. That the food they can raise or grow is not enough. That we don't hand out medicine for all. They'll try to come and take it all. They think they'll do better."*

He'd taken the mantle of Lord during the last commoners' revolt. They'd poured out of the packed alleys with knives tied to the ends of poles for spears.

"To rule Ninetha, you have to be stone."

But it wasn't just the commons who scared him.

"Watch the bountiful houses, too," he said. "They get the second blessings of the cornucopia, after the citadel. It gives them a taste for more. In the commons, they can hardly imagine the things the god-machine blesses us with. Their lives are basic and suffering. But the closer to the citadel's walls, the more they lust for what they could take."

When I walked the city, I studied it. I'd watched people in the commons haggling for spice, or thanking guardians for the daily scoops of vittle they brought from the city storage tanks. I'd tasted soups and curries made from vittle, vittle stew, vittle bread, and all the other common foods.

I'd joined the priests in the temples in the bountiful houses, giving offerings on the altar to Abe. I'd danced to the god of music, Elv, whose chariot was drawn by giant beetles that danced under the sun.

"I want to know everything," I said to the starving man in front of me. "Do you understand? The world beyond the wastes. What threats reading might bring. Why you are here. I want to know it all."

He stared at the orange. "The guard?" His voice was raspy, and he had a slight cough.

"The guardian is asleep," I smiled. "I gave him ice cream. He can't trouble us right now."

Before I'd gone to see the prisoner, I'd stopped inside the cornucopium and told the communalist on duty that I needed something to help me get to sleep, and that it had to be delectable. The guardian tonight had taken the bowl of chilled sweets. He'd never had anything like it, he said, even though he'd been inside the citadel for two years now.

Poor young thing. He'd dropped the bowl to the ground and slid down the wall just moments later. I would wake him gently, later. Maybe I'd even give him a squeeze on the arm, a kiss on the cheek. He was a tough guardian, but he was still a boy, with his eyes wide as he looked around the citadel he had been given the honor of protecting.

"Tell me what these markings are," I repeated to the prisoner, my voice firmer.

The librarian took the paper from me with thin hands that shook a little. When I first saw him on the ground, he'd looked older, with that scraggly beard and wild hair. But this close, his eyes darting across the paper, I saw that the lines on his face were from squinting and sun, not age. And despite being starved for the last ten days, his limbs were wiry and strong.

His eyes flicked to the orange, then back up to me. "It's a set of instructions."

"You can read it?"

"I can. I have," he rasped.

I took a half-step back, despite myself. I expected him to murmur incantations, or for the markings to rearrange themselves on the paper. Maybe dance in the air before us. But none of that happened, and I summoned my inner strength. "Tell me."

"Why would I do that? You have bound and tortured me, and you plan my death."

I wished I could command him like my father would, but I couldn't. I bent my head and closed my eyes. "I have risked my very soul to get these pages. I put sleeping powder in my brother Kame's wine, before he went to guard the book."

Kame had taken hours to finally slump over his musket and lean against the wall, snoring. I knew none of my siblings would be surprised to find him passed out. Certainly not Kame himself. Then, I'd had all the time in the room I needed. I'd stolen some paper from the cornucopium, where it had wrapped up pretty packages of headache powder. I'd used that paper to trace pages in the book—ones that had been marked up in the white space at the edges, as if someone had added to the incantations.

That page had seemed significant.

I had stepped back over Kame again on the way out, apologizing all the way, even though he couldn't hear me.

"If I'm found with this, I will be *killed*. I know you understand that. What are these instructions for?" My curiosity burned, as it always did. I hoped the gods would see that I did it just to understand why my family committed such a deadly sin. "I need to know. Please."

He thought about it, and I saw him look from my face back toward the orange. He licked his dry lips quickly.

"Give me that, and I'll tell you."

I needed to build his trust first, so I handed the orange over.

He tore into it, biting through the skin and sucking pulp out through the hole. I watched him shiver as he scraped every piece of flesh from the rind with his teeth.

"Now, talk to me." I sat on the bench next to him.

"It's a recipe for something called black powder," he said. "It doesn't seem edible. Do you know what it is?"

Powder. Musket powder.

Well, that cleared it up for me, like a wind cutting through morning fog. The recipe to make powder hadn't been handed down to my father by memorization, like a griot's story, so that he could teach the guardians to make it for us musketeers. It had been written down. In the book my siblings guarded.

Powder was power, and power had come from reading.

My hands shook as I took the paper back.

"I know what the recipe is," I said. "I know what the powder is for."

The stranger didn't press me for more. "My name is Ishmael," he said instead, with a slight bow of his head. The orange had reinvigorated him a little. He pulled at his hair, trying to push it into place. The scabs on his arms, from the whip, cracked and oozed a little blood as his hands darted around his face. He laughed to himself ruefully, as if giving me his name slightly annoyed him. "Yes. It's Ishmael."

"Are you truly a librarian?" I asked. To be honest, I had thought a master of the dark art would be a powerful wizard, able to kill us all with lightning bolts made from words.

He hesitated. "Well . . ."

"You're scared, I understand. I would be too." I picked up the pieces of orange peel between us, hiding the evidence of my crime away in a pocket tied to my skirt.

"You follow the old ways, out here," he said. "I knew it was a risk when I left Eufra."

"Eufra!" I gaped at him. "You've been to Eufra? Does it really hang over a river, like the griots say?"

"There's a bridge," Ishmael explained. "With buildings on it. But it's mostly just another harbor city. I took a barge down the Eufrat to reach it."

"A barge," I marveled. "On a river?"

I knew Eufra was real. People had once traveled back and forth before the land dried up. The stone road to Eufra once saw heavy traffic. Now, sand buried it, although the dirt under the Afriq Gate still had the large stones if you dug a little bit.

Still, Eufra sounded like a magical city from legend, like Boskone, Toko, or Shanri-La.

"Did you see one of the manatees when you were there on the river?"

"I did." Ishmael leaned closer to me. "We poled past one. It was like a fat cow that swam by our barge and—"

"What's a cow?" I asked.

Ishmael stared at me for a long moment. Something evaporated in the air between us, but I didn't know what it was, only that I'd lost it by interrupting him with my ignorance of exotic animals.

"I don't want to starve to death," he said, looking directly at me, so hard that I squirmed. I remembered that I'd put the guardian to sleep to unlock the cell door. Ishmael could try to attack me, maybe even try to kill me, then run.

I rested my right hand on the hilt of a dagger next to my pocket, the scabbard tied off to my belt. I didn't want to have to hurt him.

"I'm doing everything I can," I said.

"You can keep feeding me." He crossed his arms. "But eventually, when I don't die, they will figure out something is wrong."

"It's dangerous," I said, the words grating at my throat. "But I will do what I can."

Ishmael grasped my hand. "The gods curse a city that does not provide for a traveler."

I jerked back as if I'd been stung and quickly stood up. "And the gods told us we should not suffer a librarian to live."

"What do you think feels right, deep in your soul? Murder? Or care?"

"I need to leave, now," I said quickly as I pressed the papers with their dangerous writing right up against my stomach and bound them back in place with cloth. "I need to go."

Shame and fear battled within me. How could I save him? I could only prolong his misery.

Kira was right: this was cruelty.

But now I knew Ishmael had explored the world. He had seen Eufra, taken a barge down a river, and encountered strange animals like cows.

He was a human, a real person, with fear, a desire to live, and stories to tell.

I locked the door on him and fled back to my room. I stared at the silent night sky outside, my mind racing furiously. But no matter which way I imagined it, I couldn't see a way to get him out of the citadel without guardians discovering us.

Still, I couldn't stop thinking about the man in the cell.

Ishmael.

Every time I heard my siblings get up and go to change a shift guarding that room under the citadel, I knew my family was just as guilty as the librarian.

Should we be killed as well?

When I practiced firing my musket as fast as I could on training days after that, I couldn't shake the feeling that Kira was looking right through me to the stain on my soul. I couldn't stop thinking about where the knowledge had come from to create the powerful weapon in my hands.

It had come from a book.

Three days later, I took Ishmael two small pouches of vittle to hide in his cell.

"This will last a week," I told him. "And I'm sorry it took so long to get it to you. I had to wait for the right guardian."

The last guardian had enjoyed his frozen sweets, but now his eyes narrowed when I asked him whether he wanted another. After him, I'd tried the trick on two older, gruffer guardians. They pretended I hadn't asked, seeing my offer of exotic food as a test of some sort from the Lord Musketeer, delivered by his child.

"Never thought I'd be excited about basic," Ishmael said with a faint smile.

"Basic what?" I asked.

Ishmael tapped the pouches. "We call the food pellets 'basic.'"

"We call it vittle," I said.

He hid the vittle in the rags of his clothes, and again thanked me. I ground my teeth, as the gratitude felt like a sharp prick in the middle of my spine.

"What is that?" I pointed to the round symbols etched into his left arm.

Ishmael held his forearm up so I could see it better. The veins on his arms made the round symbol flex and dance as he moved. "It's the world."

I looked at the lumps and squiggles. "How?"

"It's a map."

"A map?"

Ishmael got on his knees with a grunt and pushed the bench aside. He sat back up with a tiny pebble in his fingers. "Your city. Describe the roads and gates to me."

I thought about it a second. "The citadel is in the center. It has four sides, and towers for the guardians on each corner. All the city roads lead to the one road that circles the citadel. There are the bountiful houses around it, with their own temples and roads that mainly connect house to house. Then, the commons stretch all the way to the walls and beyond."

I described the five gates, and the city walls that guarded against the wastelands.

"You said I was the first one in a generation to come here. Please explain this to me: what are the walls for?" Ishmael asked.

"I . . . I'm not entirely sure."

I had to think. We'd had walls for as long as I'd been alive. It was something I would have to put aside and think back on later.

Ishmael scratched away at the floor, until the dust and stained clay revealed what, he explained, the city would look like to a bird flying overhead.

"This is the power of symbols," Ishmael said. "I can draw

this map and give it to someone on paper a month's travel away, and they would know how to walk around your city. Writing just uses another kind of symbol, like a map, to transfer meaning by paper between people."

"But they could just ask around." I still didn't see the point of the map.

"Maybe they don't want to come and visit, but they still want to know about the city."

"But that's silly," I said. And I wondered if that's why the gods forbade writing. Maybe it was just a waste of time they wanted to save us all from.

"But is it wrong?" Ishmael asked. "Is it something to be killed for?"

I folded my legs over each other. "Kira says words spread ideas, dangerous ideas. Like a disease. That's why the gods forbid it."

"They can also spread good ideas." Ishmael scuffed at the map of Ninetha he'd drawn until the floor looked dirty again. He peered out of the small window in the cell door, his palms against the old, scarred wood.

He took a deep breath and cocked his head. "What's it like outside today?"

"Clear. I can see all the way to the rim of the world." The snow-capped rim rippled, days and days of sandy walking away.

"The rim of the world?" Ishmael turned back. "You mean a mountain range?"

"It's the rim of the world." I waved a hand. "Everyone knows this."

"Everyone?"

"Our forefolk traded with people out near the rim. There is nothing beyond them but the void."

Ishmael shook his head sadly and walked toward me. "I am sure they believed that. But those are mountains. Mountains I was hoping to map, so we can expand our understanding of the world."

As he sat next to me, I looked closely at the rounded map on his arm. "Where's Ninetha and the wastelands on that map?"

He held out his arm again for me. "I'm not sure. It doesn't seem to be anywhere we've found. And the maps we have in the libraries in my home city, New Alexandria, don't match any landmarks we've found yet. Some of us think Ninetha, and the cities here, are on the other side of the globe."

"The other side?"

Ishmael pointed at the round map with his other hand. "It's like that orange you gave me the first time you came in here. We know the world is round, just like that. This map shows the face turned to us, but we could be on the other side."

I laughed in his face. I stood up and shook my head. Because now I understood the danger of a reading man. "You're insane. That's not true. The world isn't an orange, traveler. The world is flat."

"No," Ishmael paced the cell. "No. That is what the griots say. That's legend. But we've been collecting books at New Alexandria for twenty years now, books that came from before the Exodus. Ancient artifacts that give a glimpse of what the world really was, and really is."

"It's not an orange," I repeated. And then I gasped. "You are a librarian, then. You just admitted it to me."

Ishmael crossed his arms. "So, now you will kill me after all?"

I moved to the other side of the cell. I needed to not be so close to the sin.

"How could we walk on a globe? Wouldn't we fall off?" I asked, changing the conversation.

"If it's big enough, it holds you on it. There's something called gravity. It's like an invisible glue."

"Invisible glue?"

"The ancients studied the world. They built things. Cities with millions of people in them. Buildings that stretched up into the clouds. They had a system called science. A way of verifying truths. It's powerful, Lilith. Very powerful." Ishmael's eyes shone with the light of a zealot.

I swallowed.

"Before I was born, a woman came in from herding out in the rocks for far too long. Some said she was a traveler, others a hermit, and many more saw her as a prophet. The griots say that you could see that the sun had pitted her skin, made her hair brittle, and faded her eyes. She said the sun spoke to her. People clustered around her in the commons, listening to her preach every morning as the sun rose over the walls. She also said everything we knew was a lie."

"And what happened?"

"There was an uprising. People died who didn't need to."

I moved to the door. It was time to leave. Stories about the rock witch had scared me as a child, and the thought of Ninetha burning at night still left me with an acidic taste in my mouth.

"I'm not her," Ishmael said.

"But you sound like her," I said, and slipped out the door.

Two days later Kira invited me to a meal on the citadel's roof. Four guardians set up a tray and two chairs in the grass inside the ring of small acacia trees in clay planters on the roof garden. Three poles slotted into brackets stretched a canvas triangle between the sun and the platters of chilled fruit, tarragon pie, and fried potato covered in masala.

Kira waved the guardians away to the corners of the roof, out of hearing, but within sight of their commander.

"It has been a long few weeks." She waved at the second chair. "You've been training so hard."

I sat and poured from a pitcher of cold lemonade. The cornucopia-made ice clinked against the glass.

On the roof, we could look around at all the buildings of Ninetha unimpeded. From the gleaming white walls of the bountiful areas to the muddy, cramped warrens of the commons. When the thick walls of the citadel felt like a prison, I enjoyed coming up to the roof garden.

Kira doled out these meals with her to various guardians and to my siblings as rewards for what she saw as good behavior. They were rare, and I treasured them.

"When can I go walk the city on my own?" I asked.

"Lil, you know the answer." Kira cut a slice of pie and slid it delicately off the knife onto her polished silver plate.

"Safety at all costs," I said. I'd complained about that since I had first understood there was a city beyond the walls of the citadel.

"Have you talked to your father?" Kira asked.

"Not since we found the man." I poked at some fruit and thought about how desperately hungry for that orange Ishmael had been. The fruit lost its appeal, and I couldn't bring myself to eat it.

"He's not angry with you," Kira said.

"I know."

"He's just very busy."

"I know."

It was an old conversation. She would tell me how busy he was, looking after the fortunes of Ninetha. On this day, he would have to go over the demands of the streams of petitioners coming in for the communalists. He would also walk the citadel with builders, looking at the cracks and weaknesses in its walls. There were disputes between bountiful houses to arbitrate, and temple traditions for him to preside over.

"Ninetha would fall without him at the center of it all. The bountiful houses depend on him, and the communalists look first to him before speaking to the gods themselves," Kira would say.

She was always there to interpret my father, to pass on his orders, to train me.

My father, the Lord of Ninetha, wandered the halls to keep the city peaceful. Kira, the commander of the guardians, was our protector. Without a mother, I supposed I would let Kira walk into that space where a mother would have been.

"Do you think he was angry with me?" I asked, as casually as I could.

Kira smiled. It spread no further than her lips. I could tell she was still annoyed that I'd tried to save the stranger's life. "I know you think you tried to do the right thing."

"Think?" I bristled a bit.

"Don't hold your body like that," Kira said. "It's petty. Own your disagreement. Strengthen your back and look me directly in the eye."

I looked at the years of responsibility and command etched

into the lines in her face, the heavy squint of her eyes. She
told us she came from the common streets. A street urchin,
a fighter. She'd shown me the knife scars on her arms from
brawls and duels. She knew the common ways, their desperation. She knew people.

I was still begging to be allowed to go and mingle with
them.

"The right thing for the citadel isn't always what's easy for
you," Kira continued. "Your father knows this. Anyone who
carries a musket has to come to know this as well."

"It doesn't feel good," I said.

"I'm here to help you navigate that," Kira said, reaching
forward to clasp my hands. "Do you trust me?"

"I do," I half lied to her, for the first time ever, looking right
into her eyes. Since she'd called for the stranger's death, I'd
felt uncomfortable around her. It had been so easy for her. She
hadn't hesitated, not even for a split second.

"Now we come to the reason I invited you here today. If
you do trust me, Lil, I need you to do something for me,"
Kira said.

"Anything!"

"Stop meddling with my guardians to go see the librarian."

I jerked away from her as if hit by a bucket of cold water. I
shouldn't have been surprised, as Kira eventually found everything out I'd ever tried to hide from her. It was just . . . I had
thought I'd managed to pull this one off.

Kira yanked me back by the hands, and my knees hit the
table. I gasped in pain as I panicked: What would she do if she
knew I'd shown the librarian writing? Or that he'd sketched
a map for me?

Or did she already know?

Thinking about that made the hair on my arms prickle.

"I—"

"Don't think to lie to me," Kira said evenly. "I command all the guardians, Lilith. They report to me anything that happens. I see all within my domain. Never forget that."

I was a fish caught on a hook, and there was nowhere to go. I wanted to throw up. Kira's grip made my hands numb. I waited to hear that she somehow knew what I'd been doing beyond just feeding the prisoner.

Ishmael.

"Being near that man is dangerous. He could warp your mind with his evil spells." She looked anguished. "I am not here to watch you slide into a darkness you can't come back from. There is no such thing as a little heresy. Just one printed word, read and then spoken, could doom you."

I stopped pulling against her as relief poured into me. She didn't know I'd seen a map or asked him to decipher the spell of words.

All my life, I'd thought Kira saw all and knew everything that happened in the citadel.

But she didn't know that I had asked Ishmael to read to me.

She didn't know that my father had a book hidden away below us.

She didn't know that the book's contents had built the citadel she protected.

I pulled my hands free and folded them across my chest. "He is condemned to die already. Aren't we called to be merciful to those in their last hours?"

Kira's face could have been carved out of smooth rock. "The guardians will provide that. Not you. You've been exposed enough. You will obey me on this."

I uncrossed my arms and forced myself to put my hands back on the table again. I was a musketress. A daughter.

She was *not* my mother.

Kira worked for my family.

For the citadel.

I savored that and let it roll around for a moment. But it dissolved as I recognized that she did have power over me. My father had given that to her.

Like when I faced Kira in the training room, I wouldn't win.

Kira saw the fight fade away in me.

"Good." She speared a piece of apple with a wooden skewer and held it up between us with a satisfied smile. I felt helpless against her. "No more of this then."

I bowed my head and agreed through clenched teeth. "No more."

Kira leaned back and nibbled at the apple slice. "The guardians have been told not to allow you anywhere near the cells. They will not talk to you. They will not accept gifts from you. If they do, they will be flogged. Pinet is still recovering. Your actions have consequences."

"Pinet?"

"That boy of a guardian whom you tricked and drugged," Kira said.

Poor guardian. He had such wide eyes whenever he saw me, and a little stutter.

"Do you understand?" Kira asked.

"I understand," I said.

"I hope so." Kira pushed her chair back and stood. "Enjoy the rest of the meal, Lilith."

I watched her walk away, her stride confident and long,

and a spark from my tightly clutched anger landed right in my mouth.

"Will you do it?" I asked.

"Do what?" Kira asked over her shoulder.

"Will you be the one to execute me for heresy if I keep talking to him?" I asked.

Kira stopped.

"Will you hang me?" I continued. "Or burn me alive? Or make me scream as you have me whipped from temple to temple?"

Kira turned to stare at me with squinted eyes, shocked and horrified at the defiance in my voice. "Has the sun burned your mind?"

I stood now, my back straight and strong, as Kira had taught me. I didn't know how to help Ishmael escape from his cell, but I couldn't just be cut off from him. "I know what's right. You can't stop me from going to see the man. And I will not be infected. I'm going to do what I can to help him before his end."

Kira walked slowly back toward me, slinking like a street dog about to pounce. "I've seen this defiance in many sons and daughters, but never you."

"Never me," I agreed. "Until this."

"You're going to risk a sin, ignoring not just my commands, but the gods. And you want me to let this go? Your father put your safety into my hands. I'm responsible for that."

"You've trained me," I said to Kira. "I'm safe now."

"If I trained you well enough, you wouldn't say these things." Kira reached the table. Her eyes had never left mine.

"You've taught me, pushed me, tested me, formed me," I told her. I raised the palms of my hands to her. "But you're not my mother. It was always my father's blood in these arms. That's the man you work for. Have you forgotten that?"

As her jaw clenched, I saw that I had stung her.

"I know exactly whom I serve. I stood at the front of a line of guardians when we fought the rock witch riots. I saw my own death in the eyes of the mob. Your father knows I serve the citadel, and that I serve Ninetha."

"When it comes to it," I whispered, "if you find out that Ninetha itself is built on heresy, what will you do? Burn the citadel down?"

Kira slapped me. Like the strike of a snake, it happened so fast that I saw only a blur, and then felt the hot sting.

"Don't blaspheme the city."

I trembled as the heat from the slap spread up the side of my face. "I've done everything you ask for so long. I've let you strike me in the training rooms, run me until I drop of exhaustion, and train, train, train. For the citadel."

"Yes, for the citadel."

"And during all that, I've loved you, I've feared you, I've wanted to be you." I stepped around the table. "But you are wrong about this. I will visit the heretic librarian and give comfort to the dying. Because the griots talk about sympathy, giving aid, and our duty to all living beings, not just prohibitions about reading."

"Do not put me in this position," Kira hissed.

"You put yourself there with your inflexibility." Kira could not see other paths. Too long in command, so things always had to go her way.

"If you weren't a musketress, I would have you dragged away." Kira shook her head. "We've let you stay too soft, I think, coddled by your birthright here inside the citadel. Now, you're leading yourself down a path that ends in pain and death. You risk everything. Your father himself cannot save you from the gods."

"I'm soft? You hit me with a staff every time I make a mistake!"

"To give you instincts that you would have been born with if you lived in the commons."

"A commons you refuse to let me walk around."

"For your safety!"

"Is my father soft and coddled?" I asked, and got the satisfaction of seeing Kira wince. Oh, I'd found something there. I could win this argument yet. "Would you put the Lord Musketeer to the whip if you found out he was walking down the cells to talk to the librarian?"

Kira frowned. "But he isn't. I would know."

"You think you know everything, but you don't. Kira, you can be wrong. You just can't imagine it."

"Understand, even if you run to your father to ask him about this, he will agree with me," Kira said. "You will not ever see that man Ishmael again. It is a fact you now must deal with. And if you even try to see him again, I will know. All the guardians in the citadel will be keeping an eye on you, specifically, and you will not be allowed anywhere but your rooms or in training."

The rage that came after that betrayal snapped through me like a lightning strike. "You cannot do this."

"I already have. If you so much as even try, I will know about it. I know everything that happens in the citadel. Sometimes even before it happens."

"You don't know everything that happens in the citadel. You're not as powerful as you think."

Kira smiled slightly. "What are you going to tell me? That Kame trades favors to get his favorite wines? Or do you want to educate me about the lovers your brothers and sisters snuck into their rooms? I know their names. I know their *friends'* names."

Those very secrets died on my lips. "I . . ." I had nothing.

"That's right," Kira patted me on the arm.

I yanked my hand back away from her. "I know that you have no idea what happens in the room my brothers and sisters guard."

Kira's lips parted as she studied me. "What do you *think* you know about that room?"

"Nothing," I lied quickly. The words had all just tumbled out, an attempt to score a hit on Kira. The way she looked at me now was the way a cat looked at a mouse.

"You're lying," Kira said, nodding with recognition as she studied my body language. "You think you know something I don't."

"It's not for you to know." My voice broke, and I realized my hands were shaking. The look in Kira's eyes scared me.

"Everything in the citadel is for me to know." Kira's voice sounded cold.

Nothing I could say now would be good. I had somehow gone from needling her, trying to find a path that got me what I wanted, to where I was now, standing on the edge of a horrible mistake. Maybe she knew what was in the room, and she was testing me. Or maybe this was something that she shouldn't know.

"Go on, tell me what you saw," Kira said.

"No," I said. "Stop staring at me like that. It doesn't matter what is in the room."

"Come, Lil. I have protected your father through so much. Things he never even had to tell me; I just took care of them. For a Lord, the rules can sometimes be different. Sometimes they have to do horrible things to keep a city safe."

A flood of relief burst through me. I wanted to throw my arms around her.

"You already know about the room?" I asked.

Everything started to make perfect sense. My siblings knew. My father would know. Kira had to know as well, right?

I felt as if I had grabbed the skin of childhood and started peeling it away from myself, emerging as something wiser, more educated about the truths of the world around me. "You're so pious, Kira. Is that just a false mask you hold to the world?"

Kira struggled with something, and then nodded. "Sometimes, we have to appear as something we're not to find a deeper truth." She smiled warmly at me over her soft words.

I was in on the big secret.

"You wouldn't really have killed the stranger, Kira." I was so relieved. "You let me take him to my father. You must have just been pretending. Father won't kill the librarian either; I can see that plainly. The room, the librarian, it all makes sense!"

"Of course," Kira said. Was that pride I heard in her voice? I couldn't tell. Whatever made her voice break like that, it was not something I'd ever heard before. "I've treated you like a child for so long, Lil, it's hard to remember that you're now a woman. I've been blind. We'll have to plan to let you go to the commons by yourself, won't we? Just like your brothers and sisters."

I straightened with excitement. "Finally?"

"You're old enough now. And I've trained you well. We'll

have no secrets between us from this moment. You and I are equals now. I'm no longer your guardian or your teacher. You can tell me, plainly, anything you want, and I will do the same. I won't pretend around you anymore."

"I never would have guessed you were pretending to be that pious about books all along," I said, marveling at it. "While all this time, Father had a book right here in the citadel."

Kira staggered back, her friendly, parental face wiped away by sheer shock. Her eyes widened, the clear whites of them standing out against her skin. I saw horror there, and fear. Utter fear.

"Kira?" I swallowed.

She couldn't speak. She took another step back from me, as if I'd turned into a snake.

"Child," she whispered. "Gods. Child. Oh gods, what has been done here?"

"No, no." I stepped around the table and Kira flinched. "You knew—"

She didn't, I realized, as she put a hand up to her forehead. I saw that her fingers shook. I'd never seen Kira's steady hands shake in all my life.

"Kira?" I wanted to pull my words back into my mouth. I'd been relieved to talk openly, and now I wanted nothing more in the world than to bury this secret again.

Kira staggered around to face her guardians. I stared at her back as she marched away from me.

"Kira, don't tell Father. You can't tell him," I shouted after her. It would destroy him to find out I had betrayed him. I ran after her. "Kira, what are you doing? We're equals. You pledged yourself to the citadel. Talk to me plainly, please!"

Kira stumbled away, and when she reached her guardians,

one of them grabbed her arm before she fell down the stairs. She leaned forward and put her forehead to his shoulder. I saw her body shake.

Was Kira, the commander, crying?

She gathered herself and pushed the guardians in my direction. I couldn't hear what she said, but they nodded and turned to face me. Fear rippled through me.

"Where are you going?" I shouted after her.

She didn't answer. She ran down the steps, leaving me with a growing sense of wrongness. I'd done something I couldn't undo. I'd thrown a night bucket out of the window without first looking down at the street below.

I couldn't breathe. My chest hurt. I wrapped my arms around myself and tried to ignore the two guardians at the top of the steps, who now looked at me warily.

What would my father do if Kira flew into the cornucopium to confront him about everything I'd said? Would they argue loudly? What would the communalists and advisors do? The guardians who ringed the room? Would my father have to have Kira cast out?

I'd kicked a wasp's nest.

I needed to explain my rash words to my father. If I didn't have a chance to present my side . . . I wasn't sure what the worst thing that could happen here was. I imagined Kira burning Father's book. Burning the history, the legacy that had built the citadel and Ninetha as we knew it.

She would do it. I could see it.

It would be my fault, and my family would despise me forever. And if we lost the recipe for the powder, what would we be? Not musketeers anymore. How could we protect the citadel? Or even Ninetha itself?

What had I done?

One of the guardians stepped forward as I reached the steps. "We cannot let you past."

"I'm the Lord Musketeer's daughter." I stopped before them, bewildered. "The citadel is my home."

They looked nervous, I thought. No, they looked scared. "Kira said you could not leave the roof."

"I am a musketress," I said coldly. "And I will pass."

Before they could think twice, I ran at them. They readied themselves to grab me, which I anticipated. At the last second I dropped and slid, like a spearbreaker running at a line of lowered lances. Just as Kira had taught me.

I slid on rough brick between the left guardian's legs, my head slapping against the hems of his robes, to his surprise, and I flailed as I tumbled down the stairs.

And then I stood up and ran toward the cornucopium to tell everyone that I'd done something very, very stupid.

My father wasn't there. But my brother Sinza, lean, with gray eyes and a few years older than me, leaned against one of the doors into the cornucopium. He had a cup of iced fruit in his hand. The god-machine loomed in spear shafts of sunlight behind him.

"Lil." He waved a spoon at me, a friendly smile on his face. "You should try this. It's *amazing*."

"Sinza, dogs are in the coop, and feathers are flying," I said. "I think I'm in a lot of trouble."

Sinza smiled even wider. "I can't imagine anything you could do that would match the time I—"

"I'm serious," I hissed.

"Okay." Sinza took a slow bite from the spoon and closed his eyes as he savored it. "What have you done?"

"I know you were protecting me from it; I know I wasn't supposed to know about what happens inside the room. But I accidentally told Kira."

The red-robed priests of the Nacji family faith said that confession cleansed the soul and quieted a troubled mind. Endu said they just used the confessions to control their houses with fear of revealed secrets. But I felt like I'd dropped a sack of vittle at Sinza's feet and could stand up straight again.

"Accidentally?" The cup and spoon clattered to the stone floor as Sinza grabbed my shoulders. "Lilith! What do you know about the room?"

"You're hurting me!"

Sinza looked around at the communalists in their notches, eyes closed, humming as they recited the petitions and needs of Ninetha to the cornucopia. "Quietly tell me everything you told Kira. Now."

"I saw the book. I let it slip out to Kira. She told me she knew about it, but I think she tricked me."

Sinza let go of me. "And that's it?"

"What else could there be?"

My brother suddenly looked much older, and his smile was so long gone from his face that I wondered where the gentle lover of all the delicacies that the cornucopia had to offer had gone.

"We need to go to the chambers and gather all the sons and daughters."

As he stalked out of the cornucopium, I ran after him, fear, regret, and shame roiling in me. "Sinza? I just wanted to upset Kira. I'm so sorry."

"This isn't your fault."

"It's very much my fault," I shouted as we ran down the

marble halls toward the chambers. Cornucopia globes on the walls cast yellow puddles of light on the floor, lighting our way through the daytime gloom. "Telling someone like Kira that Father has a book, it's like throwing fuel at a fire to put it out."

"Not everything that happens around here is about you," Sinza snapped.

He stopped and grabbed my arm. He stared at me with such intensity that I stepped back, startled.

"Sinza?"

"That room." He shook his head, breathing heavily. "That damned room. We kept you from it. We all did that for a reason. But we should have known you'd get curious about it. That's *our* fault, not yours."

There were no guardians at the chamber door when Sinza kicked it open and started shouting for everyone to come out. He grabbed a practice sword and beat the walls with it.

"It's the book, right?" I asked. "It's just the book?"

"Fuck the book. None of us cares about the book. But we should have prepared you for it. And told you to keep it from Kira."

"What's that about Kira?" Yusi asked, blearily stepping out of her room.

"Who's guarding the room right now?" Sinza asked.

Yusi looked at me, a question on her face.

"The *room*, Yusi," Sinza snapped.

"Endu and Thir."

"Sinza, what's happening?" I asked. What could be worse than a book and Kira's rage, I wondered.

Sinza pointed at me. "Lilith knows about the room. And she mentioned the book to Kira."

Yusi startled me with a smile. She woke up in that moment, fully, as if excited by something joyous. "Finally, it's happening?"

Sinza nodded.

Four more of my siblings staggered out into the lobby. Kame, holding a fine bottle of cornucopia red wine, wobbled in place. Then, he gave up and sat on one of the leathered couches.

"I love you, Lil," Yusi said as she glided over to me. I didn't like the look in her eyes. A jackal's glint, a predator happy to see something left out on the open plain. "But a secret never dies within you. It grows like a seed, until it bursts free of its container to show the world its strength. Many of us suspected this secret would flower someday."

"What happened?" Hetelia asked, joining Yusi.

Yusi stroked my hair, but I yanked back, unsure. My sister's joy frightened me. She felt like a stranger to me.

"We might have a rebellion. Knowing Kira, probably tonight," Yusi announced. Seven of us now milled about in the lobby.

"Kira found out?" Hetelia asked. "That's a good thing. She'll rip our father out of the citadel if she thinks he's a heretic."

"But she'll go further," Yusi said softly. "You know her. We were the ones guarding the room. She will come for us as well, as certain as the sun rises."

"She raised many of us," Hetelia protested. "She wouldn't—"

"She would." Sinza rubbed the back of his head and groaned. "Her faith is bedrock, and it comes before family, service, or who she loves. Think on it, truly think about her, and tell me I'm wrong."

Hetelia looked down at the floor. "Not having her on our side is a blow."

"That gods-damned book," Yusi said. "We couldn't have just tossed it out to the commons and told them Father was hiding it under the citadel?"

"'You shall not suffer a librarian to live,'" Hetelia said, in a mock-serious tone.

"We'll need to go talk to the guardians we've cultivated for our cause and get word to our friends at the bountiful houses," Sinza said.

I stepped between them all, horrified at what I'd heard. "What are you doing? What is this?"

"You weren't yet alive when the rock witch came out of the desert against the citadel," Yusi said.

"Her real name was Olivis," Sinza added. "We had a different commander of the guardians then. Nice man. At-Kol?"

"Ad-Kol," Hetelia corrected him.

"He died fighting in the riots." Hetelia moved over to the doors and looked out fearfully. "Kira rose to replace him."

"Olivis almost got into the citadel to kill us all," Sinza said. "She called us parasites, named Father a false leader, and I think she would have murdered us all if she could."

"What a nice story for our dear sister," Kame said from the floor. "Tell her how long it took for us to convince Olivis that we weren't her enemy, but would help from the inside if she rose against the citadel."

"If you hadn't taken so long to do it, maybe she would have caught Kira unprepared," Hetelia snapped.

"Well," Kame waved his bottle of wine. "Kira sure as all the hells is unprepared right now. But soon there'll be blood and crying once more. All because everyone in this room thinks that eventually, one day, we'll get out from under him. But the Lord Musketeer won the last time. He'll win again. You'll see."

Kame stood up with effort. He regarded everyone in the room with bloodshot eyes and drunken anger. "You should tell Lilith about our other secrets. The ones that you're so ashamed about, you can hardly look at each other."

"Kame!" Hetelia walked over and shoved him toward his room.

All my brothers and sisters had trickled out into the lobby, now, just as Kame returned to his room. "I won't fight that man from the shadows anymore," he announced. "I won't. I'm not a part of these games."

"I'm scared," I told Sinza. "I don't understand. What other secrets can you have?"

Everyone exchanged meaningful looks, and turned toward Sinza.

Sinza gently pulled me close and hugged me. "You know what it takes to have a child, right?"

"I'm not a baby," I said. "Forty days and forty nights."

Sinza nodded. "Right."

The gods were jealous, and fearful of our ability to multiply. So, their gifts came with a cost. The godly foods the holy machine gave us prevented us from having children.

To bear a child, a girl had to avoid the food of the cornucopia for forty days and forty nights. That's how long it took for the curse to fade. After thirty or so days, you bled, you became a woman, and then you could lay with a man, who had to also forsake the cornucopia, and then you could create a child together.

"Go into the wilderness with your lover. Cast yourself free of

*vittle, of medicine, and eat the wild berries. Live with the wild
beasts. Walk with the herders. Take only the fruit of the lands
around you, or eat merely the sands of the wastes. Then, you will
bear a child, or starve as you try."*

So said the griots.

"Have you ever seen our father forsake the fruits of the
cornucopia?" Sinza asked.

I shook my head.

"Nor have any of us," Yusi said.

"But I'm young," I said.

"We've never seen him do it," Sinza said. "And yet, the
youngest appear. With no mother—only the citadel's servants
to take care of us."

"We're not his children," Yusi said, her voice as cold as a
night wind from the world's rim. "And he's not who he seems.
He is a monstrous man, and if you stood guard at the room,
you would know it."

I thought about Sinza's gray eyes. No one else had that, or
his stringy hair and light sand-colored skin. We were all different sizes and heights, I realized, looking at each of my siblings,
with this revelation changing what I saw in front of me.

The world wavered. A murderous, invisible hand squeezed
my chest tight in its grip, and I started to fall. Sinza caught
me. "Hey, Lil, breathe. You have to breathe."

I shook in his hands. "Everything's falling apart," I told him.

I'd never been this confused and scared in all my life, I
thought, as someone put a cold rag on my forehead. I sat up.
Hetelia handed me some fruit juice. I drank it, then coughed
and spit it out, as it burned the top of my mouth.

"It's just a drink, to take the edge off," Hetelia said.

Still shocked, confused, and scared, I wiped my cheeks off

with a sleeve. I hadn't realized I'd been crying, but there the tears were.

"Father took us in. He gave us the citadel." I stared back at my angry brothers and sisters. "We wouldn't be what we are without him."

"That's for fucking sure," Sinza muttered.

I thought back to all the small disobediences and resentments against our father that had bubbled around the chambers over the years. Wasn't that normal, for children to chafe against their parents? Like I had chafed against Kira and set tonight's events in motion?

Screams and shouts bounced from wall to wall down the corridor toward us. I heard spears slap marble, and the floor shook with footsteps. I knew those barked commands. The sound of guardians readying a charge.

"Musketeers!" Yusi shouted.

The chamber filled with the scramble of my siblings running for their gear. I ran after Sinza. "Those are guardians!"

More screams came from past the door, nearer now.

"Guardian against guardian," I said, horrified, as I understood the meaning of the sounds. "You expected this. How could you plan this? Why—?"

"We didn't plan it; it would have happened eventually. You're not to blame, Lilith; it just got triggered early. If anyone like Kira found out about the book in the room, we knew it would trigger rebellion and fighting, just like it did when we convinced the rock witch it was safe to attack. We'll use the uprising as cover to push Father out. We'll negotiate with the rebels and take back our lives by promising them that *we* can give them a fairer Ninetha. It's the only way for us to be free of him. We can't run away: there's nowhere in Ninetha that he couldn't find us. And he'd get . . . angry. We must huddle in the citadel, plot, prepare, and wait."

I stared at this stranger, my brother Sinza, not able to understand how they had all become traitors. "I've never seen Father so much as lay a finger on any of us. He hardly ever even raises his voice."

Sinza shoved me toward my own room. "Just stay inside. Keep the door closed. Keep your musket aimed at the door, and unless it's a sibling calling for you, if it opens, you shoot."

I fought the confusion and fear ripping through me. I didn't understand how my whole world, so familiar and routine, could be blown away like sand on the wind.

"Is this how we defend the citadel?" I asked.

"No, little sister." Sinza kissed my forehead. "This is how we defend *ourselves*."

The chamber buzzed with an air of excited anticipation. A wall of long muskets bristled outside my door within a minute, and the demonic sulfur smell of black powder swirled around the air.

We had trained for this so often that my siblings' motions were automatic. They had smiles on their faces. How could they look forward to something like this?

Sinza slammed the door shut. I just stared at it for a whole minute, and then jumped like a startled dog as a musket fired. The sound shattered the buzz of voices outside.

I shuffled to the wall in shock and pulled my musket down.

"Hello, Alice," I whispered. I lay the long barrel on my shoulder, then I grabbed my bag of powder cartridges from the hook below the iron mounts.

Two muskets fired, one right after the other, and I jumped again.

I loaded Alice, the familiar movements giving me something to do. It relaxed me slightly. How many times had Kira drilled this into me?

"Rows, dammit!" I heard Yusi shout. "Stagger yourselves, and reload in sequence!"

I heard someone roll one of the barrels of gunpowder from the corner of the chamber, far from the cornucopia globes and heat, farther still from the incense burners or candles. When I was five, a barrel had exploded; it sounded like thunder. It punched a jagged, person-sized hole in the citadel's wall. Unimaginable power, and my brothers and sisters controlled it. Everything would soon be back to normal.

I wondered what happened to the ceramic vase of flowers that usually sat on top of the barrel.

Hours passed, and I could hear chaos in the far distance. Shouts, screams, and occasionally the pop of muskets. My back stiffened, and I let myself lean back against the bed. I cradled my musket against my chest and closed my eyes.

The door creaked open, and I woke up with a start. I whipped Alice about and fired. The smoke kicked into my face, and Kame ducked in after a second, his face twisted with surprise and a flash of anger.

"Gods, I'm lucky you can't aim for shit!"

"Kame!" I shouted. "I'm sorry!"

He scowled and came to sit next to me, sweeping his purple-and-gold-striped robes aside. The silk whispered across his skin, light and cheery against his deep brown.

"What happened? Where's your weapon?"

Kame snorted. "Only way to play the game is to play the game. Firing at people will not do us much good."

"Kame, I don't know what that means," I said, exasperated. "Where are our brothers and sisters?"

"They've moved on." Kame pulled a bottle out from under his robes. He fiddled with the cork a moment. "The game continues outside, as our brave siblings stand with loyal guardians against the rebels."

"And you drink yourself into oblivion to avoid everything."

"I'm winning," Kame said. He hugged me from the side, and our shoulders knocked against each other.

"I should be out there, protecting the citadel," I said.

"Oh, the citadel, our honor and heart." Kame laughed sarcastically. "Rally to it. Stand the line. Gather your powder and aim true, brothers and sisters. As you were taught and trained."

"Kira's words."

"Father's, too. He gave us the muskets. Made us the last line of defense."

"Yusi called him a monster." I struggled to my feet. I smoothed out my robes, slung my musket over my shoulder, and hung the powder bag with my cartridges on my belt. "He's only ever been kind and loving to me."

Kame looked up at me, his eyebrows arched slightly. The scrubby curls of hair on his chin shifted as he bit his lip. "Well, then I guess they must have been playing some horrible trick on you. Forget all about it and believe anything you want. It's easier that way."

"Kame . . ." I glared at him. But doubt blossomed in my mind. How many times as a child had I wondered who my real mother was, when Kira beat me in training and lessons?

When I asked about it, my father and Kira would tell me only that "she is not here anymore."

A scream died somewhere deep inside me. Why had the world turned inside out on me? Why had I done to deserve all this?

Kame put his bottle down and stood up. "What are we, if not his children?"

I didn't like how the smile had melted away from his face. Or how tight the corners of his eyes became.

"Kame . . ."

"You're smart, Lilith," he growled. "Don't flinch from this. You've lived in the citadel since you could walk."

"I've never been harmed by him," I said again, and my words sounded frailer than the glass of his wine bottle.

"Just because someone has only ever shown you kindness doesn't mean they aren't a monster to someone else," Kame said. "I'll tell you what the musketeers really are: we are his harem."

"No," I said.

In the distance, muskets fired. The screaming came from the streets outside the citadel. Far away from the chamber.

I tried to focus on that, to push away Kame's words.

"That can't be true. He's never—"

"We're another delight in our Lord's citadel of pleasures," Kame said, looking down the neck of his jug.

"He calls me *daughter*," I said.

"He calls me *son*," Kame said, turning back to pick up his wine. "You would have been initiated in a year. That's the age when he came for Yusi. We kept you from the room. We tried to hide you from him, give you to Kira, train you, put you out of sight. The book is the least of his sins."

I grabbed his bottle and threw it against the wall. Wine exploded across my tapestries. "You lie."

Kame looked at the wall sadly. "I always thought the other siblings coddled you. They were broken in their own ways, and who was I to say they were wrong? If it gave them peace, I played along, to keep them quiet. I know how to indulge and soothe my own pains. But now they lash outward, with plans to depose the 'great tyrant.' And who will rise in his place, Lil? What becomes of us, and our wines, and our iced fruits, and our medicine, when someone takes the citadel away?"

"Kame, you're scaring me."

"Good," he shouted at me. "Because it's time to grow the fuck up. Because if I were you, I wouldn't rise against the Lord Musketeer. He likes you. Maybe he'll choose you to go into the wilderness with, and you'll become a queen. Maybe he'll just hand you the citadel. You are the youngest, and the last of the musketeers he chose."

"Why are you saying such horrible things?" I slapped him, and I wept.

Kame took it with evenness, and bowed elaborately to me. "Maybe I'm wrong, Musketress. You obviously have all the world figured out."

"Damn you, Kame!" I staggered away from him and cracked open the doors onto my balcony. The wave of grief threatened to drown me. I couldn't breathe.

Down below, people were running, screaming in pain. I heard shouts from farther away, voices that I thought I recognized.

Then, I heard a voice outside that I knew very, very well.

"The citadel protects the cornucopia!" Kira shouted out on the street below my balcony. "But in the commons, you've heard the griots tell us the old gods gave it as a gift for all. Until they came to build a wall around it!"

Kame raised an eyebrow. "That doesn't sound good."

"It looks like all of Ninetha out there," I said, forgetting my rage at him. Hundreds of people marched through the street that curved all around the citadel. Not just guardians in their green robes, but commons folk in dun-colored rags and robes, cudgels and knives in their hands. The sound of the crowd's fury made the hair on the back of my neck rise.

Kira's voice bounced off the walls of the bountiful houses nearby. "Those walls must fall. The citadel must crumble. The gifts of the old gods belong to all who follow the contract!"

The people screamed back at her, an animal howl built of fury and excitement and fervor.

As Kame boozily peered outside, he said, "Well, I don't think that us musketeers will be able to shoot the entire city, do you?" As he moved to leave, he delicately picked his way around the shards of shattered glass on my floor.

"What are you doing?" I asked, my voice small against the roar of the crowds outside.

"I'm off to meet whoever wins," Kame said. He stopped in the chamber outside our rooms to pull a fresh bottle of wine from a crystal bucket full of melted ice. "I've spent my life showing that my only true love is sweet, red, and contained under a cork. Kira knows I am no threat, and the Lord Musketeer knows I'm a drunk. All the bountiful houses know it, and so do most of the commons."

"Who are we fighting for, or against?" I asked him, hearing the pop of muskets again.

"Who knows? Kira has some clear ideas. Our brothers and

sisters have schemes. But it's all falling apart. They started this morning thinking it was the guardians versus Father. Now it's the commons versus . . . whoever."

He staggered his way down the hall toward the sound of battle.

"What should I do?" I called after him.

"How the fuck should I know?" Kame replied, pulling at the wide cork and swearing as his fingernails slipped over it.

The fight fell back from the doors to the citadel, and dying guardians screamed as the crowd washed over them. Ninethan fought Ninethan, blood running down their robes to spill on the floor.

I saw women chop kitchen maids in the back with cleavers as they begged for mercy. I saw bountiful men scrabbling against commons folk, their faces like feral dogs as they snapped at each other. I saw guardians fall back in formation, spears bristling forward like thorn bushes.

Other guardians shoved against them in equally tight formations of green as Kira urged them on.

I didn't know that death could be so personal.

The screams etched themselves so deep into me. The scars, I knew instinctively, would never heal.

I ran toward the heart and center of the citadel, the cornucopium. I could hear the fighting moving closer and closer to it. And I knew my father would be there, where the gold muskets hung on the wall.

From the second floor of the cornucopium, I could look down at the god-machine and the communalists gathered nervously around it. My father stood with families from the bountiful houses, guardians, and several of my brothers and sisters, who must have changed whom they were fighting as they realized this had spun out of control into something worse than they had planned for.

Temple guards from all the colors of bountiful houses stood in the corridors leading into the cornucopium, all with their swords or spears out.

All of this was my fault.

I'd told Kira about the book. And I'd done that because I wanted to save a stranger from a horrific death.

All I'd had to do was stand back, keep my mouth shut, and let the world pass on as it had planned. Let the more powerful than I do what they wanted.

Why couldn't I have just let one person die?

You shall not suffer a librarian to live. Well, it seemed that the gods would have their blood, one way or another.

"Urik!" Kira shouted, using my father's name. It made me shiver to hear it so casual on her tongue. No one used his name, as if they were calling out a friend. He was the Lord Musketeer, or Father. Not Urik.

"Urik of the Inichuktalla," Kira called out. "I have your sons, and I have your book."

My father had taken the gold muskets down from the wall. One of his most trusted from the bountiful houses stood next to him with powder cartridges in a polished wooden box with brass latches.

I shivered. He didn't look like a monster. Just the man who picked me up to his shoulder and rubbed his beard against my face while I laughed and asked him to stop. The man whose hand I held. Surely, he was our father, and the things my brothers and sisters said weren't true.

"You were literate all this time, you liar," Kira shouted.

I couldn't see Kira from this side of the gallery, so I started to walk counterclockwise alongside the marble balustrades while looking down at the floor.

"Kira," my father said coldly, not giving her a last name. But then, Kira came from the commons and had no lineage. He'd found her in the guardians, a scrappy recruit with nothing but zeal and belief fueling her.

A flaming mess of paper flew through the doorway and into the cornucopium. It splattered against the floor, burning pages flying up into the air over the startled communalists.

Our family book.

"You held yourself and your family up as the protectors of the holy bounty," Kira said.

I could see her now. She stood in front of her guardians, a wall of green and seriousness, their spears piercing the air around and above her. And farther down the hall, the grimy commons folk milled behind them.

Kira's face quivered with a rage that I couldn't quite place for a second, until I recognized it as betrayal. It was not just hatred but sadness that showed in her damp eyes.

"Surrender," Kira said, "and I will give you an easy death."

For an answer, my father fired a golden musket. The sound of it cracked and echoed throughout the cornucopium. Blood splattered the guardians' faces behind Kira, and she dropped to her knees.

"Ahead!" she screamed, her face distorted by rage. She clutched her shoulder, where blood leaked through her fingers, and one of her guardians dropped his spear to grab her.

She disappeared behind the wall of implacable guardians, whose robes kicked up into the air as they charged their enemies—the bountiful folk and their loyal guardians surrounding the Lord Musketeer.

Spears clattered against spears, and then found skin.

The screaming I'd heard earlier started again. Men were being pierced by metal, feet and bodies straining to push back against the mass that was shoving against them.

I wasn't sure where to go, or what to do. I could shoot into the throng, but what would that accomplish?

Nonetheless, I'd been trained as a musketeer.

I got to a knee and opened the powder bag to pull out a cartridge. I bit, spat, and began the process of loading.

Seconds later I stood back up, with Alice ready to fire in my hands, and I saw Kira's forces break through the defenders.

My father fired into the crowd, and the nearest guardian fell. Then, the next reached him, a sword flashed, and the Lord Musketeer of Ninetha disappeared under the mob of commons folk who surged in.

I ran.

Rebel guardians ran up the stairs after me, and I turned to run the other direction. But spears blocked my way.

The citadel was overrun by our enemies.

I had one shot.

I looked down the barrel at my nearest foe, a tall man with scarred hands and a butcher's apron. His locks were pinned back with a hand-stitched ribbon, delicately embroidered. Made by a wife, or a daughter.

I lowered my musket, and callused hands ripped it away from me, beat me, ripped at my robes, then dragged me off down the obsidian and marble tiles.

For a moment, I thought I tasted death. But guardians beat the common folk away and took me to a cell, where they stood guard as the chaos raged through the citadel.

"Hello?" said the prisoner in the room next to me after a

moment. "Hello? Who's there?"

"Ishmael." I recognized the voice.

"Lilith. What's happening?"

"It's the end of the world, librarian," I told him, and I curled up on the hard, wooden bench on the far wall.

He kept trying to talk to me, but I closed my eyes and tried as hard as I could to make everything go away.

Someone tapped softly at the door to the cell.

I limped away it as it squealed open, and I shivered, expecting a mob to come in and seize me, but only Kame stood in the light of the cornucopia globes, with a stupid grin on his face.

"Hey, little sister," he said. "You're alive!"

"Kame!" I wobbled over to him and squeezed him with the strongest hug. I ached all over. I suspected I had a broken rib, as it hurt to breathe too hard, but I wrapped my arms around him anyway, glad to see a friendly face. "They got you, too?"

"Shhhh," he whispered. "No, I have found a way for us to flee Ninetha. I thought I'd spring you out with me!"

"Flee Ninetha?" Shocked, I let go of Kame and looked up at him.

His grin faded. "Lil, everyone's dead. Do you understand? Everyone."

"What?" I couldn't handle the words. They struck me, but my mind didn't want to let them stick.

"They're even executing people who served us, Lil. Hanging them from the cornucopium's walls. The floors are a pool of blood; you can barely breathe in there. They were torn apart by the mobs, or killed by guardians loyal to Kira."

Every word hit me hard. I felt like I could fall apart, like a sand-ant nest in a high wind. I could waft off into tiny particles, swept away, because I couldn't find the will to even stand.

I took a deep breath. "Father?"

Kame winced. "The Lord Musketeer is dead. There is nothing you can do for him."

I shook my head. "No."

Kame stared right through me. "I saw him."

"Anwago?" I could see his concerned eyes, my rock, my calm older brother who whispered lessons in my ear about which communalist was most loyal to my father, and which bountiful house we needed to ignore for displeasing our family.

"Dead. They hung him in the corridor."

"Gods. Yusi?"

Kame sighed and shook his head.

"Endu—"

"Dead, all dead. Sinza—run through by seven spears. Hetelia—dragged off and stabbed. Ume was thrown from a balcony and then trampled. Song speared through. Yamie, he took so many out, but they got a rope on him and strangled him, I hear. Vikkor tried to run, and they chased him down. Thir locked himself in a bathroom, and they set it on fire. Zo, I don't want talk about. They're all dead."

Every name had struck me like a fist to the stomach. My face felt numb, and my arms felt so far away I couldn't imagine using them again. I wobbled.

"But if they killed everyone," I hissed as hot tears ran down my cheeks, "then how in all the hells are you free and walking about?"

"Pearl," Kame said. "I'm free because of Pearl."

"What's Pearl?"

"I'm Pearl," hissed a voice from by the door. "And we don't have time for little conversations. We need to go. We need to be on our way before any other of Kira's guardians come."

I looked past Kame and saw a thin woman with her hair braided back with gold snaplets, and thin purple silks draped over her shoulder in the style of a Venkamist, although she didn't wear them comfortably. It was a disguise. The Venkamists were the most pious of the old bountiful houses.

"Pearl joined Kira when she saw the direction of the fight; she even pledged her own personal guards. She's a close friend of mine."

"Kira lives?"

"Oh, yes." Kame shuddered.

"You said she would know your only allegiance was wine."

"My plan failed. She just hangs anyone she's suspicious of, I'm told. I thought I would hide with Pearl. We, uh, share indulgences I didn't believe Kira would stand for, so I knew Pearl had only pretended to ally with the new rulers. She doesn't care who's lord of the citadel, as long as her lifestyle is not affected."

"But that bitch is talking about breaking the bountiful houses apart, casting the petitioners out, and letting chaos be the road to the cornucopia," Pearl said.

"You must swear to Pearl that we will flee into the wastes." Kame put a brotherly hand around my shoulders. He was serious now, no forced jolliness. "And swear to her that we will come back with powder, and musketeers, and that you will retake the citadel, and you will restore the bountiful houses to their station. Do this, and she'll help us."

"You swore this?" I asked Kame. Then, I lowered my voice so that Pearl couldn't hear me. "Kira burned the book. I don't know how to make powder."

"But you have copies of the pages," Kame said, raising an eyebrow conspiratorially.

I was shocked. "How do you know?"

"Why else would you go to see the librarian? Kira complained about it to Father." Kame tapped my head and leaned closer. "I know you, little sister. I know you well. You can't read, but you know about the book, and you kept visiting the cells. I searched your room for it, but I can't find anything. Where is it?"

"Why were you searching for it?" I looked suspiciously at Pearl, who stood in the doorway. With everything changing so fast, knowing Kame and his wine, could I really trust him?

I felt instantly horrible for thinking the worst of my own brother. But they had called my father a monster. Kira had turned against us. Ninetha had turned against us.

I did not know as much about the world as I had thought.

Kame's smile faded, and he said softly, "I see you're thinking down the right path. I'm sorry your mind has to be like this now."

"And what path is that?" I hissed.

Kame laughed, no shame in his eyes. "You're right. I did think I could use the copies you made to gain favor with Kira. To show my own zeal."

I pulled away from him and pushed his hands away. "I give you that paper now, and then what happens?"

Kame sighed. "I see the fear in you, and I'm sorry."

"Do you blame me?"

"Do you blame *me*?" Kame countered.

"Yes," I said.

"If the page copies are not in your room, I guess you have them on you, right?"

I stared at my brother, and he at me, until I looked down at my sandals. "I will gouge your eyes out before you can try to take them from me. And I'm not a drunk like you. I've been training every day of my life."

"That's fair. But you're trapped in a cell as Kira seizes the rest of the citadel." Kame's voice broke slightly, and I could see for the first time that despite all the smiles and jokes, he was as terrified as I was. "You can stay here until Kira turns her attention back to you, or you can come with me."

"He's right," Pearl said. "We need to leave!"

Kame swept his hands out. "Little sister?"

"You swore yourself to her?" I asked.

Pearl couldn't see Kame, since he faced me, so she didn't see him roll his eyes at me in frustration. "Of course, I swore it. We will avenge our lord and father, and we will destroy Kira for violating the citadel. Swear it also."

"I swear on my life that I will come back with musketeers and retake the citadel," I promised. "I swear the bountiful houses will take their position again. I swear that Ninetha will have order."

"Good enough for me," Pearl said quickly. "Now come."

Kame looped an arm under mine.

"Wait," I murmured. "Wait."

"What now?" Kame asked, tugging me along.

"The librarian," I said.

"Fuck the librarian," Kame said.

"He can read," I said, loud enough for Pearl to hear. "I can't. Can you?"

And who else had survived the wastes? Ishmael knew the other cities out beyond our walls. We needed that knowledge.

Kame looked over at Pearl, who looked down the hallway, then back. She nodded. "Take the librarian."

"And we have to get our other brothers and sisters," I said to Kame.

Kame cocked his head. "Lilith? I told you they were dead. I didn't lie."

He helped me out through the door as I numbly considered his words. Yes, he had said that. I remembered it. It had slipped away from me.

"It doesn't seem real," I wailed. The world swam about me, and I had to grab at the wall.

"By the gods, hush yourself." Pearl looked back at me, fear quite clear on her face. She unlocked the librarian's door and yanked it open. Ishmael stepped cautiously out, his gaunt frame silhouetted in globe light. His eyes softened when he recognized me.

"Lilith," he said.

"Ishmael." I raised a hand in greeting.

"Are you well?"

I limped forward. "No, Ishmael. I am not well. But thank you for asking."

"Are they here to kill us?" Ishmael nodded at Pearl, Kame, and the two bodyguards.

"No," I said. "At least, I don't think so."

Pearl had some slightly grubby guardian's robes, which Kame and I pulled on.

"You look like you spent the day fighting in the streets," Pearl said, looking us over. "You, though, prisoner, are a problem. Kavin, strip and give him your robe."

The bodyguard she pointed to sighed, and Pearl snapped her fingers. He grudgingly pulled off his thicker, purple robes and handed them to Ishmael.

"Here," Pearl said, laying some of her own purple silk

around his neck and knotting it. "House Venkam's been tying these on their necks because they're out of robes for the fighters they hired to help Kira. They've felt pushed out toward the commons for long enough, so they saw an opportunity. But Venkamists aren't the only people with some purple wardrobe items, thankfully for us. There you go; Kavin, quit pouting. I've always taken good care of you."

"Thank you," Ishmael said softly.

"Stay on either side of me. You are now my bodyguards. Do look the part, or we'll all be killed. Kavin, Lika, go break stuff in the cornucopium and have fun. When you're bored, head back home. I'll meet you there."

The two bodyguards took off, grinning, which unsettled me. It was the end of my world, but they were having fun.

"Let's go," Pearl ordered. She walked out of the small corridor as if she owned the citadel, and we matched her on either side, with Ishmael at the rear.

We skulked down the corridors. We'd straighten and stiffen our backs, acting the roles of Pearl's personal guards when we were spotted by guardians or random commons folk in rags. Chaos reigned, though, and we were ignored. Too many looters and people wandering around, staring at the murals and the pure-white walls.

Kame suggested that a less-trafficked way out of the citadel would be the kitchen. It was now bare, ripped clean of anything that could be picked up. Not a single pot or table remained.

Someone smashed a clay jar in a nearby storage room and laughed wickedly, and both Kame and I flinched. But we kept moving.

Outside, in the gloom of night, we moved through the tight

rows of bountiful houses, our way lit by the distant flicker of a temple on fire.

"Is that the House of Anda?" Kame asked.

Pearl nodded. "They barred their doors and fought, so Kira's guardians threw bottles of oil with burning rags over the walls."

Distant screams occasionally pierced the air above the houses. Each time, I reached out to squeeze Kame's hand as he helped me along.

The walking, while painful, started to stretch out my beaten muscles. My ribs still hurt, every breath seared my side, but my legs found a rhythm.

Pearl stopped us near the boundary to the Afriq road, where one of her men waited against a wall, with supplies wrapped in a gray wool blanket by his sandals. "Now, we change."

I pulled on a stained and muddy commons cape and heavy leather boots, and grabbed a herder's stick. Kame rubbed mud on my face to disguise me, and I returned the favor. Ishmael shrugged off his heavy purple robe and rubbed dirt into his clothes.

"Here." Pearl handed me another long stick wrapped in cheap burlap, tied up with coarse husk rope so that I could carry it on my back.

"I already have a walking stick," I said.

"It's a musket," Pearl said. "From the training rooms. It's not yours, but it fires. Kame, I have one for you as well."

Crowds celebrated in the public squares between the three- and four-floor-high tenements of mud brick. Some of the structures had slumped over after builders had made them too high. Fires burned everywhere—some in the middle of streets, where people had dragged trash out to light on fire. Musicians played horns that cracked the night, and drunk revelers offered us barley wine in ceramic cups as they staggered past.

"It's a new day in Ninetha," a man shouted at me as I tried to hide my trembling hands. "You won't have to goat-herd anymore, friend. We'll have access to the cornucopia, as the gods intended!"

"We will drink chilled ambrosias!" a woman at the fire behind him screeched.

"And eat chocolate!"

All those savage, angry faces—underlit by fire—cheered. They all celebrated the deaths of my sisters and brothers so easily. I couldn't help but hate them.

"How could Kira do this?"

I'd tried to grapple with this in the cell, but I could hardly face it. How long had she been waiting to pull down the citadel, while teaching me how to live, fight, and protect it? Some part of me had expected that Kira would come down to the cell and let me go and that she would have an explanation that made all of this make sense.

I'd pledged to come back with muskets and powder, as Pearl wanted. I'd said it to save my life.

But now, it took hold of me, as I thought about everything Kira had taken from me. My brothers and sisters, murdered. My father. The citadel.

Everything.

She'd taken it from me in an instant because of her hatred of books. No mercy, no explanation. Just instant, feral murder.

"Never hint at the punch that's coming," she said, when throwing me off my feet while we trained.

I hadn't seen it coming. But I had seen how she believed

in killing when she'd looked at the librarian. I just could never have imagined it directed at me.

That fucking backstabber. She'd sworn to protect the citadel, and now it was being looted.

I would come back. I would come back smelling of sulfur, steel in my hand, ready to blast every murdering traitor clean of Ninetha.

Oh, my poor family.

My knees buckled, and Kame noticed me stumble.

"Hah. I think she's already been to the citadel for some strong drink!" One of the celebrators clapped his hands and giggled loudly. I glared at him, but Kame stepped in between the crowd and me as he held a hand up in the air at them.

"We've had far too much and are headed back to sleep it off with our cousins," Kame said, his voice so easily light and merry I hated him as well.

He pulled me up straight and walked close beside me. "Don't draw attention," he growled from the side of his mouth.

"They're cheering their deaths. Endu, Yusi—"

Kame slammed his elbow into my side. "Don't say their damned names here!"

I gasped as the pain shot through my side and dizzied me. I couldn't breathe or talk for long seconds as we walked on.

"Sorry," Kame said, as I wheezed on.

I had nothing to say to him.

The Afriq Gate loomed ahead. The flash of green against the walls warned us that guardians stood watch.

"And here is where I must leave you," Pearl said. "I can't get you past the walls. I do know this is where they have the fewest on guard."

Kame let go of me and walked over to her. "Pearl . . ."

"I don't need your gratitude," Pearl said coldly.

"My gratitude is my own to do what I want with." Kame grasped her forearms and kissed her cheek. "Here it is, whether you want it or not. I know this wasn't just self-interest. It's too risky."

"My family has always known a good investment," Pearl said with a small smile.

I realized that she didn't really expect us to come back. It was something she'd said to convince herself to help Kame, a friend. A true friend.

She was going to be shocked when I came back with an army at my back. I made a vow to myself, there in the dark, with the commons celebrating the destruction of my family.

"I'm a drunk and a fiend," Kame whispered back to her. "You know exactly how useless I am. Gods, you've said it often enough."

"And since when have you ever listened to me?"

"You'll miss me," Kame said.

"Not as much as you think. I need to save what wine I have left in my cellars; there's a new ruler, and I don't think the communalists will have time to make me any more, with Kira as the Lord of all Ninetha." Pearl turned away from us all and headed back toward the bountiful houses as I considered her words.

Kira as the Lord of all Ninetha.

Just like that.

Kame stood in place and watched her fade away into the shadows, until I yanked at his cape. "We should go!"

"I know."

We slunk toward the gate, and after a few steps, Kame passed me and the librarian.

"Slouch as if the world weighs heavy on you," Kame said, now leading the way forward. "That's how they look in the commons."

The guardians at the gate looked over at us as we approached.

Ishmael spoke for the first time since we'd left the citadel. His breath sounded thin. "Why are there even walls? I've never seen walls around a city in all my travels."

"Never?" I asked.

"Never," Ishmael said. "There's nothing but the wastes out there. Is there something out there I should worry about? What do the walls stop from coming in?"

I shook my head. The wastes held nothing that I knew of, or that Kira had trained me for. "The things you need to worry about are inside the walls. They're to keep things in."

That's why the guardians at the wall faced inward toward Ninetha. What did it take for people to bear children? Forty days in the wilderness. Not everyone could be allowed to leave. Ninetha groaned under the weight of its commons already, always shoving against its mud-brick walls. The walls kept Ninetha from breeding even faster than the communalists could ask for vittle to shovel into the barrels that were dragged out to the distribution squares.

If the guards didn't stand on the walls, the commons would spread out farther, and then the real starvation would start. Not just the unpleasantness of getting by on the constant dreariness of vittle every day, sustenance poured by guardians into the hands of the unfortunate. People would starve until they were just walking skeletons, Father had once said.

"What kind of people would we be," he had asked me, "if we let that happen?"

When Father was young, he'd let the commons eat nothing but food from their own gardens and the meat of animals. Without the cornucopia's blessings, they lived as if in the wild, for far more than forty days and forty nights.

"They are like rabbits if not tended to," Father had told me. "That is why leaders must be careful of the commons folk."

He'd said that while Kira looked proudly on from where she stood under the golden muskets. Had she dreamed about murdering him even back then?

The three guardians on the road under the Afriq Gate raised their hands. Their spears leaned against the inside of the stone arch that curved over their heads. More guardians stood on the small parapets built out from the wall. They were looking over at the dancing women in a nearby courtyard of packed dirt that opened onto the road.

"Who are you?" the nearest guardian asked. His gray beard jostled in the warm wind.

"I am Jerit," Kame said. "This is my brother Ishmael, and his daughter, Iva."

"And where do you think you are going?" the guardian asked.

The two other guardians behind him moved over to their spears, and my heart sped up. They didn't look hostile, just careful. But as they moved closer to the wall for their spears, they opened up more space between them. Space we could run through.

"We're headed for our herds," Kame said. "Where else would we go?"

"No one leaves or enters tonight," the guardian said. "Go back to the commons and find a fire. Dance the night away, celebrate. A new day will come tomorrow."

"The celebrating wore us out," Kame shook his head somberly. "We just need to get back to our animals and make sure they're well."

Herders and foragers, hunters and tree farmers in the plots outside jammed up against the walls, they could all leave Ninetha. Their extra food supplemented the cornucopia's bounty, and helped the rest of the city survive on more than just vittle, even though Father had reduced the amounts. Kame and Pearl had planned our escape around this, but it looked like Kira had thought about all the people who would try to leave Ninetha.

Including us.

"The goats'll keep for a night," the guardian said. "Tomorrow, they'll all be close to where you left them. So turn around, join in the reveling."

Kame stood between the guards. I could see him search for a word, a phrase, something that could talk the guardians into letting us through.

"I don't think," he finally said, "that the goats will be able to, uh, find their way back home if we aren't there to help them."

The guardian tilted his head and frowned. "You really don't know much about goats, do you?" For a moment we all stood there and stared at each other, until the old guardian held out a hand and shouted, "My spear!"

"Run!" Kame shouted, and grabbed my hand.

I ran through the gate out into the wastes, my legs reaching as far as they could with each stride. My side burned, my lungs heaved, and bramble ripped at me from the dark, while Ishmael and Kame pulled me along so hard that my shoulder popped. A spear hit a rock to my right and clattered.

The farther we ran from the gate, the darker it got, and the more we stumbled over the gnarled scrub and rocks. I could hear spears hit the dirt nearby with soft thuds, but I couldn't see them.

Kame stumbled and jabbed an elbow hard into my back.

"Kame, dammit!" I yelled as he tripped me. I smacked into the gray dirt. I coughed and spat the earth out of my mouth as I sat back up.

"Lil . . ."

"That hurt!" I said. My ribs creaked with every breath. A sharp point had jabbed at the side of my hip when Kame fell. I patted at it and felt blood down the side of my leg. "What the hell, Kame?"

"Sorry," he said. The wet-sounding cough of his voice scared me.

"Kame?" I crawled over to him, my eyes only now fully adjusting to the dark. "Kame? Kame, what's wrong?"

A spear slapped into the dirt several feet away, and I flinched.

"Shit," Ishmael hissed. He dropped low to the ground. "They're still throwing spears at us."

Kame lay on his side. I could see the long shaft of a spear on the ground behind him. Where was the point?

"Kame, Kame," I repeated my brother's name in a panic as he pulled me closer. I ran my fingers down his side, my hands shaking because I didn't want to find what I found next: the metal spear point that had gone right through him and then grazed my hip.

"I'm sorry," Kame said again.

The spear had hit him at an angle as it dropped out of the sky.

"What do I do?" I asked him, panicked. "Kame, what do I do?"

"Sorry," he repeated.

"Stop fucking saying that," I yelled from between my teeth as another spear struck the ground near us. The guardians clearly had a general idea where we'd run to and were throwing spears at us, but they were not coming out into the dark after us.

Yet.

Ishmael pulled himself over to us. "What happened?"

"Spear."

The librarian moved around to Kame's back. I saw his shoulders slump under the silhouette of the cape as he kneeled to examine the spear. "Lilith—"

I could hear from the tone of his voice that he knew it was bad.

"Break it off," I told him. I'd heard stories from Kira about how she had done this in the rock witch riot so she could carry wounded guardians back to the citadel.

"Do you know any medicine?" Ishmael asked.

"Break the shaft as close as you can to his back, so that he can walk, but don't try to take it out." I ripped at my cape, trying to make long strips. We couldn't beg a communalist to ask for a miracle from the cornucopia. We were on our own.

A spear slammed so close to us that the dirt hit Kame's feet. Hot tears dripped from my chin as I held the cloth around the spear tip.

"Don't scream," Ishmael said, and then stood up. He put a foot under the spear, near Kame's back, and then kicked down with his other foot.

Kame groaned between clenched teeth, bottling the scream that wanted to break out.

The kick only splintered the shaft; it took Ishmael three more tries until it broke free.

"You have to run with us, Kame," I said, as I bound up his bleeding wounds in figure eights, using the spear's shaft as a hitch.

"I don't know if I can," he whispered.

"You can," I said, and willed him the strength in my words. "I know you can."

"Gods, I could use a drink to take the edge off this," he said.

"I know a place." The words tumbled out from me. "I know a place where I can get you a drink and someone to look at you. You just have to keep going."

Back at the Afriq Gate, I could see the glow of torches being handed out to the guardians.

"We must go now," I said.

We pulled Kame to his feet. He whimpered. It sounded so pathetic that my heart skipped a beat. My ribs hurt so badly, I wanted to faint from the pain. Blood continued to drip down my leg, and my robes slapped wet against my skin.

I looked up at the stars and constellations that Kira had taught me during wilderness training. "This way," I guided us.

My eyes had adjusted to the night. The great belt of the Milky Way above us lit the wastes just enough that I could see the way to lead us toward a herding path I'd run on before with Kira. The torches behind us bobbed this way and that, but they were falling farther behind. The guardians couldn't see us, so they were crisscrossing about while we made progress in a straight, but slow, line.

We'd escaped.

As we walked, I tried to find the confidence within me that

I had faked just minutes ago when I'd told Ishmael and Kame that I knew where to go next. But the truth was, I felt like a broken, hunted animal trying to paw its way toward a hole to hide in.

TWO

THE RIM OF THE WORLD

I always found it strange that, despite the heat of the sands and the fierce sun, I shivered as night gave way to the early amber of morning's arrival. I wrapped my commons cape tight to my body as I watched Ishmael come over the herding path.

He'd changed clothes. He wore a brown hide jacket that hung to his calves. It had a slight cape on the shoulders and large, polished-bone buttons on the front. The edges of his wide-brimmed hat kicked slightly in the wind, and the flasks that were strapped to the sides of a traveler's sack on his back clanked as he moved.

He picked his way across the grooves in the dirt, new boots digging into the ground.

"I thought you'd just leave," I said, as relief washed over me.

"I said I would be back to help you."

"Not everyone in my life has been who I thought they were," I said.

Last night, after we'd banged on the door of a stone hut to wake up the confused, bleary-eyed shepherdess inside, Ishmael had grabbed my hand and told me he had to go back out into the night. He said that before he'd approached Ninetha, he had buried his traveling possessions in the hard ground, by a tree outside the Afriq Gate.

Ishmael wasn't my family. The librarian owed me nothing. My hands were wet with Kame's blood as he lay on the floor, slowly dying, so I had more important things to think about. I'd just nodded and said, "Goodbye." I'd assumed I would never see him again.

He'd said he would be back, though.

And here he was.

Ishmael looked back toward the hut. "Kame didn't make it through the night."

"No."

For a long moment, I listened to the wind. Steel grass in the cracks between the stones danced and whipped about. I blinked out the grit that constantly stung my face.

"I'm sorry," Ishmael said.

I wiped at the corner of my eye and didn't say anything.

I followed Ishmael in, where we each took one side of the canvas that wrapped my brother's body. We walked past the shepherdess, whom we had tied to the end of her own bed, and out into the morning sun.

I spread Kame's body out on a sky frame that I'd built in a nearby ravine; I'd just finished it before Ishmael returned. I'd needed something to focus on, something I could *do* for Kame after he stopped breathing. The scrap wood and twine structure wobbled. It was no more than a cot at the bottom of the cut in the ground behind the hut, not a grand platform that the son of one of the bountiful houses would normally get.

We cut the twine and unrolled the canvas. I used a porcelain pitcher of water to wash Kame's body, and I sang the song of endings as I washed him with a scrap of cloth, my voice breaking when I came to the last words: "And when the final thread is cut, our tapestry is complete."

"That was beautiful," Ishmael said, standing over us on a small rock, like a priest. His coat flapped heavy against his feet.

"Your people don't sing it?" I asked.

"This is my first time hearing it." Ishmael crossed his hands behind his back, looking respectful. "You'll have to tell it to me again when you can. I want to write it down so others may know of it."

It made me feel uncomfortable to talk about writing at a funeral. Something profane.

"Walk tall in the gardens of the gods," I told Kame. "Because they will know you did great things here in the preserve of humanity."

We waited respectfully by the platform until the ground stirred. Oily tendrils reached up and caressed Kame. They probed and tested his skin. Sniffing. Making sure he was dead.

Once assured, they reached up and spread themselves around him. Hundreds of strands wrapped around the cot and pulled the body down toward the ground.

The tar covered Kame's skin, replacing the deep brown of it with a smooth onyx, so polished that every surface reflected a warped image of me, the librarian, and the blue sky above.

Then the ground sucked his body down into itself.

I let out the deep breath I'd been holding.

"You were worried?" Ishmael asked.

"The grasping hand of death? I was worried Kame would be judged a sinner and left by the ground to rot. We have to burn the bodies, then, when the ground refuses to take them."

"But the ground always takes the dead." Ishmael looked horrified. "Always."

"Not here in the wastes."

"Things are different here," Ishmael agreed. "Is there anything else you want to do for your brother?"

I looked down at the diminishing black-mirror pool by our feet. "There is no passing feast, no paid life singers, no priests. There will be no plaque, no cornerstone. I guess there is only a memory carried by me and the friends he drank with, now."

The ground crumbled under my feet as we clambered back up the ravine to our temporary home. Smoke rose from the distance, and Ishmael glanced over at the muddy path we'd tripped our way up in the night.

"They're still celebrating back in Ninetha," he said. "So many of them. I've never seen so many people before in all my travels."

I frowned. "But you've been to Eufra. I thought Eufra was a bigger city than Ninetha?"

"No. Ninetha is much larger."

"But isn't Eufra the largest city on the Eufrat?" The harbor city loomed large in the tales I'd heard as a child.

"It is, but Ninetha is easily ten times the size."

We walked on as I digested that. The griots called Eufra the father city to Ninetha. Gilgamesh from Eufra had found the Ninetha cornucopia far back in the fog of legend, and he'd wrestled with the angel Enkidu for the right to live by it.

"We shouldn't stay here long. Kira"—I spat her name in bitterness at the sand—"knows about the shepherds' places."

Ishmael said nothing.

"I will go back." A fire burned inside me, and the words

threw fuel onto it. "I will make her feel what it is like to lose everyone she loves, everything she's had. I will rain hell onto Ninetha."

I swore it.

For Kame.

I would scream his name from the top of the citadel one day, or die trying. And I would scream the name of every one of my brothers and sisters. Kame, Anwago, Yusi, Endu, Sinza, Hetelia, Ume, Song, Yamie, Vikkor, Thir, and Zo. Their names would never be forgotten by the world.

We filled two sacks with dusty, plain vittle nuggets from the pantry and poured water into the librarian's flasks from the barrel in the corner of the room. Ishmael gave me a bag to put my pages in, so that the sweat wouldn't damage them from where I kept them against my body.

"Please don't kill me," the shepherdess begged when I pulled away the cloth we'd jammed into her mouth. "Please."

I felt a little bad about what we'd done to her, sneaking up in the night and scaring her with a bloody, dying Kame between us. Ishmael had held her down, and I had tied her to the bedframe.

"We just need some of your vittle," I explained. "Then, we're letting you go."

"You can't untie her," Ishmael said from beside the table. He pulled books out of his pack. Book after book, stacked in piles around him. The shepherdess's eyes grew wide with horror. "You need to leave her here. Let someone else find her."

"What? She could die!"

"Untie her, and she runs to Ninetha."

The shepherdess held her bound hands up. "I swear. I'll bind myself to Inkun's word."

I pointed at her and looked at Ishmael. "She'll swear to Inkun."

"I don't know Inkun," Ishmael said. "I think someone who fears death will swear to any god to save their own skin."

I glanced around the small single room.

"I'll give you a dull knife," I said to the shepherdess. "It'll take you a while, but you can cut through the rope with it. How about that, Ishmael?"

Ishmael shrugged and started to repack.

"You can't take those books," I said. "They're too heavy."

"The books," Ishmael said, "are the whole point."

"Surviving is the whole point," I said.

He finished pushing the yellowed, unholy old books into his traveler's pack, and then cinched the buckles and straps of the top flap.

"There is more than just survival. There has to be. There must be meaning to the world," Ishmael said. "And there is meaning in these books that I will carry to new people."

In the end, he carried the pack, and so I couldn't argue with him about what he put in it.

We left the leaning hut before the sun got too high, as we didn't want its heat to suck away our energy. I could hear the shepherdess grunt as she started sawing at the rope. Once out from the ravine, we climbed up a low hill with a gnarled cedar tree that stood proud against the barren dirt and wind at the crest.

With my musket looped comfortably over my back and a bag of vittle tied to my waist, I felt like I was on yet another of Kira's weeklong adventures outside the wall. The shepherd-ess's boots, which I'd stolen along with her food, didn't fit as well my sandals. I'd bound my feet with extra cloth, hoping it would work. My sandals dangled from the butt of my musket, though, just in case.

Ishmael stopped at the tree and got his bearings off the sun.

"This way," he said, but I did not follow.

"Eufra lies in that direction." I pointed behind us.

"We're not going to Eufra," Ishmael said.

My face dropped, and then I felt it tighten with anger. "Why?"

"We'd die before we reached Eufra," Ishmael said. "It's far too dangerous to go back."

I reached my hand behind me to rub the musket's cold steel. I needed to comfort myself a moment with that small familiarity.

"I lost everything because of you." Anger at Ishmael bloomed easily in me. It gripped my chest so hard, it left me breathless. "If you hadn't been dragged through those gates, and I hadn't pitied you, then my whole family would be alive. I wouldn't have just buried my brother. I'm a fool."

"And who dragged me through those gates?" Ishmael asked acidly.

"People who cared about the warnings the gods gave us." I grabbed one of the straps of his pack and the books inside. It pulled Ishmael off balance. "These books, they don't bring anything but death and grief. And you as well. I understand why you're feared."

"I brought nothing but knowledge," Ishmael snapped. He twisted away from me, ripping his pack out of my hands. I stumbled after him, a wave of grief rising up through me so suddenly, I felt like I was about to lift off the ground into the air.

"You give us knowledge like the serpent that slithered up the Bifrost with the apple. Coming up from the frozen earth to give us the knowledge of sin!"

"Maybe the serpent had the right fucking idea," Ishmael said. "Maybe the serpent didn't get to write down his side of the story after he was killed by people who only memorized stories and let them fade away, change, and become bastardized legends."

"You are a blasphemous heretic!"

"You fling words around, but you barely understand them," Ishmael said. "You so easily point them at others, but turn around and look at that perversion you call a city."

He pointed back to Ninetha, which we could just see from the top of the hill we'd walked up.

"Perversion?"

"You built a wall around it to keep people in. You built a castle around the cornucopia. Did you think the gods made something like the cornucopia to allow one single person to take it for themselves?"

I looked at the mud-brick walls and, for a second, I saw them as something more menacing than comforting. I saw them as Ishmael saw them.

I did not like it.

"You sound like Kira. I heard her tell the mob that the cornucopia was a gift from the gods."

"Everywhere else, it's known that the cornucopias are for all of humanity, even those who don't come from your city."

My father had said that his father's father's people had built the cornucopium to protect it from the rioting commons, fearing that the half-mad, starving Ninethans who packed up against the walls would destroy the machine in their desperation.

The bountiful houses had worked hard with my forefathers, digging ditches to take the cornucopia's clean water out into the city so that the thirsty could drink, and so that the gutters would take the city's filth out into the silver pits, where the god-machine would dispose of it.

"Our hard work made this city mighty," my father would tell me. "Always know that hard work rewards the hands that do it."

Because some day, that hard work, those hard decisions, might have fallen on me.

I pointed at the gates. "What's that?"

Ishmael squinted. "I can't quite see."

He reached back for one of the metal objects dangling by his canteens—a simple spyglass with spiral glyphs carved into the brass. Writing. Maybe it allowed him to see more clearly with spells carved into it.

"Guardians," Ishmael said. "Lots of guardians."

"Maybe they fought Kira," I said. "Maybe they're looking for me and Kame. Father shot at Kira; I saw it. Maybe she's dead."

The librarian considered me with pity. "Will you risk talking to them? Kira has the cornucopia and medicine to heal herself. If Kira's not dead, then she has to kill you. A dictator can't risk leaving any open claims to the throne."

"A dictator? What's that?" I asked.

"A king. Like your father."

"He was no king. He was the protector of the cornucopia."

Ishmael clipped his spyglass away. "King. Dictator. Lord Musketeer. Whatever you call it, Kira rules the city now."

I grabbed my hair and squeezed it, soft and springy between my fingers. "Then Eufra."

"I told you, we won't make it. That way is death."

"Fuck!" I straightened myself, forced to look the situation in the eye. "Then where are we going?"

Ishmael pointed to the hazy slopes in the far distance, visible in the crisp morning air. "The mountains are within reach."

"The rim of the world," I said flatly.

"There's no such thing. The world is a sphere. I told you this already. We've read about it in books. I've been sent out to find where our maps and the world maps we've found line up. When we do that, we'll understand so much more. We can take that knowledge back to New Alexandria and create a better map of the world than the one the ancients passed on."

"There'll be nothing but the void," I told him wearily.

Ishmael started to walk down the hill. "There's only one way to find out."

It was madness to just strike out into the distance without knowing the land. But then, Ishmael was a wandering librarian. He hid his books away and smuggled them into cities, trying to spread words, like a disease. Like Kira had warned.

"There used to be a city near the rim." I ran to catch up to him. "Nudasi. In the old days, you could walk from here to Nudasi under a canopy of jade trees. The trees had all died in my grandfather's day. Victims of the blight. It must have taken Nudasi, because no one has come from there since."

"Do you know the direction?"

"I can show you the markers," I said. "But what if we get to Nudasi and it's a dead city?"

"See the green fringe around the mountains?" Ishmael

pointed. "The wastelands end at their feet. We can forage."

Kira had taught me to forage out in the dry lands around Ninetha, too. You needed to know how to survive forty nights to have children. I'd never been out from the walls that long. That was a full woman's quest. But I had managed to pass her tests for up to ten days.

I didn't want to grill lizards for their meat. I'd rather chew dry vittle. But I knew how to hunt, and I knew the ground roots, bitter fruits, and tastiest insects, if it came to that.

But I didn't volunteer that to Ishmael.

I had to keep some of my secrets close. I didn't know Ishmael. We were recent and maybe temporary allies. What would a man beaten, almost killed, and now given his freedom do to keep it? What had driven him across the wastes when so many years lay between him and our last visitor?

I'd thought I knew my own father. I'd thought I knew Kira. Even Kame, who I thought was a wastrel and a drunk, turned out to be noble and brave in the end. And his friend Pearl had risked her life to save him.

Kame and Pearl had loved each other, in their own way, I realized with a start.

So, what lay deep inside Ishmael that I couldn't see right now?

Hells, what obvious things had I already missed?

"Keep on the rock and firm ground as much as you can," I said, after many minutes of following Ishmael. "We don't want to leave footsteps for them."

Kira could track a sandmouse for her dinner, and she could well be leading those guardians we saw leave the city. After a lifetime of training me and mentoring me, my teacher could now be hunting me.

Well, fine, I thought. If that was the case, only one of us would live.

Ishmael and I didn't risk lighting a fire after our first full day of walking out into the wastes. We ate crunchy vittle, tasteless and odorless, without any spices to cook it in or soups to soak it in, and we washed that down with warm water from his canteens.

"When I was in training, we could at least have a fire," I grumbled. But I understood why we didn't want to give away our location.

I watched the sun slip away, back behind us, toward Ninetha. Night crept toward my back, and then enveloped us as we ate silently.

Kame's absence ached within me.

All of my siblings had been silenced. It hit me hard so hard that I toppled over into the sand.

Ishmael crawled over on his hands and knees. "Hey, hey," he said.

"Everyone is dead," I wept. "I have nothing and no one, and everything is gone. And I'm trapped in the wastes with a blasphemer carrying around a pack full of books."

He wrapped his arms around me. "I am so sorry."

I shoved him away.

A hug didn't fix anything.

And I hated him so much. He could see that, as he sat back, arms draped on his knees.

I wiped the tears away. "I'm tired. That's all. This has been too much."

He gave me a blanket from his pack. "Then sleep."

"We shouldn't," I said. "Kira says, 'Sleep in the day, when the heat saps you. Move at night, when it's cool.'"

That's when all the wasteland creatures would be out, and you could hunt them for your sustenance.

The librarian leaned back against the pack, propped up against a furrow in the dirt. "Fuck Kira," he said nonchalantly. "I was your prisoner until yesterday, I starved while in that cell, and then I was freed and ran for my life. Then, I unburied my belongings, buried your brother, and spent my whole day walking. I need to rest."

He pulled his wide-brimmed hat down over his eyes and settled in.

And that was that.

I couldn't sleep. I watched the stars come alive and sprinkle the sky with their light.

"They call it the Cross," Kira once told me, after she'd wrapped my shoulders in a blanket. "If you find it in the sky, you can always get back to Ninetha. It may just be a more convoluted path than you imagined."

I wasn't leaving, I promised myself. Not forever. I would just be taking that more convoluted path home.

Questions raced through me. How did one raise an army? What would I even tell people that would make them leave their homes and walk across the wastes to join me in attacking Ninetha's walls?

The cold settled over the warm ground, and wind tickled everything this way and that. I jumped at random sounds, convinced I heard guardians about to leap out at us from the dark.

But no green robes or desert cloaks flapped out of the night. The guardians would probably zig-zag about for a while longer, trying to find our trail. Or maybe they'd be kicking in the doors of herders' huts outside the walls of the city.

Kira likely wouldn't command them. If she was now the Lord of Ninetha, she'd stay in the citadel, like my father had.

My head weakened, my eyes closed, and I dreamed of screaming people as they died inside the citadel I had sworn to protect with my steel and with my life.

I coughed dirt out of my nose as a hand slapped over my mouth. I kicked and fought against the blanket wrapped around me, and panic blasted away sleep as surely as a bucket of cold water.

"It's a guardian," Ishmael whispered. "Stay still. I just didn't want you to make a sound."

I stopped thrashing.

Ishmael pulled the blanket back from my face, but remained crouched over me as he looked toward a cut in the hill behind us. "See?"

I twisted to follow his gaze.

"I see him," I panted. A green twitch, and a figure that hopped from rock to rock as he looked down at the ground. As I watched, my heart gradually slowed from the shock of waking up with a hand over my mouth.

Then I rolled out from under Ishmael to reach for the musket Pearl had given me.

Dreamlike, I followed the usual sequence. Cartridge, bite, tamp, flintlock pulled back, and then I rolled back toward the rock that offered the only protection we'd found.

The guardian loped over the hard dirt, kicking up the upper layer as he approached.

I sighted down the barrel, hands shaking slightly.

When I pulled the trigger, I would take the man's life before he even realized what had happened.

"If I do this," I whispered, "others will hear it."

"I'm not as strong as I used to be." Ishmael rested his head on his hands. "That man will be well trained. And well fed."

"Then, we should run," I said.

Ishmael scratched at his stubbly cheek, where the beginnings of a curly silver and black beard had started to become apparent. "He'll go back and gather the others if he sees us."

The guardian kept moving closer.

"I'm still a protector of Ninetha," I said. "As stupid as that sounds, I was trained for it. I can't build my return to Ninetha on ambushes and trickery."

"Lofty ideals from someone on the run for her life."

I stood up from behind the rock and threw the blanket off my shoulders as Ishmael scrambled to try to hold me down. I aimed the musket straight ahead, as if I stood in a row of my brothers and sisters.

"Hold!" I called out grimly to the guardian.

He'd been focused on the ground below him, not up ahead. I startled him, and he glanced around like a trapped animal.

"I am loaded and ready to fire." For once in my life, my words snapped crisply into the air, with the authority that I'd never mastered inside the walls. I walked around toward the guardian, and he stepped back as I advanced. "What is your name?"

"My name?" Confused, he pulled his spear from under his arm and held it forward.

He could try to throw it, but I would shoot him down before he could get halfway through the motion. We both knew it.

But I also kept my distance, well clear of a killing thrust.

"What do you call yourself?" I asked, a little frustration in my tone. "It's a simple question, yes?"

The guardian shook his head. "She *said* you didn't even know us. And I still could not bring myself to fully believe it."

"Believe what?"

"I stood at the door of the chambers three nights of every week. Can you really say you don't know me?"

I stared at him, trying to find the face and the name in my memories.

Nothing came to me, just an emptiness.

"I'm Torit," the guardian spat, hatred in his voice.

I flinched at the obvious disgust on his face.

"Torit," I said slowly. But holding the name in my mouth didn't bring anything back to mind.

"You piece of dogshit." Torit took a step back. "I thought you and your family were like gods on Earth. I lined up with the other guardians in the kitchens, ready to die to protect the citadel."

"You seem very alive to me."

"I saw the hundreds gathered with Kira. I thought, look at them all. We can't stop them. She's inevitable; she clearly has the gods on her side."

"And now you're here to kill me." I looked down the sights at him. My hands started to tremble from the weight of the long barrel ahead of me.

"It was hard to put aside my belief in the Lord Musketeer. That piece of me that wanted to believe in you screamed that I was a traitor. But now here we are, and you don't even know who I am—"

I let the musket drop to point at the ground between us both. "Kira will take Ninetha and rule it for herself! Join me instead."

"And how will that be different from the Lord Musketeer's

rule?" Torit took another few steps back.

"The citadel protected Ninetha. That was your job, and mine, until Kira"—I had to pause for a moment, as my voice broke and my vision wavered; I took a deep breath—"did what she did."

"I truly think Kira freed us," Torit said. "I think she gave us back something that you stole."

"I stole nothing." I raised the musket again, and Torit kept backing away from me.

"Your family did."

"If it wasn't for the work we did, they would have all certainly starved. What do you think will happen now? That every Ninethan will just walk in and take what they need from the cornucopia?"

"I don't know what the future holds," Torit said. "But Kira told the truth. You are a tick sucking off the gifts of the gods. You hoarded the bounty of the cornucopia for yourselves while the commons starved."

"Stop," I begged him. "Don't let her poison you. Join me. I'm going to go to another city and build an army. I'm going to come back to Ninetha and restore the citadel. You could be at the head of that army. You could—"

"What? Have a home in the bountiful section?" Torit shook his head. "This is why Kira's hunting you."

"She killed my brothers and sisters. Hung them from the walls of the cornucopium!" Hot tears ran down the grime of my face.

"They shot into the crowds of regular people," Torit shouted at me. "Fired into them like they were nothing but targets, and reloaded calmly without even flinching. Cut down families without a second thought."

"She's no different. She'll hide away in the citadel, with you to guard her."

"No, she's with us. She led all twenty of us out into the desert after you," Torit said. "She never asks us to do anything she wouldn't do herself."

"Please, stop walking away." I wiped at my tears, and the musket bobbled about, aiming at the sky, a rock, the ground nearby, then back to Torit. "I don't want to shoot you. But I can't let you run back to her."

"It's my duty," Torit said, "to at least try. Besides, if you fire that gun, they'll all hear where you are anyway."

He spun about and ran.

Ishmael struck him from the side, his long coat flying behind him as he leapt from behind a nearby rock. He'd taken advantage of our standoff to move around without being noticed.

Both men rolled around and scrabbled for the spear, hoping to try to lever it away from each other. The librarian managed to twist himself with a strange flip to pin Torit against a reddish boulder. He pushed the spear's shaft flat against the young man's throat.

Torit choked and gasped.

Slowly, ever so slowly, Torit's face moved from red and furious to pale, and then confused.

"That's enough," I said. I uncocked the flint on the musket. "He'll see reason now."

Ishmael never looked at me. His voice cold, he grunted, "If he gets away, he'll tell Kira, and anyone else looking for us, what direction we left in."

"Don't do this."

"It's him or us," Ishmael growled. Fear and anger crackled in his voice.

"Please." Torit had stood at my door for years. I had never paid him attention, or even bothered to ask his name.

But I knew it now.

I knew it now.

"Ishmael!" I shouted as I approached. "Stop!"

"You're not my ruler."

Torit's eyes rolled up toward the sky. All I had to do was stand still, and the problem would be solved.

"Dammit." I flipped the musket around and hit the librarian in the back of the head with the butt of the weapon. The feel of wood and metal striking someone's head startled me. The practice dummies had wooden heads that kicked back hard when I had drilled the motion with Kira squinting at me.

"Fuck!" Ishmael staggered off to the side, a hand on the bloody back of his head.

Torit gasped, his wide eyes rimmed with tears as he sucked air.

He grabbed at me, but only weakly. I stepped back and pointed back in the direction he'd come. "You're right. I won't fire the musket. You should run, though, or the librarian might cast a reading spell on you to suck your life away. Go tell your new ruler where I'm hiding. We'll be gone when you get back here."

Torit coughed and wobbled away.

Ishmael moved to stop him, but I raised the musket. "Let him go."

"We can't, it's too dangerous."

Torit's senses returned to him and he ran away from us, moving faster and faster the more he caught his breath. He disappeared into the distance.

"We need to pick our stuff up and run," I said.

Ishmael sat against a rock and stared at me. He let go of the back of his head and wiped his bloody hand against his coat.

"You may have just killed us," he said.

I looked about the dead land around us, as my hands trembled. "Ishmael, I don't think I've ever felt as alive as I do right this second."

I had broken an amiable trust between us, and I knew it. I had to do it. I couldn't regret it. But after I helped Ishmael wrap a strip of cloth around his head, he only spoke to me when needed, and he spent the rest of the day trudging ahead of me.

It shouldn't have shocked me that a hit to the head with the butt of a musket would change a relationship. But Ishmael's cold anger only fueled mine, because I couldn't convince him to see this through my eyes.

He didn't respond when I told him I had to set an example. That the responsibility of protecting people meant that I couldn't kill Torit any more than I could have let Ishmael die when he had lain in the dirt, surrounded by Kira and the herders. I knew it put us in danger, but how could I expect to ever come back to Ninetha if word spread that I'd murdered my own guardian?

I might have to fight in self-defense, someday soon. Apparently Kira was hunting me so that she could order me killed in front of her. I would fight when it came to that.

But not until then.

There was no reason for it.

The librarian said nothing when I explained that. He just walked.

We passed over hard ground with little greenery, and we scrambled over hot sands that kicked up into the air and made every breath scrape my throat. We picked our way through scraggly, gray bushes and through folds in the land that made gentle valleys where thin sand-flowers hid in the shade. We pushed on all day, and then into the night.

I stopped us in the late night at a pyramid of stones on the edge of a rocky hill. I walked over to a red pebble. One that I'd placed on the pyramid two years ago, after carrying it all the way from the street outside my window.

"We all bring a stone here," Kira had said. "Every visit. There used to be markers all the way to Nudasi. We maintain the farthest one we can reach, in case a traveler needs to see it in the distance."

"This is as far as we've ever come," I said to Ishmael.

He stepped out past the pyramid marker.

I watched him walk away, the heavy pack shifting from side to side with his steps. I squatted and picked up my pebble. I squeezed it as hard as I could in my hand.

"Why are you lying to me?" I called after him.

Ishmael ignored me.

"You're scared of going back to Eufra. But you won't tell me why." I couldn't read a person like Kira, but I'd had time to think on the long day's walk. "It's not just Kira you fear, but something else. And you can hate me for what I did to you so I could let Torit go, but we are bound together, yes? I'm not a child. Do you understand?"

Ishmael stopped. He wearily looked back at me and the pyramid.

"What are you scared of?" I asked.

"Archangels." Ishmael stared into the distance. He turned and started to walk again.

"What do you mean?" I asked. "What archangels?"

After a moment, I realized he wasn't going to stop. I took a moment to retie the outside of my robes, and I took a step past the pyramid.

It was the farthest I'd ever strayed from Ninetha.

Another step.

Then another. Still farther.

I looked back as I ran out well past the final marker, my heart in my mouth. Every step from now on carried me into new places. Every single movement meant something new, something strange, and something profound for my new life.

Was this how Ishmael felt every moment of every day when he wandered the land?

Surely not; it would be exhausting.

Eventually, one had to adapt, I felt. But I marked the thought to come back to later when Ishmael was talking to me again.

"What are these angels?"

"Archangels," Ishmael said.

"Why are you so scared of them?" I asked, and ran to catch up.

Ishmael kept just far enough ahead of me that talking was pointless. Every time I tried to gain on him, he sped up. Even with all his gear rattling about, I could barely keep pace.

He was a stringy man, lean from his last journey and leaner still after his time in the citadel. But with each hour in the open air, his steps grew more confident.

I lived in his world now.

"I've shown you the marker," I shouted at him. "I've given you the direction in which Nudasi lies. You don't need me anymore. Are you going to abandon me out here for Kira to find?"

It wouldn't work. I would live out in the land. I wouldn't be a wild, hairy man like the tales of old-man Enkidu. I'd be a wild and hairy woman, eating insects and honey and attacking anyone who came upon me in the wastes. Kira had taught me how to survive here.

But I didn't want to live wild and solitary. Doing it even for forty days and forty nights hadn't sounded any good to me. I certainly did not want to do it for the rest of my life.

"For the love of the gods, Ishmael, be plain with me."

He wouldn't talk. He kept walking until the early hours of the morning, until the sky slightly brightened and I could barely walk any farther.

"Here," he finally said, many hours after I had given up trying to talk. We crawled under an overhanging slab of rock that looked like it had shoved out of the ground into the air just to create shelter for us.

Our breath blew clouds of steam in the cold air, so we wrapped ourselves in the two blankets that were rolled and lashed to the top of Ishmael's pack. His knees jammed against my stomach as he scrunched himself up into a ball, but I didn't complain.

"I'm sorry," I finally said to him. "I'm sorry."

"For what?" I could see the anger and hurt on him in the dawning orange light.

"For hitting you in the head."

"With your weapon," Ishmael said.

"Yes. I did that." I'd spent so much time explaining why I'd done it at first. Justifying myself, explaining the logic of my decision.

I'd never apologized, though.

"You sure as hells did," Ishmael grunted. "My head's still ringing."

I winced. "You didn't deserve it."

"No one deserves a strike to the head. Never." His breath filled the air. After a whole day of walking, it reeked of stale water and the handfuls of vittle we'd grabbed from a second smaller bag that hung from his waist.

"You're right," I agreed. "I won't do it again."

"Damn right." Ishmael massaged his feet and grimaced.

"Tell me about the angels," I said. I could feel the seriousness on my face.

"Archangels."

"I saw the terror in you." I pulled the edge of the blanket closer to my neck. Now that we'd stopped walking, my body was no longer providing heat. The cool nibbled at my flesh and seeped deeper into me.

Ishmael nodded. "They hunted us, when I was a child."

He slid the blanket down—with a burst of cold air that made us both shiver—and pulled the front of his shirt up.

"What are you doing?" I asked, nervous.

He pointed at old scars that ran ragged down his side, ones I hadn't paid too close attention to in the citadel. The ones his tattoos swirled around. "The archangels attacked librarians. My first memory is of one dragging my mother out of our stonehold while I screamed for her."

Thou shall not suffer a librarian to live, I thought to myself. The tales of glimmering angels walking the land, hunting books and heretics, had chilled every listener in Ninetha since childhood. Although angels hadn't been seen in generations, we had all heard the stories about them. And we had all been told how reading could bring the holy vengeance of angels down on us.

"What happened to her?" I asked.

"Something no child should ever see," Ishmael said softly,

and my heart broke for him a little as he looked over my shoulder into some other place.

"They say angels used to walk the land here," I said. "Before it died and became the wastes. Their shining skin would dazzle your eyes."

"The archangels usually just destroyed the books," Ishmael said. "They'd burn them. But my parents, and their parents before them, were not just librarians; they were from Special Collections. They traveled the world, saving fragments, texts, anything they could find. It was dangerous work. They were hunted—by people, but also by an archangel. One of the few surviving ones."

"It killed your mother?"

"And my mother's mother, and her father. And while it did that, my father swept me up and ran. Renounced his calling right there. I hated him for that, later. I called him a coward so many times over the years. For leaving my mother. For abandoning Special Collections. But he never looked back."

"After all that, you still became a librarian."

"I found an underground chapter and joined. I took up the robes, and started copying my first book when I was thirteen. That's when it came back."

"The same archangel?"

"Just as I remembered it," Ishmael said, his lips tight. "A full head taller than me, and silvered. Its face like a mirror. You could only see these reflections of yourself sliding across it. A god-machine."

"How did you know it was the same one?" I asked.

"Across the forehead, its name was seared in a red ink that has never scraped away," Ishmael closed his eyes. "Arbet."

"Arbet?"

"It's an ancient word for the number four."

"The number?" I held up four fingers, my thumb closed against my palm.

"Yes. I called my father a coward for all those years after my mother died. But when Arbet kicked in our wall and came for me, my father leapt to fight it without even a second thought, screaming for me to run."

"I'm so sorry."

Tears threatened to leak out from Ishmael's eyes as he squeezed them shut. He opened his eyes sadly after a moment and smiled. "I was a child. An arrogant, ungracious little creature who didn't know the world."

At that moment, Ishmael didn't seem like a well-traveled man twice my age, but a sad little boy who missed his parents.

"But you're so far away now," I said. "You're in the wastes."

He shook his head, his hair springing off the rock by the blanket as he did so. "New Alexandria flourished as the archangels died. Over several generations, we have built archives, heavily fortressed of course, but actual archives where we collect the books instead of hiding them. Our people spread out across the land to try to share the magic of words with all, even when we are persecuted for it. But I have cast myself out from that. Arbet lives, and it chases me. It killed a lot of people who tried to protect me in New Alexandria. I had to lead it away."

"Why you?"

Ishmael pulled his shirt back into place, and wrapped the blanket back up around us. I shivered as warmth returned. He shifted onto his back and looked up at the rock wall just over our heads. "Something happened to the archangels, just a few generations ago. They began to return to the earth, pulled down by the tar. But Arbet survived whatever killed all the others. It lives because it's driven to exterminate my family's line, to try to stop literacy in us."

It sounded like a song written about the ancients. An epic chase across the land, a bloodline struggling to survive, loss and heresy and adventure. But adventure turned out to be horrible up close, not nearly so grand as the stories.

"You sleep for the first half of the day. I'll watch," I said.

Ishmael grimaced. "Don't close your eyes."

I pulled the musket from under my side. "I won't."

"That won't stop it," Ishmael said. "Nothing stops it."

He closed his eyes.

We moved through the night and slept during the day, splitting the watch between us. I slept nervously the first two nights, expecting his hand at my mouth again.

Then, the routine set in and I slept deeply.

We ate handfuls of crunchy vittle as the sun set. We griped about our chafed feet and tired legs. And we looked at the rim of the world every evening, trying to determine if the wall of rock had grown larger over the previous night's walk.

"There's a formula to determine how far away we are by the apparent height of the mountains," Ishmael told me as we trudged on.

"We've walked five days," I said. "We have seven more to walk."

Ishmael stared at the rim. "According to the books, that would make these taller than any mountains in the world. I thought these might be the Ever Resting Mountains, which the maps mark as the highest."

I shrugged. "All I know is that Nudasi is nestled in the rim, and that we have seven more days to walk. That is what the griots say."

"But those are just stories passed from person to person," Ishmael said. "You can't trust them any more than you can rumors, or children playing the whisper game."

"In all my life, we'd never seen a traveler until you came along, yet the griots told stories about the people who used to pass through on their way to the rim of the world," I said. "Those are stories told out loud, not whispered from one person to another. We all hear them, and we can correct the teller if they forget a detail."

"If it hasn't been pressed to paper, it is not permanent," Ishmael objected.

"Paper burns," I said. "Paper rots."

"But if you copy the words, or even duplicate them with machines like the ancients did, then they are forever."

"Obviously not forever." I waved my hands at the world around us. "Those books died during the exodus."

"I've read enough of the ones that survived to know that we don't live in the 'garden of the gods.' This is a world. Earth. We've just forgotten it. Knowledge was ripped away from us by the archangels."

"'The gods looked down at humanity squabbling and slaughtering each other in the old world.'" Griots' words. Words I'd heard many times while watching them call out in Ninetha's square. "They saw us debate meaning and text, they saw conflagrations and suffering. So, they offered us a tended preserve to retreat to, but if only we would agree to leave the written word behind."

"And now you will tell me, 'Thou shall not suffer a librarian to live,'" Ishmael said bitterly.

"That's right. You're heretical."

"I have another stanza for you," he said. "One that your griots have conveniently forgotten."

"What's that?" I asked.

"'So that you will not suffer, we give you a gift. Ask from the cornucopia what you need, and we will grant it to you if you lay down your books and swords. We will let no person go hungry ever again.'"

"There's no such commandment." This time I started to walk ahead as fast as I could, trying to outrun the words, and Ishmael had to hurry after me, his pack clanging as he wobbled to get up to a half jog.

"All that work your forefathers did to build a wall around the cornucopia, that could only have been started after the archangels stopped enforcing the will of the gods. After the librarians took New Alexandria for themselves."

I kept walking, and stared defiantly ahead.

"I guess that makes us both heretics," Ishmael shouted after me.

We didn't see the cleft at first because we had been walking at night by the stars and the moon. But on the eighth day, Ishmael had his spyglass out as we crested another set of warped hills as the sun rose. He handed the device to me and pointed.

"There. Do you see it?"

The foothills of the rim stretched up into the clouds. The great stacks, heavy with rain, constantly fetched up against the stone and ice, except in one place. Clouds spilled into a great gash in the rough shape of a V carved out of the rim.

"What do your griots say about that?" Ishmael asked. He had a book out, but the pages were all a soft yellow with no markings on them. He sketched the rim, with particular focus on the destroyed section of it, into the notebook. Then he added little markings, words.

"I've never heard of this thing," I said.

It disturbed me. Maybe even scared me a little. It looked like a giant had thrown a rock through the rim. Debris and scorch marks, now grown over with trees or covered in snow, had been scattered in a great backsplash across the mountain.

Gods, the scale of it all.

I turned the spyglass around, back to where we'd come from. Nothing.

Wait. A glint flashed in the setting sunlight.

A spear?

Or a librarian-obsessed, silvered creature hunting my companion?

"What do you see?" Ishmael asked, noticing I'd turned around.

I strained to look at the far-off morning shadows, until I finally caught a glimpse of green.

"Guardians."

Something in me had hoped that they would stop at the last marker and turn back. It was as far as anyone from Ninetha had walked out into the wastes since Kira was a child. Or so she said.

Ishmael heard the despair in my voice. "She's scared of you."

That surprised me. "How strange, because I'm terrified of her."

I thought of Kira fighting in the training room, unstoppable, unable to ever give up. I'd never beaten her, never outrun her, and never been able to match her.

"You still want to go back?"

"I will," I said firmly. But as I spoke, I thought about the rock witch. I'd be another wild, dangerous woman who stumbled in from the wastes to throw myself against the citadel. "I just don't know how I'll do it yet."

All I had was one musket and the pain that I clutched against the back of my throat. Was that enough to avenge my family and restore the citadel?

"There's a whole world out here," Ishmael said. "You don't have to go back."

"They murdered my family. I held Kame in my arms, Ishmael. I watched the life leak out of him because Kira decided to hunt us." I trembled as pain whipped through my soul. "She has to pay."

"And then what?"

"Everything goes back to the way it was. It goes back to normal."

"After what happened, do you really believe that?" Ishmael asked.

I didn't say anything. I knew he was right, but it wouldn't stop that growing fire for vengeance that was burning deep inside me.

Ishmael awkwardly shifted the pack around on his shoulders and lowered it to the ground. He removed food and blankets to uncover his precious books.

"I think you would like this one," he muttered, and handed the second one in the pile to me.

I took it, but by a corner, ready to drop it in a split second if the markings moved, or the book did anything suspicious.

"What is it?" I asked, scared of it, and yet drawn to the wrongness of it all. The forbidden had a lure all its own, and here the forbidden smelled faintly of dust and mildew.

But was it any different than the pages I'd kept bound against my stomach since the citadel?

"It is a saga called *The Count of Monte Cristo*. All written down on these pages," Ishmael said as he repacked everything.

"I can't read. I shouldn't." I thought a moment. "I wonder if everything that happened is because of the book my father kept. His sin, our family's sin."

"I don't agree," Ishmael said, tying his pack shut. "What happened to you was tragedy. Created by human hands. Kira's hands."

I agreed. I bit my lip. "What's in this story that you think I would like?"

"It's a story of vengeance," Ishmael said. "And redemption."

He pulled his pack back on and took the book back from me.

Before I could stop myself, I asked, "What happens?"

"It begins on a ship, where a loyal man has lost his captain to a fever. Our scholars in New Alexandria don't understand all the concepts in the book, but I think we can still understand its soul. And it's a glimpse of the world the ancients once lived in."

Ishmael opened the book and looked down at the figures scratched into the paper.

"Think about it," he said reverently. "How many of our ancestors' hands have these words been passed on through? And how many people have heard this tale?"

I led, and Ishmael followed. He began to read from the

pages. It made me shiver in fear to hear the words come from his mouth. Words that were not his own. Words written down onto the page by another mind, somewhere back in time behind us, a mind reaching out across the depths to give us its words.

What could it be trying to slip into my own mind?

Just in the first lines of the story, there were words that I didn't know. Like Smyrna, Trieste, and Naples. Were they a spell?

Like a griot, Ishmael started the story of a young man coming into a harbor of some kind. There were men who held malice toward him, although he couldn't see it. Like Kira had brooded without me ever realizing, planning my harm like Dante's enemies planned his.

"Stop," I said. "Stop."

Ishmael closed the book. "What?"

"It's too real," I said. Hearing those men speak through the page, even if so many of the words remained alien to me, made my hands shake. It felt like it was happening to me in the moment.

We dug a trench into the light dirt to lie down in and covered ourselves in branches from what few tangled gray bushes braved the searing sun. As the dirt formed itself to the back of my head, I squinted up into the blue sky.

"If you just renounced the books, would the archangel still chase you?"

Ishmael pulled the last branch over and wriggled down into the dirt as well. I waited for his reply, and then waited some more.

"Ishmael?"

He grunted. "I tried that once. I was still young, and terrified.

And it peered right on through the desperation in me and saw my true heart."

"What was that?"

"I want to know," Ishmael said. "Where did we come from? What happened? We forgot the entire world of the ancients. How?"

"We made a pact."

"With the gods. Yes. But is that really the truth, or is that just what we tell each other?"

"'In this land, you will want not,'" I recited.

"And yet, I see so much wanting in my travels that I have come to think the gods fucked up." Ishmael crossed his arms.

I sat up at the blasphemy. The wizened branches clattered off my head to the side. "You can't speak against the gods. Humanity made a contract with them."

"That's what we're told. But you wouldn't know, because you can't read. You can only trust what you're told, and you have little that lets you verify what is real around you."

"And you do?" I crawled out of the hiding hole.

"Yes. That's what this is all about," Ishmael snapped. "Knowledge, and the verification of that knowledge, and the classification of that knowledge. That is what we do. That is who I am. We can examine what someone else once wrote down and learn things, more than we could have learned on our own."

"And that's why an archangel is chasing you." I staggered away from him and sat down a few paces away. I would sleep in my own hole today. When the gods struck him down, I wouldn't get hit as well. "You wept about your parents and your hardships, but they're all self-inflicted."

"Says the spoiled scion of the citadel," Ishmael said.

"I don't know what a scion is," I snapped back.

"Exactly my point." Ishmael pulled the branches back over himself, and I lay down in the full glare of the rising sun.

Four more days of dreary walking, my feet raw with blisters from my boots, and Nudasi appeared as a distant glitter in the night. We'd eaten the last handfuls of chewy, stale vittle by this point, and I'd started to worry about whether we would end this journey eating off the land rather than our own supplies.

Ishmael spent a few minutes with his spyglass, studying the horizon behind us, looking for Kira, or something worse, before we set out. But so far, the guardians hadn't caught up.

Seeing the lights was a relief. We would have starved if there had been no city.

Now, I could abandon Ishmael at the city gates and turn to finding an army. With an army, I could fight Kira and return to Ninetha.

I could avenge my family.

The fantasy constantly played at the back of my head the farther I got from home. The first days, I'd been numb. I'd expected grief, but I'd had to focus instead on climbing the furrowed hills in the wastes, or trudging across the mud as small wisps of dust whirled and danced around us.

I laughed as I saw more buildings appear. "Nudasi. My grandfather knew many travelers from this city who passed through Ninetha."

There were so many buildings outside Nudasi's walls. That had to mean it was a vast city. I would recruit people from throughout its nooks and crannies. If Kira approached, or even came inside the walls, I would hide deep in the city. Here, no one would know me, even though I'd walked all the way across the wastes.

"I'm a traveler," I realized in shock.

I'd dreamed of it when listening to griots recite the stories of trading parties that had journeyed to Nudasi and Eufra. I wanted to be an adventurer and see the things they spoke of. I had imagined myself standing on a barge and poling along the gentle Eufrat River to distant cities.

What child didn't?

I'd let go of such things in my formal training as a musketress. I learned how to defend the citadel. I learned my duty.

Maybe I'd make a better adventurer than a musketress.

"Is being a traveler everything you'd hoped?" Ishmael asked.

"I didn't think it would be this smelly," I said. "Or dusty. I haven't taken a bath in so long, there's dirt in every crack of my body."

We approached the white-walled Nudasi buildings at dawn. A small crowd of people approached us. They wore leggings and shirts, not a single comfortable robe on any of them. The women wore patched, blue shawls with a ring of stars at the front, and cloth bonnets. The men had white, curled wigs tied back with black bows.

"Travelers!" one of the women shouted. "Welcome to Nudasi! Tell us your names! Where did you came from! Are you hungry?"

One of the men pressed a small pie into my hand. It smelled so good, I couldn't stop myself. I bit into it without answering a single question.

Someone else shoved a wooden cup of juice in my other hand. A nasty, cherry juice. I drank it greedily. The hand pie was cherry as well, I realized.

"We come from Ninetha," Ishmael said and introduced himself. "And I'm headed for the mountains."

He pointed at the rim, and the small gaggle of folk looked over at the great gash in the rim of the world. Long streams of clouds funneled into that gash. This close, as the sun rose and we didn't hide from it, I saw boulders the size of houses tossed clear of the gash to land in the wastes. We'd walked around many of them over the last night, I realized.

We'd crossed a scarred land to get to Nudasi.

I wondered what that maelstrom of clouds and the destroyed land around it had to do with the wastes.

A woman draped in a blue sash covered in white, five-pointed stars split the crowd. "I am Priscilla, and I'm the current president of Nudasi. Senators, make room for our guests and don't crowd them!"

Everyone moved back.

"We are a little overexcited," Priscilla said, and bowed gracefully to each of us. "We haven't had a traveler in almost ten years. The Cleft was a curiosity for many, but the wastes have gotten even worse since I was a child. But we welcome you openly, and let me assure you, we do follow the traveler's code."

"Thank you," I said, relieved.

Priscilla took my hands. "Come, join us for a morning meal to celebrate your arrival. You will stay with me. I want to hear everything about your journey."

I could barely see through the tight crowd around us, but I noticed something as we walked out of the dust of the wastes and onto cobblestoned streets. "Where are your walls?"

Priscilla, who led me by my hand, glanced over her shoulder. "Our what?"

Ishmael leaned over to me. "There are no walls beyond Ninetha, Lilith."

I stood tiptoe to try to see over everyone. Nudasi nestled against two sweeps of rock on either side, where the rim's arms reached out around the city to protect it. The farther in, the more the rock hills hid our view of the Cleft.

The strange square houses all had marble columns out front and dimming globes that hung from chains in the air over the entryways. Folk stood in front of their houses as word spread, and children ran alongside the welcoming committee, trying to stare at us through the senators' legs.

Cherry trees littered the garden spaces between the blocky, columned houses. Fallen, ripe cherries stained the carefully maintained ground under the trees.

"We have clothes if you need, and food is waiting," Priscilla explained.

"And the cornucopia?" Ishmael asked.

"At the heart of our great city. You can join the people's line whenever you wish."

"The people's line?" I asked.

Priscilla let go of my hand as we all swept into the largest columned home I'd seen yet, twice as tall and with three times as many columns holding up the roof that hung out over the whitewashed frame. Bronze doors twice my height creaked open as a crowd crammed into what must be the president's home.

A burly man with a great beard and a tall black hat gently intercepted me. "I am Slammin' Joe, Priscilla's husband. We have a room waiting for you."

The press of people who were interested in touching me, talking to me, asking questions about my travels overwhelmed me. Their excited and exuberant faces popped up everywhere I turned.

Slammin' Joe pulled me away from the crowd, around the doors to a corridor, and from there into a quieter area of the house.

"Here is your room, traveler."

I looked at the marble floor and hand-woven wool carpet, then over to the luxurious bed with soft covers and pillows. I'd been sleeping on hard earth so much that my neck felt bent.

"I don't know how to thank you," I stammered, with total honesty. The simple luxury I'd taken for granted as a daughter of the citadel returned to me after all that dust and grime.

"The bathing room has a tub, and the water comes from the god-wells, where it's warmed. I assume you're familiar with it all."

I stepped inside the room, set the musket down on the bed, and unbuckled my powder along with the few things I had in the bag at my side.

I sniffed the contents of a small marble bowl on the top of a hand-carved set of drawers.

"That's toasted basic," Slammin' Joe said, "with lavender and coconut oil."

Something to nibble on before the feast. And here, they used the same name for vittle as Ishmael had. *Basic.*

I crunched on some fresh, flavored vittle as I looked to the door, excited about scraping the travel off my skin. I was enjoying the quiet moment, as I listened to the distant buzz of people still talking farther down the corridor.

I noticed something. "Where's the lock for the door?"

"Lock?" Slammin' Joe asked.

"I don't—" I paused. "Right now anyone could enter through that door."

Slammin' Joe grimaced. "You're not a follower of Washtun."

"I don't know that god," I admitted, a little nervous. Slammin' Joe's bulk almost filled the doorframe. I could not get past him if he decided to stop me.

"Washtun is the god of utter transparency. Honesty is our highest calling here. You don't need to bar your door."

I struggled to find the words to protest without insulting Slammin' Joe and the rest of Nudasi.

"Aren't you comfortable?" Slammin' Joe's words felt like a challenge.

I changed the subject to give myself time to think. "Do you follow any other gods?" I asked.

"We celebrate the Blue Shoe Festival of Elv and his songs," Slammin' Joe said matter-of-factly.

"I've been to one of those!" I said, relieved to find something in common. "I came close to being a deejay once." Only the best dancer from the previous year was picked by the priest to choose the songs the choir would sing.

Slammin' Joe grinned. "Priscilla was the step-deejay two years running."

I forced myself to relax a little. These people seemed so nice. "The god of utter transparency?"

"Ask me anything." Slammin' Joe radiated pleasantness and smiles.

"You have such an interesting name," I said tentatively.

"It's from the list," he said.

"What's the list?" I asked.

"We plant the cherry trees to honor our god's greatest trait:

honesty. But gods are often capricious, and we'd be lying if we didn't accept that our veneration needs to be tempered with the truth of their nature, no matter what gifts they gave us. Zayus trickled into women's rooms as a beam of golden light to lay with them against their will. Washtun gave us honesty and the foundation of rotating presidencies that we pass from senator to senator. We take the names of the ones our god enslaved while he invented honesty and freedom."

I didn't know what to say to that. It made a chill touch the back of my neck. So, I moved on from the topic, not sure what to make of it.

"Why are you really having this welcome feast?" I'd been to enough formal events at my father's side to know that something was always happening in the background.

Slammin' Joe tapped the corner of his eye and smiled. "We're trying to keep you in eyesight at all times. You're strangers. We might honor the traveler's code and believe in Washtun's freedom, but if so many of us surround you, what trouble can you get up to?"

"Oh." Transparent honesty.

"Wash the nasty dust off, and come join our party. I can stand right outside this door, the only door in or out, and make sure no one enters. If it makes you feel any better."

I bit my lip. I looked at the bathtub just in front of a half-wall that I assumed hid the toilet and bidet away. I nodded. "Please do that."

I took the musket from the bed with me, went through the steps to load it, and then balanced it on a marble shelf next to the clean stone tub. I checked that the recipe pages were folded away in the small leather bag Ishmael had given me so that my skin and sweat didn't destroy them.

When I turned the water on, I could hear the pipes gurgle, and I splashed my hand across the hot water coming up from below. I wondered if only the president's house had access to water from the city's cornucopia, or if all the houses had it.

I would ask tomorrow.

Tomorrow, when I would need to figure out what to do about Kira. She'd be here soon, and Nudasi didn't look anything like Ninetha so far. There were no tight streets and anonymous markets near here to hide in. Maybe I needed to explore farther into the city later.

When I threw my clothes onto a stool at the foot of the tub and plunged into the water, it felt like the last weeks washed away from me. The tub was massive enough that I slid under the water and held my breath. I blew several satisfied bubbles and laughed. I was alive and taking a bath.

It was a simple act that felt surreal. My problems faded away to a haze in the back of my mind.

I came up for air. A dark-eyed man with silver hair and tattooed arms sat on the wooden stool across from me, with towels on his lap. The corners of his eyes crinkled with age and sun.

He held a finger to his lips. "Don't scream, Musketress."

I stared at the long dagger in his right hand, my eyes unable to break away from following the etched swirls, the glint of light from a window that played off it as he shifted, and the way he gripped it so hard I could see his hand tremble.

He continued, "You can't load it fast enough—"

Water poured out onto the floor as I reared out of the tub to snatch my musket. He stood up, horror on his face as he realized he'd made a fatal mistake. He must not have seen me load it. Where'd he come from? Around the stone wall, by the toilet. A small part of my brain spotted dusty sandal prints.

Naked, vulnerable, my heart beating so fast it felt like a hummingbird's wings thrumming away, I swung the musket.

"Fire it and they'll all come running," he said. "Then, they'll know you for what you—"

I pulled the trigger, the lock snicked, and the musket kicked.

The crack exploded through the room and bounced off the walls. Smoke spat into the air all around us, and the smell of powder gagged me.

The man stared, stunned to still be alive.

"That was a warning. The next one will be to your heart," I said. A bluff, as I couldn't load another round before he attacked me with his knife, but he wouldn't know that. No one in Nudasi could know that.

"You haven't reloaded," he said with a smile.

Shit. He did know more about the musket than I assumed anyone here could know.

He swung at me, and I jumped back. I knew the knife could pierce me naked just as well as through cloth, but there was a terror added to being so exposed.

Forget modesty, forget fairness, forget rules! Kira shouted at me from memory. *There is only life or death in this kind of fight. Bite, club, throw, attack, do anything, but do not give up before the fight is truly started.*

My soapy feet slid on tile as I kept away from the evil edge of that knife, but I felt the wall behind me in a second.

I flipped the musket and used it like a club.

Confusion lit his eyes for a second as he dodged back, the metal-capped end of the musket's butt missing his head by a finger-width. A wild arc, but I'd just wanted to push him back.

Another obvious swing and he'd grab it from me, and although he looked wiry under his simple clothes, I could see the cords of muscle in his forearms.

He came for me again. I held the musket in front of me like a spear. It was an old, familiar grip, learned from years of training next to the guardians. I hit him in the throat with my feet planted, and then pushed like I was trying to force a spear through a wooden plate.

The strike unbalanced him. The shove took him off his feet, unsteady on the now wet floor. He fell, struck the bathtub with the side of his head, and bounced off the tile floor.

He lay still, not so much as a twitch.

Slammin' Joe ran into the room. He slid on the water as he approached.

"What have you done?!" Slammin' Joe shouted. "Darcus?"

Slammin' Joe ignored me. He pushed past me to crouch next to the sprawled-out man who'd tried to kill me. I scuttled away into the room, one hand between my legs, the other holding the musket as I tried to cover my chest with the crook of my arm.

I grabbed a towel and backed off toward the bed. I wrapped the towel under my arms, and then grabbed my bag of cartridges. Soapy water dripped off my hair and stung my eyes.

Reload.

I smacked the musket against the floor and had it up to my shoulder, pointed back into the bathroom. Kira would have been proud of my calm and speed.

"Don't you move," I hissed at Slammin' Joe. "Don't you dare fucking move."

Fear choked my mouth. It was so dry, I couldn't swallow. I heard footsteps off to my side at the door to the room as people ran to the noise. Was Darcus dead?

He'd tried to kill me. I'd had to defend myself.

I swung the musket away from the bathroom and at the people who burst into the room. "You stay back from me."

More curious faces crowded the corridor just outside, bobbing about as they tried to peer in.

"Give her space," Priscilla shouted. She pushed past everyone and into the room. "Slammin' Joe, Slammin' Joe, is that blood?"

"It's Darcus's." Slammin' Joe pulled Darcus onto his lap, and a whirlwind of rage swept across his face as he looked up at me.

"He tried to kill me." My voice sounded small, and it broke a little.

Two men tried to step past Priscilla toward me. I pointed the gun at the wall next to them and pulled the trigger.

They dropped to the ground right away, terrified at the explosion. Priscilla crouched and looked over at the wall. Pulverized stone dribbled out of the hole that had appeared.

She looked at me through the powder smoke. I could see her rethink her impression of me. "Everything Darcus and his people told us was true. You have ancient weapons."

"And the next time, I'll point it at the door if they don't stay out of the room."

Priscilla stood up. "Leave us," she ordered them.

"But—" one of the men started to protest.

She cast them out with a dark glare. They retreated into the corridor and out of my sight. I could hear them murmuring, though.

"You're the leader of Nudasi?" I asked, trying to remember the strange word she'd used to introduce herself. How, I wondered, would I get out of this building, let alone the city? I couldn't even get dressed right now.

"I'm the president," Priscilla said, as if that answered my question, even though I still had no idea what that was.

"I didn't try to kill him," I said, gesturing at Darcus. "He came after me with that knife."

Darcus's dagger lay under a polished stone sink that stood on three legs, with flowers carved into them. I used my toes, careful to grab the handle, to slide it across the floor toward Priscilla.

"You recognize it, Slammin' Joe?"

Slammin' Joe nodded. Darcus stirred in his arms and groaned. That sound sent a flutter of relief through me.

"I had to hit him," I said firmly. "But I could have shot him. I didn't."

Priscilla held the dagger lightly and shifted it this way and that. I tightened my grip on the musket.

"Savary's dagger," Priscilla said after a long moment. She looked wistful.

"Savary?"

Priscilla set it down on the bed. I backed up, putting it between us. "Darcus came to us out of the desert. He came from Ninetha, he said, and told us it was a walled prison where people lived in small rooms jammed together and starving on basic."

I started to correct her, and then realized Darcus came from the commons. That was Ninetha, in his eyes. I swallowed.

"Darcus had five of his people with him, and they begged to make a life here. They told us such awful tales about your people." Priscilla sat down on the bed. She looked to Slammin' Joe and Darcus sadly. "We didn't really believe the worst of it, but Savary did. She walked out into the wastes to give Ninetha the good news that there was another way—a city where anyone could visit the cornucopia, as the gods intended. Darcus helped guide her."

I could feel the words that would come next, like a prophet predicting the future. But I interrupted her. "Who was Savary to you?"

"My daughter. She went out into the wastes, and that was the last time I saw her. Ninetha killed her."

"She was the rock witch." I pulled the musket back and started to casually reload.

"Rock witch?"

"The commons folk, they called her the rock witch. She preached in the streets. They named her Olivis, after the prophet."

"Don't do that." Priscilla pointed at the musket. "You're safe here." I stopped reloading. "Just tell me about my daughter."

"She turned the commons folk into a mob. They stormed the citadel."

"And then you killed her?"

"I was a child," I protested. "I didn't kill her."

"Your family stole a cornucopia away and hid it from the gods. You tricked it into giving you weapons."

"So, where did Darcus get that blade?" I asked. I pointed my musket at the dagger on the bed. Metal came only from things the cornucopia made. They would have recycled something, or asked it for something that it didn't recognize as something that could kill.

Priscilla raised a finger, then froze. "That's fair."

"What are you going to do with me?" I asked after a moment.

"Your companion wants to climb the rim to see the edge of the world," Priscilla said. She looked tired. "Go with him."

"No!" Darcus shouted. Slammin' Joe had wrapped a strip of his sleeve around Darcus's head. Rust-colored blood stained it.

"Darcus, I'm sorry," Priscilla said to the old Ninethan. "I thought your stories were extravagant and bitter. You didn't come from a place that honored the Washtun way of honesty, so I suspected you were pulling tricks on us."

Darcus shook his head sadly. Priscilla turned back to me.

"Some small part of me even hoped that you would tell me Savary lived in Ninetha. The mother in me that kept that light lit for her yearned for that. Now, I can let her go."

Priscilla stood up, and I thought that she looked like she had aged in the last ten minutes.

"You'll be safe in here tonight," she said. "But you leave at dawn."

Slammin' Joe struggled to help Darcus to his feet. "I'll still come for you," Darcus said, leaning on Slammin' Joe's shoulder. The hatred on his face made me flinch.

I licked my lips nervously and watched them push past the half-open door. A babble of concern rose from the crowd outside.

Two men and a woman stayed outside the door to guard it.

"Are you keeping me safe or making sure I don't leave the room?" I asked, before they shut the thick, wooden door.

I was as much a prisoner here as I had been back in the citadel.

Left alone, I let my hands shake. My forearms had started

to burn from keeping my fingers clenched so steady all that time. I dropped the musket to the bed and slid down to the floor as I tried to control my panicked breathing. I'd come to raise an army, and already I'd lost.

I still had my musket.

I still had the powder recipe.

But I had nothing else.

Ishmael raised a hand, but I'd already spotted him in the long snake of a line that passed between the cherry trees. He'd shaved, and someone had styled his hair, cutting it close to his temples and braiding it along the top. He looked younger and rested.

Green moss sprung lightly under my boots as I walked. Two men in Nudasi garb had escorted me out of the room and out through the town to get supplies, and then to make sure I left the city.

"Your companion, Tariq," one of them said to Ishmael.

People in line glared at me.

"You didn't tell them your real name," I whispered. "Why?"

"I always give a false one in cities I visit."

"Is Ishmael really your name, then?"

Ishmael nodded. "I was so sure I was about to die in that cell when you came to me. I figured either Kira or the archangel would come to end me. So, I thought I could give you my real name, so that when I died, maybe someday a librarian would pass through, and if they heard about my real name, they'd know I died in Ninetha, and they could write it down for New Alexandria's histories."

"You think highly of yourself, that your name should live on," I told him.

"Oh, I'm sure this name will last." Ishmael grinned. His pleasant mood irked me so soon after I had fought for my life. I still felt jittery and on edge, and the strange shapes of the buildings, the different clothes, even the smells, they all pressed in on me.

"They won't let me stay here," I said.

"I was told. The senators of Nudasi have also made sure to tell me how highly they think of you." Ishmael waved his hand at the people around us. He picked up his pack and moved it forward.

I ignored his jab. "Are they all senators? They look well fed and rich. They must be from bountiful houses?"

"Everyone I've met is a senator, and they choose a president to live in the palace once a year." Ishmael nodded at the woman in front of him. "Senator."

"Senator," she smiled back. "A beautiful morning."

"There are no bountiful houses here," Ishmael said, and he moved his pack forward four spaces as the line shuffled along. "Certainly none on that mountain. It'll be a cold, tough journey. It would be better to leave you."

"I don't want to go," I spat. "But what choice do I have? I think they'll kill me if I stay. Someone tried last night. Do you know there are people from Ninetha here?"

"Couldn't recruit your army?" Ishmael asked, the tone of his voice flatly amused.

"Will you let me come with you or not?" I asked. I hated doing it. It felt servile, desperate, and humiliating. Back in a nice room, back to that familiar comfort, and a haughtiness had come over me far too quickly.

"I joined hands with you because I didn't know this area, and because you saved my life twice," Ishmael said. "I've helped you once; I'll help you again. But after that, we stand clear of any debts to each other."

"Thank you," I said, my voice small, even as I simmered. We'd shuffled out onto one of the stone-paved streets. I looked down it toward a central circle that the inner buildings clustered around. Four roads led to it, a spoke pattern I found slightly familiar.

I gasped. At the heart of the paved circle, the familiar shape of a cornucopia stood over the people of Nudasi, utterly naked to the sky. Four bulbous trunks, like fat baobab trees, and the nest of tangled limbs overhead that writhed with god-black veins. Each trunk had niches carved smoothly into them, with their tongue-like tables that jutted out from them. Three of Nudasi's senators picked up food from its tables, and the fourth took a silvered staff.

"Where are the communalists?"

"There are none."

I stared at the people putting their hands to the nooks and closing their eyes. It looked all wrong to me. A senator approached them and shouted, "You have one minute, so have your needs clear in your head as you approach! After you commune with the cornucopia, move on quickly. There are one thousand and four hundred in line in any given day. Do not harm those waiting behind you by dallying."

Priscilla and her entourage hung back at the edge of the crowd, watching us with suspicion and hostility in their eyes.

"I can't believe just anyone is allowed to approach and beseech the cornucopia," I said, looking away from Priscilla and back to the god-machine.

"You're shocked," Ishmael said, ignoring their glares. "But this is a city the way the gods intended it. The cornucopia gauges how many children a city can support, and it blesses us. The only way to avoid its control is to eat off the land for forty days and forty nights. But who would do that when the cornucopia takes care of all? Ninetha is the only city I've ever seen that ignores the gods on this."

"You rebel against the gods," I whispered. "There are angels hunting you."

"I've done nothing your family hasn't done. If anything, they've taken heresy far further than I could have imagined. How many people did it take to build the citadel? Did they even wish to do it, or did they have to work in order to beg for food, which meant their lives? How long did it take your ancestors to trick the cornucopia into making steel tubes and powder for your weapons?"

I hadn't thought about any of that before. I'd never been confronted with it.

"That was done long before me," I told him.

"But as that boy back in the wastes said, you lived off the gains like a full tick on the back of a starving dog."

I didn't like this rested and well-fed Ishmael.

"These other cities are paradises?" I asked bitterly.

"No, but yours is certainly a hell." Ishmael looked over at me, saw my hurt expression, and sighed. "There was a man in the old world who lived in a land where the rulers hoarded the food for themselves in greed, even though there was plenty for all. Close to starving, he fled to a nearby land that he'd heard rumors about but could not believe. But what choice did he have, other than a last desperate gamble?

"He faced many challenges, until much later, on his hands

and knees, almost a walking skeleton, he came upon a house in that fabled land. He crawled, near death, until he saw a bowl of steaming food on the back steps, and he wept in gratitude for his luck in finding people so generous as to leave this bounty out for him. He devoured it. But then a chained dog snarled at him, and he came to realize: he was eating a dog's scraps.

"This taught him that he had breathed corrupt air all his life, but until then he had not seen it around himself. He had to travel to understand the way things stood in his old land. That is often the way of humanity. Remember this, and tell it to all you see. The contract with the gods to wander their preserve commands us to be gentler creatures."

"I'm shocked to hear a griot's words from you," I said. I knew the story. But maybe I'd never understood it.

"I copied the words down to paper," he whispered conspiratorially. "And they sit forever in New Alexandria. Someone will read them long after that griot or I return to the tar in the ground."

We shuffled closer with everyone else.

"How does it work? What should I do once I reach out and touch it?"

Ishmael looked over at me. "You can imagine what you want. But it would be better to tell it what you are going to be doing, and it will try to anticipate your needs. It's like daydreaming."

We moved again, and I came face to face with the cornucopia. It felt so familiar, the clover-shaped mass of obsidian plumbing and ancient machine. I approached the shadow of a niche, glanced nervously at Ishmael, who walked on past to a niche of his own, and then I stood alone.

The mumble of the crowd all around the machines faded away. I could only hear a faint hum.

I stepped even closer and closed my eyes. I reached the palm of my hand out until it pressed against the warm surface, which yielded, like flesh. I wanted to yank my hand away, but I couldn't.

Panic rattled me slightly, but like the sound of the people, it faded as well.

Daydream.

I could have sworn a massive presence lay just beneath the surface of the god-machine, patiently waiting for me to gather myself.

"I'm going up to see the rim of the world, the Cleft, and journey to the next city. I need provisions."

As I imagined our journey, my hand slid off the niche as it hardened.

Sound rushed back into my ears, and I blinked. Tubes shivered, things gurgled from inside of the cornucopia, and a bag fell out from the petals above the flat table.

I grabbed it and looked inside. Packets full of vittle. A thin, crinkly cape with a silver lining. A mask with bug-like glass eyes. I took it out and looked at the straps.

"What's this?" I asked as we moved away from the cornucopia.

Ishmael had one out as well. "I don't know."

"You wear them if you go to the Cleft." Priscilla had moved closer to see what I'd been gifted. After looking my items over, she continued, "When the world rained boulders on our ancestors, half of Nudasi died. Some of the brave in those days climbed the northern pass to make for the Cleft. Before then, no one could climb the rim. But the air failed them.

Two heroes died that day, and the others had to turn back. Nudasi senators approached the cornucopia for help, and the gods gave us masks to breathe with. We use them still to this day. You'll know when you need them."

I looked up at the rim of the world, then over to the Cleft and the torn-up clouds being sucked into its gap.

What an ominous thing to live in the shadow of. I didn't want to die up there.

"President Priscilla, let me stay. I can teach you how to make muskets. I can give you power that you can't imagine—"

"I don't want your weapons." She brushed her arms, as if washing away my offer. "We've heard enough about them and the pain they bring in Ninetha. We stay here, away from your troubles and ideas. The cornucopia provides."

Slammin' Joe stepped in front of her and pointed toward the slopes of the rock wall that reached impossibly up into the clouds. "Head that way. There's a path marked with painted cairns to take you to the Cleft."

I put the strange bug mask into the pack and pulled it onto my shoulders, all the while thinking about what I could do to change my fortunes.

"There will be people chasing me," I said to Priscilla. "They'll wear green and carry spears. Ask their leader about the rock witch, but don't tell her that she was your daughter. If you want vengeance for your daughter, they'll tell you how. And keep your weapons close at hand. These people are dangerous."

I turned my back to Nudasi, and maybe also to my childish dreams of raising an army to return to Ninetha.

"That will spill a lot of blood," Ishmael remarked after a long moment of silence.

After we had walked for a few minutes, I turned back and saw that Priscilla still stood there with a small crowd of senators.

"If I can't be at the head of an army for Ninetha, I can still try to kill Kira for my brothers and sisters."

Ishmael nodded. "Are you sure you want to carry that on your soul?"

"I've written words, saved a librarian's life, and been read to. My soul is a lost cause," I said bitterly. "What is adding another death to whatever judgments I'll face after I return to the ground?"

"You shouldn't think like that," Ishmael said. "A soul is never a lost cause."

"Where will we go after the Cleft?" I asked, changing the subject. I felt a bit adrift. I'd focused all my plans on getting to Nudasi and then seeking revenge. But the ground had shifted under me yet again.

"Priscilla gave me directions to Tamarlane. It lies just under the Cleft. From there, we can follow the land before the mountains to see how far they sprawl. I'll make notations for New Alexandria."

I glanced back at the small party of people. Stony faces stared back. "You sound cheerful."

"I've walked more of the land than any other librarian I have heard of. When I took the vow of Special Collections, I knew my life would never be the same, but when I hand over my notes, people will read them for years to come. I'll be immortal on the page."

I couldn't share his bright mood. I could only dwell on my latest failure. At first, fright had driven me out toward Nudasi, kept me moving at night, kept me sustained. Now,

I frequently thought about Kame dying as I tried to keep the blood from leaking out of his body, and how scared he'd looked on the ground beneath me.

Again, I had failed my family. Failed by being the only one alive, by not firing my musket to protect the citadel, and I'd failed by running away again.

My mind wandered a lot as we walked, and sometimes I felt like a taut rope vibrating in a strong wind. My jaw hurt because I kept it clenched so hard, and loud sounds made my heart jump. No longer out in the hot sands, we returned to sleeping at nights and forging on in the light. We needed daylight, or we would likely plummet off into the abyss that was always to our right. At night, as we camped in the shadow of the rim of the world, I woke up in a sweat, and sometimes I'd choke on a scream that arose in the back of my throat.

It all exhausted me.

And above it all, the Cleft loomed over us. Clouds poured into it like water into a drain and then were shredded by its jagged, splintered edges.

The air grew cold when the path zigzagged its way up the rocky cliffs. We pulled on the crinkly capes, exchanged our shock at how warm they kept us, and pushed on. The slope had grown steeper, and we had to be careful to follow the line from cairn to cairn. In some places, chain had been hammered into the rock face so we could pull ourselves along the path.

On the third day, Ishmael woke me early. "Come, look."

He handed me the spyglass and pointed to the bottom of the trail. I hadn't really understood how far we'd climbed, because I'd focused ahead, and up, worried about loose rocks that could slip and kill us. The path sloped away, and off to both sides; we stood hundreds of body lengths over the ground.

I stared for a bit at the rocky debris scattered around the ground under us. All shattered by their falls. If I fell, my body would get dashed against them.

All the way back to the first cairns that marked the way along the rim, I saw a small clump of movement. I squinted through the spyglass and saw the green robes of guardians.

"I had hoped they'd get delayed at Nudasi."

"They're three days behind now, not one and a half."

The rocks on the steep trail and switchbacks, along with our heavy, well-stocked packs, made our travel a snail's crawl. And it seemed to me as though the higher we clambered, the harder it got to move my feet one in front of the other, and the less walkable the trail became. Three days on foot in the desert, and we would be far out of sight. But here, we could look all the way back and see the tiny dots of our pursuers.

Ishmael took the spyglass back from me and braced an elbow against a flat rock face to use it again. "That boy said Kira had twenty guardians. I count nineteen now."

I leaned against the solid wall of rock behind us, away from the edge. Once out of the foothills, there was a reason this was called the rim of the world. The rock was often sheer. "She won't stop. Not until I'm dead. Why?"

My eyes burned. Kira had loved me, hadn't she? How could she discard that so easily to stalk me to the edge of the world? She could turn around at any point and go back to Ninetha.

Why wouldn't she leave me alone?

"You listen to the griots. How many stories are there about orphan children who set out to avenge a parent's death? How many to regain birthrights?"

"Many," I had to mutter.

"You can't be allowed to live. As long as you live, Ninetha is at risk."

"But—"

"Didn't you plan to build muskets and return with an army?" Ishmael asked. "Is she wrong?"

I picked my cape up off the ground, where it had been an unsatisfactory blanket, and wrapped myself in it.

"You don't know what it's like . . ." I trailed off as I saw his face and realized the utter thoughtlessness of my words. I'd seen his scars. Maybe I hadn't truly believed his story, that a man had fought an archangel himself. But clearly, Ishmael was haunted by something.

Ashamed of myself, I pulled my pack on and started to walk ahead.

Ishmael scanned the land all around until he was satisfied, then scrambled after me.

"They're moving faster than you," he said.

"This pack is full of vittle, and my shoulders burn," I complained.

"Climb faster," Ishmael said, his mouth tight.

We ate vittle stew over a simple fire kindled with scraps of woody, thistly bush that grew on the path.

I held my fingers out toward the fire, my stomach full in that way that only vittle makes you, and burped.

"What happens when you walk as high as the clouds?" I asked.

Ishmael stared off into the night at the long strands of cloud that reflected the silver light of the moon.

"I don't know. I've never been up this high."

"And what do your books say?"

"That they're mist. Water mist."

"But they looked like whipped cream," I said. They had to be like a soft, feathery pillow.

"The books say different."

"And they're never wrong?"

Passion filled Ishmael's eyes, lit by the flickering fire light. "The ancients had a system of interrogating the world around them. They called it science. It's in a lot of the surviving texts that have been copied down. They did experiments to see how things worked around them, and they used deduction to reason out why. For example, an ancient philosopher measured the size of the Earth using a rod and some shadows."

"How?" I couldn't picture it.

"If the Earth is round, then a pole raised up into the air will cast a shadow by the sun." Ishmael drew a circle, and then a triangle in it, making it look like a pie with a section cut out of it. "Now, if you wait until the solstice, when the sun is directly overhead at its farthest point north, you also measure the angle of the shadow it casts when a pole is raised at the same moment in another city. If you know how far apart they are, and the angle, you can determine the curve. From there, you can determine the size."

It made no sense to me.

"Science is a series of steps," Ishmael continued. "You propose an idea, and then try to create a way to test it that would prove it wrong. Then, you write the idea down so that others can try to prove it wrong. The longer it holds, the more likely it is to be correct."

"I guess," I said. "But why would you do any of that?"

"For knowledge," Ishmael said.

"But what is the point of knowledge?" I looked at Ishmael

and saw that we were on the opposite sides of a river from each other, staring across the water in a lack of understanding.

"What do you mean?" Ishmael shook his head with frustration.

"It won't make a cornucopia work any better," I said. "You can't use it to build a city of your own, away from the bounty of the gods. It won't bring back the old magics, because we gave that up. We made a pact with the gods that we would give it all up, and now it's lost. The griots said it took hundreds of years for science to work. I don't have that much time, do you?"

"Even without all that, don't you just want to know the stories of our kind, before the written word died?" he replied.

I reached into the bag he'd given me for the papers I'd carried all the way from Ninetha. I held them out between us. "I'm tempted to throw them into the fire, right here. All these markings have given Ninetha is misery and death."

Ishmael snatched them away from me. "Don't do that."

For the second time ever, he looked down at them.

"It says that first you must task someone ignorant of your designs to go to the cornucopia for certain materials, minerals not found in the earth of this world. You are to gather potassium nitrate; the cornucopia will give it to a person who imagines a tree stump they need to kill."

"Do you know what that is?" I asked.

"I've seen the word *potassium* in books of science."

I moved over to his side, curious, despite myself, at the way he could pull meaning out of nothingness on the page.

"Where is all this? Can you hear it somehow?" I asked.

"Gather charcoal from your many fires," Ishmael muttered. "And last, sulfur, which you must trick the cornucopia into giving to someone by—"

"All that is on this paper?" I interrupted.

"Yes." He stopped to look up at me. The dancing red light of the fire cast shadows up on his face, a demonic effect that shifted and danced. "Do you want to know how?"

I felt like I was reaching forward to steal the forbidden secret of language from Ra. A way to trick the cornucopia into giving us the raw material to make powder.

"A little, show me a little," I said, my voice wobbly and too frail. "No more than that."

Let me sin with words just a little, I thought. If you *could* sin just a little.

Ishmael held up the paper and pointed at some squiggles. "That's a word. You can tell by the space between this one and the next."

"I suspected that," I admitted. As I'd copied it over, the thought had snuck into my head.

Why was I being so tentative? I had started so much of this by being goat-headed enough to steal in there and copy the pages. I'd known it was wrong then, so why had I done it?

Because Father couldn't have been wrong?

"Now, these are letters." Ishmael moved from shape to shape. "And each letter is a sound, basically. This is *sssss*. This is *uhh*. And here we have *luh*, or *llll*. Now, *ffff*. Then, *uh*. Then, *rrrr*. Those are the parts of the word sounds. Chain them together, and you have *sulfur*."

I looked at the word. Still squiggles.

But I could see that the *uhh* squiggle repeated itself.

I knew *uhh*.

It wasn't a spell. It didn't reach up through my eyes with ink and drill itself into my brain, and nothing happened when I said it. It was just a letter.

Still, I took the papers, folded them back up, and put them into their protective bag. Enough dark magic for one night. My hands trembled a bit.

How could I stray so far from the dutiful musketress who had listened to the stories the griots told me when they came to the citadel and my father blessed them with bounty? I had ended up an enemy to Kira. An outcast.

I rolled myself up into the crinkly cape and stared at the fire.

"Tomorrow, we reach the Cleft, and the slope is even higher there," Ishmael said. "Rest. We will need it."

But it was hard to sleep knowing that Kira and her guardians were running up the slope to catch us. When I stared out into the dark, down toward the god-lights of Nudasi on the plain beneath us, I could feel them approaching us.

I pulled the musket and my powder bag, mostly full of cartridges, into my cape with me. The cold steel in the crook of my elbow comforted me, and the faint smell of powder tickled my nose. It smelled of home, and comfort, and hard training, and certainty.

I fell asleep with my cheek against the barrel, homesick.

Late in the morning, as we started our climb again, dizziness struck me. I felt faint, and Ishmael stumbled on a rock and almost pitched off the trail. The gravel would have slid, and he could have fallen clear off the side of the rock.

I caught his pack before he slid away, but when we scrabbled back to the safety of the path, we took a moment to lie against each other as we panted.

"Yesterday," I said, "I noticed we got slower, but I thought we were tired. And now it's worse. I can't focus."

"The air is bad," Ishmael said. "It's the air itself!"

I didn't understand him until he pulled his pack off with effort and reached in for his mask. He shook it in the air between us and laughed. I took my own pack off and dug around for my bug-like mask. I pulled it on and snugged the simple straps on the back.

With just the first few breaths, my head cleared.

I stared at Ishmael, who looked like a monster. A human body, with an insectile head with two glass eyes that bulged comically large out of the mask.

"Are you well?" he shouted, his voice muffled.

"Better!"

I could still see the path through the glass eyes, although the image was slightly warped at the sides.

"Keep moving!"

With the mask on, I found my strength again.

"Slow," I called out. Fog had rolled down onto us. Wet dew trickled down my neck and gathered in my hair. I had to wipe the glass eyes of my mask.

"Ishmael! I can't see you."

I didn't want to walk off into the abyss. I moved on my hands and knees, looking for the next cairn that marked the path. Then, the next.

"Damn you," I muttered. "Damn you."

And then I broke out of the mist and realized we had walked through clouds. I looked across at the very tops of the clouds that surged their way into the Cleft. I had turned the corner of the rock and into the great catastrophe that had happened here so long ago.

Ishmael stood on a shelf of rock that thrust itself out over the clouds. The wind yanked at him, and his clothes fluttered as hard as a kite's tail.

I crawled my way to him, looking out over the clouds, terrified the wind would snatch me away.

He stared into the distance. He hadn't moved this whole time I'd struggled toward him.

"Ishmael!" I touched his shoulder, and he jerked away from me. I shouted at him again as he staggered a bit, the fierce wind almost shoving him off his feet.

He pulled his mask off, and I saw tears stream down his face. He crumpled to his knees and sobbed, a broken man. I had to push my face to his to hear him over the thundering around us.

"I don't understand," Ishmael said. "I don't understand."

I looked over in the direction he faced. The clouds streamed off out into the dark abyss, and there they glinted as the mist turned into snow. Or maybe ice.

The glittering trail extended off into the dark nothingness.

"We really are on the edge of it all," Ishmael said.

"Not quite," I said. "We're on a shelf in a cut in the rim of the world."

Where the clouds spilled off into the void.

Ishmael crumpled in on himself and hugged the mask. I could not shake him into movement. The sight of the edge of the world had broken him. I knew the feeling. I'd had my own world turned upside down and shaken.

But I think Ishmael valued being a know-it-all far more than I had.

On my hands and knees, I crawled out farther on the slightly tilted shelf to look at the other side of the Cleft. How far from the very rim were we? Could we keep climbing upward?

I didn't see a way to do it. After this shelf, I couldn't see a way up the sheer cliffs of rock.

This was as far as a human could go.

I scuttled about the edge some more, curious, and then stopped.

"Well, shit."

I scooted all the way back down to Ishmael, and I only screamed once, when the rock under me shivered from a particularly nasty gust.

"Ishmael, put your mask back on."

He didn't respond, so I yanked it out of his hands. That got his attention.

"What's the point?" he said.

"Put it on!"

I pushed it at his face, and he pulled back. But he put the straps on.

"Come." I took him by his hand, like a reluctant child, as I carefully crouched and moved us both out toward the tip of the shelf. Every extra gust put my heart in my mouth. I didn't want to die by being flung off this piece of rock out into the clouds. Or, worse, into the abyss.

"Here!" I shouted as loudly as I could.

We sat as high as I felt safe.

Ishmael pushed his mask close to mine. "What should I look at? Are you mocking me?"

"Look down."

I pointed at the very bottom of the far edge, toward a maelstrom of clouds that covered it, and the abyss just beyond that edge.

"I see nothing!"

"Wait!"

I grabbed his head and forced him to face the right direction.

"Wait!" I repeated. My throat hurt from shouting.

Then, the clouds broke, and Ishmael saw through them. I heard his startled yelp. He began to stand to try to see better, then quickly changed his mind.

We stared at the break in the clouds.

It looked just like the tattoo on his hands, but blue. A ball of a world, the size of my fist, far below the rim. I could see tufts of clouds, and I traced out the shapes of the land that Ishmael had carved in dark ink on his body.

"There's your world," I shouted to him as I pointed. I laughed. "There's your Earth!"

Our ancestors had crossed that great, dark void to come here. They'd left behind all their knowledge, books, wars, inventions, histories, and much more, just as the griots said.

The Old Gods lived there. I shivered as I gazed down at it, because it was said that the grand god Set hid at the heart of the Great Pyramid by the Great Canal. Zayus reigned from Mount Lempis. The great and shining cities made of glass, like Nuva-Jor, Ikra, or Jing, had been built down there, and then abandoned to nature. That small blue ball was where so many of our stories came from, and yet we did not know that world. The gods had taken it away from us, and we had agreed to their terms.

A wondrous ring of sparkling silver shards circled the blue and green world, like a bracelet. A structure so large, I knew the tiniest little notch in it would be larger than all of Ninetha. One of so many details that I could see the storytellers had left out. Massive lattices trailed off the ring, and as I watched, a brief flare of light suggested something had hit the section I squinted at.

I felt like an ant studying a vast and tremendous city from a crack in the street, barely able to comprehend what it looked upon, and yet still struggling to comprehend it all.

Only, judging by the debris and twisted shapes of the structures, everything I saw had been abandoned far in the past, much like Earth itself.

THREE

THE
ARCH
ANGEL

The gods delivered us from strife and pain, starvation and struggle, plagues and destructive weather. All we had to do was to give up knowledge.

An easy trade for the bounty of the gods. Right?

Ishmael staggered out from the howling winds, hand on my shoulder, and we slid and stumbled our way back down to the main path. He said nothing the whole time.

I didn't mind the silence. It gave us both time to let the immensity of what we had seen slowly release our minds from its dizzying grip. We'd been struck dumb, and I had to imagine it was because Ishmael's mind swirled with new perspectives, and not a few new questions that we may never find answers to, just like mine. And, as I reemerged into myself, I knew that walking downslope with a heavy pack on my back was dangerous and needed my focus. Even more so in the thick haze of the clouds, hardly able to see ahead. I could envision myself slipping forward and then tumbling over my feet. I would bounce my way down the rim, picking up speed, until I flew off a sheer rock face.

It wouldn't do, I thought, to die right after seeing something like the edge of the whole damned world.

Every time I contemplated the heights we stood on, vertigo threatened me, so I took to focusing on just my feet. Something tiny, inconsequential, and easier to focus on.

We finally broke out of the clouds.

I had to face the horizon and come to terms with the fact that I had walked along rock paths so far into the sky that I could look down on birds. Far below, the ground stretched out toward the distant horizon, brown and desolate. But I could see a distant band of green on either side of the wastes.

That was because the destruction fanned out from the Cleft, and I thought I could see groves of trees off in the distance to either side of the desolation's path through our lands. The brown dirt and scrub grew in width as it got farther from the rim. It was a cone of devastation that emanated from where something must have struck the Cleft. Or from whatever had created the Cleft, shattering the very rim of our whole world.

There was a lushness to the green color that bordered the scarred land. I'd never seen a hue like it. All those stories of forests and trees the griots had talked about, and I'd always pictured gray and towering gnarled scrub. My imagination alone could never have conceived of such a vibrant green, so full of life.

If this took my breath away so, what would a river be like? Or an ocean?

The rich blue of the world we'd seen from the shattered rim slid back into my memory. I'd actually looked down upon vast oceans that took the heroes of the oldest stories we passed around so many weeks to cross.

"Stop!" Ishmael ordered. He leaned against a rock as he ripped away his mask and tied it to his pack.

"He finally speaks!" I spread my arms in mock surprise.

He pulled out a book of blank pages, possessed by an inner urgency. "I need to make notes."

I stared at him. After the shocked silence, Ishmael, never one lost for words, had finally found his tongue; and yet he still wouldn't admit to being wrong. "What are you doing?"

"I have to write all this down while it's yet etched into my mind's eye," he muttered.

His back firmly up against the rock, he marked down letters to make his words. I saw the *uhh* symbol, and many more. It wasn't spell-casting, but he was creating a way for his thoughts to be shared with a stranger who could then decode his symbols to hear his thoughts, and wasn't that a magic all by itself?

But it still felt sinful to watch him do it, so I turned away.

"You were wrong," I said. But was like a defeat to have to be the first to point it out. I felt none of the triumph that normally came with being able to say those words.

"Wrong, right, it doesn't matter," Ishmael said. I glanced back, outraged, and saw nothing but an excitement that had taken him over. He scribbled at his paper, hastily and sloppily, the shapes hurried and wobbly. "We both *know* more about our truths, and the nature of the real world now. We must preserve this."

While he scratched away, entranced, at the paper, I took off my mask, then my pack, and I soaked vittle to make us a cold porridge. I couldn't scavenge anything to burn and heat it up, so I waited for the tiny nuggets to soak up the water as I stirred them. We had a little sugar to sprinkle on top, and I savored it.

After we ate, he wrote some more, until I finally pointed at the sun on the horizon. "We should keep moving."

The path back to Nudasi lay below us and stretched off along the rim to our right. Shadows from boulders crept up onto the rim as I kept glancing over. I wanted to spot any flash of green that would let us know we needed to scurry down faster.

I didn't want Kira to beat us to the fork. If she did, we would never see Tamarlane, or even Nudasi. She would trap us in the clouds. I worried that Ishmael had taken up too much time up here in the Cleft.

After he'd tossed the remaining vittle porridge out behind a rock, Ishmael finally packed everything away, and we started down. He had a serenity to him, now that his words lay forever carved on the thick pages of his book.

"My mind still reels," he said. "The Earth is a sphere below us, and we're in its heavens."

"It looked like we were far beyond the heavens," I said.

After a moment, Ishmael agreed. "I think you're right. We are several worlds away from it. I could block it out with my hand, like the moon."

We were like another moon, flying around the old, original world we'd come from. Only this world was flat.

"Ishmael?" A small smile crept up into the corners of my mouth. "You told me about science and experiments. All that ancient philosophy?"

"It was the tool they used to learn about the world around them."

"Did you yourself ever try to replicate the poles-and-shadows experiment to verify it?" I asked innocently. "Or did you just read and read, but never check for yourself?"

"No," Ishmael said, his voice tight and annoyed. "I never tried myself."

"I wonder what those shadows would have told you?" I mused, as if talking to myself.

"Your point is made. Our world may be flat after all."

Boulders slouched around the fork in the path ahead. We crunched closer over loose rock and some dirt. The path down supposedly took us to Tamarlane and then into more lands unknown to us. But those were also directions given to us by the leader of a city who would be happy to see me dead.

Well, Kira hadn't lied to us so far, I reassured myself. We'd gotten to the Cleft, after all.

Shadows rose up from behind rocks. I squinted against the setting sun at them. Both Ishmael and I slid to a stop as we realized the shadows wore green cloaks.

I backed up several steps to a more solid piece of ground while I unslung my musket. I had my hand in my cartridge bag when one of the shadows raised both hands and stepped out into the open.

"Kira?" I called out. I knew the answer already, but I still had to go through the motions.

"Lilith?"

Shit. I pulled the cartridge free and bit. Tap, drop, smack the cartridge into place, because I still didn't have a rod for it. Then, I raised the barrel.

She remained in place the whole time, not even trying to rush at me, even though I expected it any second.

"Can we talk, Lil? I have no weapon."

She sounded tired, her voice small and weary.

I wavered.

"She's tricking us," I said to Ishmael. She had to be.

"Throw your spears down," Kira shouted to the guardians gathered around the fork.

I flinched as spears clattered to the rocks by their sides.

Right now, I could fire. Rip a hole right through her body and avenge Kame, my father, and all my brothers and sisters. A tear trickled down the side of my face and clung to my chin.

"You can do it." Kira nodded toward the musket. She always could look at my face and see my thoughts. "I wouldn't even blame you for killing me right now. But if you do, please lead my guardians back alive. They don't deserve to die here on the rim of the world, alone and hunted."

Kira blinked a puffy, bruised eye and scratched at the dirt on her ashy forearms. For anyone else, that movement would have signaled nervousness, I thought. But not Kira.

No, I realized, not dirt. Blood from a wicked cut on her shoulder that stained her sleeve before it dripped down her forearm.

"I count only ten guardians with her," Ishmael hissed at me. From the corner of my eye, I saw him back away as he glanced all around him at the shadows.

I tensed again, expecting the attack at any moment.

Wind whistled through the crags and rocks, ice cracked in the distance, but no footsteps ran across the rock toward us.

"What happened to you?" I asked. I kept the musket aimed steadily at her. From this distance, the shot would punch right through her forehead. "Where are the rest of your guardians?"

Kira's shoulders slumped. Such a slight gesture, but the woman in front of me was not the same person I had always looked up to in fear and awe. She had become an older woman in pain, her eyes tired and focused off into the distance.

A kicked dog, I thought. The bitch that killed my family.

"Nudasi welcomed us," Kira said slowly. Her lip twitched with suppressed anger. "They sat us at a table and brought out chilled wine, fresh fruits, and ice cream from the cornucopia."

She laughed at the memory, but her eyes remained hard as mountain rock.

"After so many days of eating nothing but handfuls of vittle, it seemed like a dream. We . . . relaxed. They told us where you were headed, and I could see that if we refilled our packs and made good time, we would catch you. I felt confident. I felt like I understood the world, even after something as strange as leaving Ninetha. All was right with the world, and then the ruler of Nudasi asked about the rock witch."

I met Kira's hard eyes and felt a small kick of sickness. My conscience tugged at my soul to remind me that I had told Priscilla about her daughter's fate. I'd known it could cause spilled blood.

I had hoped it.

What a coward I was, to hope that someone else would take my own vengeance onto their shoulders. Just because I wouldn't have seen it happen didn't mean the gods wouldn't weigh it against my soul in the underworld.

Kira nodded, a suspicion confirmed as she saw my face. I expected rage to crackle and leap up. Instead, she continued: "I described how I came across the rock witch in the griots' plaza, how I led the guardians against her, and how we dragged her across the cobblestones before we did . . . what we did to a heretic. And all the while, Priscilla stared at me, never once looking away."

I took a deep breath. The guardians behind Kira regarded

me with blank stares, and nothing else. I couldn't understand it. Like reeds near a pool, they wilted and swayed from exhaustion.

Kira closed her eyes, and I winced at the sight of her purpled eye and battered cheek. "When I finished, she pulled a sharpened knife out from under the table and stabbed me in the shoulder before I could react. I could see the murder in her eyes. She only missed my heart because she'd never tried to do it before. That's all that kept us alive in the confusion of the moment—their lack of training."

She stopped and gathered herself, to my surprise, as she found a second wave of strength.

"They tried to kill us all. What the fuck did you tell those people about us?" Kira asked, direct as ever, even in this strange new state.

"I told her a truth. You executed her daughter."

Kira opened her eyes. "I'd never even been to Nudasi—"

She stopped. I saw the kindling of understanding.

"You confirmed it for her," I said. The last of the sun faded, and only purple and orange twilight remained around us. "You described her daughter's death in detail. And you showed her the bloody hands."

"The rock witch." Kira looked up toward the stars. "I thought you'd left some trap, but I actually set it for myself long ago."

"Where are the others?" I demanded. I couldn't believe that nine guardians had been killed facing Priscilla and her people. Not guardians from Ninetha, trained by Kira. "Did they die there?"

"Torit died in the city," Kira confirmed. "I wish we could have given him back to the ground, but we had to run or die ourselves. Once we fell into formation and got to our spears, we scattered our opponents like leaves in a wind."

One of the guardians said, "We were burning with anger. We tracked you. We were going to run harder than we'd ever run in our lives, and for longer. We wanted to get revenge for Torit. But that plan died in the night."

I thought back to the young guardian as he had stared me down. Poor Torit. All my mercy had given him was days more of life, not a whole future. I'd murdered him. I just hadn't had the stomach to do it with the musket while I could see his face.

"Zulian was the first to hear the screams from Nudasi." Kira pointed at one of the guardians.

The screams? I stopped thinking about Torit.

For a moment, Zulian struggled to find the words. Then, he nodded and squinted with pain, recalling the moment. "It's something I'll never forget, that sound. So many of them."

The guardian shook his head at the memory and slumped forward.

Ishmael instantly turned to face the path back toward Nudasi.

"Ishmael?" I asked.

Despite the gloom of twilight, he pulled out his spyglass and peered through it. He wasn't worried about the guardians anymore.

"Almost as soon as the rest of us could hear them, they stopped," Kira continued. "We couldn't figure out what they were. But they stopped. We kept going in the morning. It was cold. So cold we struggled to breathe. Banda fell over twice. His lips were blue. I didn't want more guardians to die. I turned back. I thought we could sneak around Nudasi and head back out into the land. We'd eat lizards and drink cactus, but we would return home. But my plan was a deadly mistake."

"Priscilla attacked again?" I imagined a crowd of senators with sharpened knives running up the mountain at Kira.

"She did not," Kira said, and looked down at the ground. "It was not Nudasi."

"It was an archangel," Ishmael said.

"It was," Zulian said, with all the strength of a mouse in his voice. "The Lamentations of the Exodus describes them as glimmering. But this one's body was pitted silver, corrosion across its flanks. It had shoulder blades of knives, and broken fingers like mangled daggers."

Ishmael shivered.

"It dragged its left leg like a wounded dog," Kira said. "It wasn't making good time up the path, but then again, neither were we."

"We thought we were saved," Zulian said. "Emmi over there wept when she saw it."

"I thought, surely we were on a holy quest now," she said.

"We hailed it," Zulian said, as he slid down the rock. Another two guardians sat down near him as well. And Kira did nothing about it. "We were in awe at seeing it with our own eyes. An actual archangel. Surely, it came with gifts."

"But as we closed on each other, I heard it keep asking one question," Kira said. "Over and over."

Ishmael lowered the spyglass and gloomily turned to Kira. "It asked for me."

She turned to him, heavy with the weight of her story. "Your name is Ishmael?"

"That is what I am called."

"What abominations have you unleashed with your spells

of literature, or was there some greater sin against the gods that they had to send an archangel to hunt you?"

"My only crime is literacy," Ishmael said. "I tried to renounce it once, and still the archangel came for me. I think it's broken."

What a heresy, I thought, to call a god-machine broken, but after all the sins and horrors so far, it didn't cause much of a ripple among the guardians. Some of them even nodded.

"It grabbed one of my guardians, Dina, and threw him aside." Kira took a deep breath. What came next hurt her, as the words made her live it again. The pain made me feel sorry for her, which I didn't want. It was a traitorous feeling, and I fought it. "I heard his back break against a rock. We were screaming, confused. Why was an archangel killing us?"

Ishmael nodded knowingly.

"Our spears were useless," Zulian added. "They just broke against it. It threw more of us off the side of the mountain. I heard them scream all the way down the rock face."

"Banda and Sed saved the rest of us," Kira said. "They pulled out a rope and fastened it to a stone as the archangel slashed us to pieces like a whirlwind. It took the two of them to pick up the rock and leap to their deaths so the rope could surprise the creature and yank it right off the rim with them. Leaving us bloodied, almost half of us dead, and those who survived beaten."

The surviving guardians looked hungry, tired, and cold. A couple of them looked vaguely familiar. I would have seen them guarding doors at home, or maybe walking with me out onto the roads to watch the commons gather for their vittle.

"I'm a pious woman, librarian," Kira said. "You've seen what I did in the citadel, what I would have done to you, if

I'd been allowed. And yet the archangel would have sliced my head off without even a second's consideration. What does that mean?"

"It's a dangerous machine," Ishmael said. "Maybe the gods made it and left it here, but I think it lost its mind a long time ago when it stumbled across my family and we became its one target. Or maybe the gods just hate me above all other sinners. I don't know."

He slid his pack off and pulled out a packet of vittle. Kira glanced at it, then forced herself to look away.

"I looked over the side of the cliff. I watched it stand up," Kira said. "Still covered in their blood and entrails. Then, it just started walking back toward Nudasi like nothing had happened. I didn't want to face it again on the trail, so we kept running."

Ishmael threw her the packet of vittle.

I felt ashamed to see how quickly the guardians descended on it with a flurry of green cloth. The guardians already sitting on the ground crawled to Kira's feet and looked up at her with desperation.

"Eat a small portion only!" Kira growled as she opened the packet for them all. "Or your stomach will revolt. Alpheus, slow!"

I leaned over to Ishmael and whispered, "Do you trust her?"

"You've known her longer than I have. She wanted to kill us. She could still want to kill us."

"But you gave her food." My arms ached, so I lowered the musket a touch.

"I was distracting her," Ishmael said. "They're clearly starving. We could run around them right now and head for Tamarlane. I doubt they could catch us, in their state."

The guardians paid almost no attention to our small conference. Even Kira had turned her back to us.

I'd never in my life seen her do that.

"They don't know about Tamarlane," I said. "If we leave them, they might die."

"That may not be the worst thing," Ishmael whispered. "Remember when she tried to burn me alive, and she murdered your family?"

"I will never forget. I can still taste the bile on the back of my tongue," I hissed at him. "But do you believe you could leave those guardians by her to die? Do you want to carry the death of ten souls to be weighed with yours when you stand at the entrance to the underworld? What kind of life would you have to live to balance against that?"

"It might not be any life at all if we help her."

"I'd push Kira off the side of the rim. I still might. But only her. The rest of them, they were trained to follow her." And my family had taken that for granted. Abused that. Trusted that they didn't have to gain the loyalty of the guardians because they had Kira's.

As I stood there in the growing night, I realized that I was not the person who could return to Ninetha and gain revenge with the blood of everyone who stood against my family. If I couldn't kill Torit myself, if these ten more lives weighed this heavily on my conscience, then I could never live with the murder it would take to sit in the heart of the citadel again.

So, if I didn't care to rule Ninetha, what could I do here?

"Kira," I called softly, like reassuring an alley dog and holding out a treat. "Kira."

She chewed slowly on a mouthful of vittle as she turned.

"What are you doing?" Ishmael grabbed my shoulder. His fingers dug deep into my muscle, and I had to wrench myself free.

"Saving our souls," I told him.

"Damn it." Ishmael glanced around. I could see him trying to decide whether to run past the guardians and head to Tamarlane on his own, or trust me and help the woman who had tried to kill him. But I knew his heart wasn't in it. As we left Nudasi, he'd asked me if having Kira's single soul on my conscience was worth it. I had to believe Ishmael still walked that true path, even if seeing the round Earth had shaken him.

"We're headed to a city called Tamarlane." I pointed at the cairns leading straight down this section of the rim. They used the destroyed edges of the Cleft to help a traveler get quickly down to the ground. "Ishmael has directions. They'll have a cornucopia."

"I didn't see any god-lights last night," Kira said.

"I don't know how far it is," I said. "We can sleep the night here while you recover. Send some guardians with flasks to walk up the path a ways; they'll find pools of water from the clouds."

"What else is up there?" Kira asked.

"The edge of the world," I said flatly.

Kira looked at me, trying to tell if I was toying with her. She couldn't find a satisfactory answer on my face, so she turned to two women in green. "Emmi, On-ja, follow the path up to the clouds and fill as many flasks as you can."

They gathered flasks and, with a wistful glance at the bag of vittle that Kira now bundled away into a bag, started the climb.

The last of what little glow remained in the sky would fade at any moment. They'd be coming back down in the dark.

"Do you have anything to burn, so they can see to return?" I asked.

"The moon will rise soon," Kira said. "And they have the best eyes."

The spears remained on the ground to the side where the guardians threw them, and I still held the musket in my hands, although it pointed to the ground now.

"Ishmael, take one of the spears," I said.

Kira waved carelessly over at them. "Take them all, Librarian. Move them over to where you'll camp for the night, so that you feel safe. They'll do nothing for us if that god-machine comes for us tonight. If that happens, we'll run. You should too, Lilith."

I set the musket against the side of my leg. "Maybe."

I took the first watch, made sure to sit behind a boulder, and listened to the murmur of the guardians. For the first time in my life, when Kira had introduced them, I did my best to hold their names in my head: Nichael, Xiona, Li, Dumuzi, Inanna, and Ishkur were new to me. On-Ja and Emmi had left for water. There was Zulian, who had told us some of their story. I heard Alpheus by a far-off rock, throwing up what little he had eaten.

I sat with my musket across my lap, my back to the rough stone, and listened as a small chuckle rose from a guardian as Alpheus staggered back to them.

With just a touch of food, a little cheer had returned to some of them.

Emmi and On-Ja came back two hours later, and I listened to the guardians all sigh happily as they drank cold, fresh water. On-Ja sighed loudly as she lay down in a soft patch of ground.

Footsteps crunched across the gravel toward me, and I raised the musket.

"It's me," Kira said.

"I know," I said. I didn't lower the musket. "That's why I'm pointing this at you."

Kira smiled as she sat on a rock several lengths from me. "Before Nudasi, Torit said you had him at the tip of your musket, but you didn't fire. Why?"

"I didn't see the point in wasting a life. Yet he still died. I killed him by leading you into that trap."

"We both share the blame." Kira folded her arms. "This started long before that."

"I don't know how to do this," I said. Even with death between us, I didn't have the strength for anything but honesty when I heard her speak. "To stand near you. To see you. My fingers tremble."

"We're both trying to survive, Lilith. That's enough for now. Answers, or a new path—that can come later."

"New path? I can't forgive you," I said. "Never."

"I know."

"I'm so tired, Kira," I confessed. I lowered the musket. "Since the citadel fell, I've only slept in small shifts on the ground, and when I finally got a real bed to relax in, a crazy man with a knife attacked me because of things you did when I was just a child. Then, I climbed the rim, walked through the clouds themselves, saw the old world from myth itself hanging in the void at the edge of the world, and there's an archangel chasing us, and here you are, sitting in front of me."

"It's been a fucking strange series of events," Kira agreed.

"What do you mean when you say you saw the old—"

"You killed my family." Because, wonders aside, that scar throbbed far more than any cares about cosmology or histories.

Kira lowered her head and stared off to the side at Ishmael, who slept soundly, wrapped in his cape.

"I can't undo that," she said, her voice almost lost to the wind. It didn't thunder at us here, but it still moaned across the rocks.

"I can never forgive it," I said again. Tears stung my eyes.

"You shouldn't. It was a ghastly thing."

"You took everything from me," I cried. "Everything."

I hated myself for not being able to kill her, and I really, really despised that tiny part of me that enjoyed talking to her again. I wanted to scream and let the pain rush out of me into the air.

But that wasn't how it worked, was it? I had to carry this dull, aching horror with me until it could fade away on its own.

I thought back to the moment in our quarters when Sinza and Hetelia had argued with Kame. They'd played in the shadows and tried to goad Kira. Like teasing a cat with a scrap of meat, but keeping it just out of reach. You couldn't be mad when it hissed and came for you with claws out.

I couldn't forgive Kira. But I knew that my brothers and sisters had lost control of a fire they didn't have to set. I could blame them as well. Even though I would do anything to have them back. To have my old life back.

"Ninetha belongs to all of us," I said. "I have the right to return to it. I don't want to rule; I just want to go home."

I may have lost my family, but I could walk the streets again. Smell the familiar mud brick and sand kicked into the air with a hint of curry and stale basic. I could live in the commons, I thought. It would be a small life, but I could make it work.

Kira didn't reply to that. No need to voice a refusal. We both knew that if I came back and was discovered, the bountiful houses would revolt to try to regain their old status.

I hated it. But I understood why she would never let me step past the Afriq Gate.

Kira pointed at the sleeping form of Ishmael to push the conversation in a whole new direction. "You and the librarian?"

"What? No!" My denial came too quick for her. An eyebrow twitched, and she cocked her head at me.

"He's pleasant to look at," she noted.

Said the woman who would have burned him to death when she first saw him, I thought.

"He's far older than me."

"That can be its own fun," Kira said. "Or haven't you—?"

Was this a game of hers to keep me off my balance? Despite my suspicion, embarrassment rose up through me.

"I've been busy staying alive, Kira."

"You don't want to die with regrets."

"I won't." I rested the musket on the point of my knee. "My brothers and sisters had few regrets when it came to lust and love. I am not naïve. There were boys who came to me. But I think—"

I stopped. I couldn't handle looking directly at her. I put a hand over my forehead and rubbed it.

I hated her.

I had to hate her. Talking about my brothers and sisters to their murderer? It was a dishonor to their memory.

"I used to think those were real loves," I said in a broken

voice, as I followed a treasonous line of thought that had only occurred to me just this moment. "Now, I'm wondering, how many of those people threw themselves at us because they wanted, or needed, something only the cornucopia could give them?"

I looked back up at Kira and saw the answer on her face.

"Dogshit." I turned my head from her. I thought about the boys I'd teased in the courtyards with ice cream, the ones I'd kissed and handed slices of star fruit, apples, or honey-soaked dates. "We abused the god-machine."

And what I couldn't admit to Kira was how much I missed it. I missed the soft beds, clean water, and servants. I missed cold sweet treats, and well-spiced, hearty rices. I wanted to walk along the whitewashed corridors again, with my hand trailing the cool surface.

"I helped," Kira muttered. "Abe will balance my soul in the underworld, and some nights I think the scales may tip me into one of the hells."

"Either way, Ninetha is all yours," I said. "I hope it brings you peace."

Kira said nothing. I saw no peace in her eyes.

"Get away from me, Kira," I said. I raised the musket. "It hurts me to see you."

Ishmael woke me in the dawn. I'd been dreaming of small globes, worlds spinning about each other and god-machines stirring around them like insects around a hive. And I'd dreamed of my siblings, laughing on armchairs as they drank too much. Now, tiny droplets of mist beaded my face, and the rock I slept against dripped with even more moisture.

"Time to go," Ishmael whispered.

The low clouds covered us in gloom as we quietly rear-ranged our clothing, tied our boots up, and pulled on our travelers' packs. We gave the guardians their spears, but forced them to walk in front of us.

"I won't turn my back to that woman," Ishmael said. "Just because the two of you are talking doesn't mean—"

"I agree."

Walking down a mountain sounded easier than going up, but I found that facing downward made it easier to pitch for-ward. The backs of my legs hurt before long, and when we had to walk along hard rock cliffs, it felt like I might stumble right off the rim's craggy sides and into the air.

When we paused for lunch, Ishmael climbed a boulder and peered up the path we'd spent the morning on. He waved me up, and I struggled up the stone to his side.

He handed me the spyglass and pointed.

"By the cloud line," Ishmael said softly.

An archangel crouched over the ground next to the same boulders we'd slept against last night. I watched as it picked up a stone, hunched over, and sniffed it. Shoulder blades fanned out from its back like shattered winglets, and the silver metal skin, mottled and mangy with pitted spots, slid as mechan-ical muscle moved. Impossibly thin, it stood up, silhouetted against the soft gray light under the clouds.

"It is Arbet," Ishmael said, his voice flat with suppressed emotions.

I gasped when it turned to look right at me with black eyes too large for a human face. Shadows slid over the mouthless jaw, and the neck of steel cords flexed as it moved.

"Those hands," I whispered. And I thought about the tale of the bandersnatch. Those claws that catch . . .

The archangel took a strong step forward, and dragged its left leg behind it.

"What mangled the leg?" I asked. "Was that you?"

"No," Ishmael said. "Something else long ago. It's always been like that."

"We need to keep moving," I said. I'd known it was out there from Ishmael's story while we were out in the wastes. But I'd treated it like a mirage, far out on the horizon and unreal. Kira's story prickled my back. The archangel hunted us, and I could feel that new knowledge deep in my bones now.

"Oh yes, yes we do," Ishmael said, and slid off the rock to the ground.

We hurried as fast as safety allowed. Occasionally I'd glance back up, expecting to see the archangel, but it remained half a day behind us, dragging itself across the rim.

"In the old days, they said the archangels didn't kill," Ishmael told me. The guardians climbed down a tough slab of rock ahead of us, using a rope. "They would slide a finger through your nose up into your brain, and after that you couldn't read. You would sit around, tell strange stories, and stare off into the distance for no reason. The cornucopia would give you what you needed, but you lost the ability to make anything, to invent, or even just to be curious."

I thought that sounded worse than death.

After I clambered down, Ishmael untied the rope and climbed down the rock. He saw no point in leaving it there to help the archangel. At least twice, I thought Ishmael would fall off and die, but he made it down to us and jumped to the ground with a grunt.

We stood and regarded the world in front of us. From here, foothills stretched down toward flat land. I'd never been so happy to see an even expanse of dreary desert dirt and sand.

"We can make a better pace now," Kira said. She wiped sweat from her forehead with a sleeve caked in dried blood. She'd gone without food and walked the rim so hard that her cheeks poked gauntly from her face.

The guardians used their spears like staffs to help them walk. The Kira I had once known would have yelled at them, as it would warp the weapons to lean on them like that. But she gripped her own spear as well.

Even with that help, Li slipped and broke his wrist an hour later. On-Ja found a straight stick in her pack, wrapped the fabric and stick tightly to splint Li's hand, and we moved on.

We slept with our heads on our packs that night. We didn't open them or take our boots off. We all wanted to be able to get up and run quickly if necessary.

I had barely closed my eyes when Ishmael shook me awake. I blinked. "I just fell asleep."

"It's your watch."

"No. Not enough sleep," I groaned as I pushed myself out of the dirt.

"It's never enough." He pushed a timepiece into my hand. I stared at the smooth, cornucopia-made brass oval in the moonlight. I felt the tick of each second in it. "Two hours."

I rubbed my crusty eyes. By the time I opened them again, Ishmael was snoring softly on the ground.

Had I fallen asleep? For a second I panicked, but then I glanced down at the timepiece's hand. No, I hadn't.

I crawled up onto a mound of dirt that gave me a vantage

point over the sleeping guardians, and I peered up the path toward the hard walls of rock that we'd struggled down all day. No glint of menacing silver.

Yet.

The moon imperceptibly crawled across the sky as I stared at it and let my mind flutter about. If I no longer wanted to raise an army against Ninetha, what was there for me to do?

I felt cut off from everything as I sat there alone, with my knees up to my chin to keep warm.

No people to call my own.

No plan.

Vengeance had congealed into an uncomfortable lump inside of me, and the roaring fire had guttered out.

I was stuck between an archangel that wanted to kill my companion and the people who'd killed my family. I realized I'd been so tense for so long that my muscles hurt. My jaw throbbed.

I kept forgetting to breathe. I felt like a little desert animal, all scrunched up to take up the least space as possible as it shivered, hoping no one would notice.

Please don't eat me, world.

I missed Kame. Hells, I even missed Anwago. Endu's small kindnesses. Yusi's brush. I reached up to my hair. I'd been twisting it every night to form small locks. No braids anymore. No time.

I wondered if I would ever see a mirror again.

It seemed like a silly thing to miss. But it still reminded me that I could never go back to the way things had been. That world had died. The citadel as I knew it, even if I could get back there, would only contain the ghosts of people I could no longer talk to.

And without the people, the walls and luxuries were just unimportant, lifeless things.

When I woke Ishmael up, he grumbled at me. We took a moment to wake the others, sip some water, eat a handful of vittle, and start our walk again. Here, in the foothills, we could safely navigate at night without worrying about falling over a cliff or into a deep cut.

"The Milky Way will guide us," Ishmael said.

"I still don't see any lights from Tamarlane," Nichael said. He'd been worrying about that for hours now, even after Kira told him to stop. I noticed that Kira made sure to stand between Nichael and me. He wouldn't let it go, though. "We can see out onto the wastes. Where is the damn city?"

"I don't know." Ishmael pulled out his spyglass again, but this time he scanned the horizon and not the rim. "But we have to move forward and follow the cairns. They were left here for a reason."

We could give up, I thought, and just sit down and wait for the archangel to put us out of our collective misery.

Ishmael slid the spyglass away. "We can split from them at Tamarlane," he said quietly to me. "I know you don't want to walk next to Kira any more than you have to. Neither do I."

"I keep expecting them to rush us," I said.

It exhausted me to watch for any holes, rocks, or bushes to trip over while at the same time keeping an eye on everyone up in front of me.

"I keep waiting for them to attack as well," Ishmael whispered.

When the morning sun began to paint the lands orange, we took a break to sip water. Canteens clinked softly in the morning air, and the guardians muttered softly to each other.

"I don't think I'll sleep properly until I deliver my notes to New Alexandria," Ishmael said. I'd noticed that his excitement grew the farther down the foothills we walked. "What we found changes everything."

"But does it?" I'd reached the end of my patience for his strange knowledge.

"What do you mean?" He looked wounded.

"The griots said the rim was the edge of the world. You dismissed it. Yet there it was. I wonder, did you even believe in archangels before you saw one?"

Ishmael looped his thumbs into the straps across his chest as he clanked along beside me. "No. I didn't think archangels were real. But don't be so smug. You and I know that you would never have hunted for the truth yourself. We are different that way. I was wrong, that's correct, but I was the one who decided to come and see if I was right or wrong."

We slipped into a light bickering again over the value of written words versus stories, until I happened to look ahead and realize Kira could hear us.

"We should stop," I said. "We'll go round and round, and never agree. We don't want more reasons for Kira to try killing us again."

"In New Alexandria, you don't have to hide your curiosity like this," Ishmael said. "You can talk freely."

"We're not in New Alexandria; we're in the wastes with Kira and her guardians."

He wanted to tell me more about the city of his birth. When I thought about how Kira had ripped Ninetha away from me, I realized the archangel had done the same to Ishmael. It had forced him to flee his home and everything he had ever known. And it was clear that, as he talked about the library at the heart of the city, Ishmael missed it.

I took off my crinkly cape and hung it over my head for some shade against the sun.

I had just started to wonder if Tamarlane really existed, and if Nichael would lose his patience and kill me soon, when a guardian—Dumuzi—shouted in excitement. "I see buildings!"

"Be wary!" Kira shouted.

We had no idea what the people in Tamarlane would be like. Were they hostile or friendly? Did they follow the code?

No one came out to regard us.

A large bird made out of twisted, rusted metal glared at us as we approached from the rim's foothills. It perched on a black arch into the city as we passed underneath.

The guardians lowered their spears and stepped cautiously through the main street.

"It's covered with the sands," Kira said. She dug at the road with her boot until she hit stone. The sand came up over her ankles.

"Maybe there was a storm," I said.

The rectangular buildings had shingled roofs in a triangular shape, a strange shape to me, but similar to Nudasi's homes. I peeked between the doors of the nearest one.

More sand was jammed up inside against the walls.

"Commander!" On-Ja shouted from farther up the road.

She and Dumuzi shoved the doors of a great temple open, and we all gasped. Hundreds of corpses lay inside, their skin dried and pulled tightly over their bones.

Dumuzi stepped away from the doors and leaned over, sick at the sight.

"They didn't return them to the ground," Ishmael said, as shocked as everyone else.

"I've seen animal carcasses out in the wastes dried up like that," I said.

"I think I know why they died," Kira said from around the corner. She'd moved around to the other side of the temple, toward the heart of the town.

I stepped out after her. And my heart fell as I came around the corner.

The rotted cornucopia that rose at the heart of Tamarlane slumped in on itself. Sheets of dried tar stuck to the melted roots. It looked like a tree I'd seen slowly wither away after lightning struck it and it burned from the inside out.

I grabbed my stomach. It felt like the sight had kicked me in the ribs.

"Have you ever heard of a dead cornucopia?" I stared at it, utterly rooted in place. I didn't want to go any closer. "Librarian, is there anything like this in the world?"

"I've never read of it, or heard of it, and certainly I've never seen it," Ishmael said, just as shocked as any of us.

"They starved to death in there," I said, horrified.

The wind shifted, and I gagged at the smell of putrefaction that rolled over us. I wrapped my cape around my face, neck, and mouth so that I could approach the god-machine.

Splotches of iridescent sores pockmarked the veins and roots that shimmered as we all cautiously approached the guts of the cornucopia. The shadows inside its body hid the maw of the well at the heart of it. I approached as close to it as I dared and looked down. The shaft under the cornucopia burrowed far into the ground, maybe all the way down into the underworld itself, where the spirits of the dead wandered.

As if reading my mind, Ishmael said, "We shouldn't stand here. Ghosts may come for us."

"This is wrong," Kira whispered from next to us. I saw a tear in the corner of her eye. "We shouldn't look into the heart of the holy works."

But she didn't move away. She reached up to touch a strand of melted cornucopia, a curved rib of obsidian material that rose into the air over the debris pit, but Ishmael grabbed her wrist. "If something infected the god-machine, what do you think it will do to human flesh?"

Kira pulled her hand away. She flipped her spear forward in a smooth movement and tapped it with the point.

The entire rib slumped, shattered by the mere touch, brittle and frail. Pieces flaked off into the wind and flew out over Tamarlane, but most of it slid down into the shaft.

We all jumped back nervously and listened to the echoes of pieces of cornucopia as they shattered and bounced off the walls.

A distant moan rose from the depths.

"We've provoked the dead," Kira said. "We should leave."

"I should write this down," Ishmael whispered.

"Don't you dare pull out a book near her," I hissed at him. "She will kill you. We cannot provoke her."

"I know," he said. The grimness on his face matched the tight fear in my jaw. "I said *should*, not that I was going to do it. I'm interested in preserving my life as well."

"Says the man who wanders from city to city to find books. Or teach literacy." ·

We backed farther away from the cornucopia.

"It doesn't matter, I guess," Ishmael said. "Without getting any food here, we'll starve. We don't have enough to feed all of them. We're as dead as the cornucopia."

"No," I said to him. "On the rim they would have starved,

but Kira and I know how to live out here. All women know how to survive out in the wild away from the city, or there would be no children in Ninetha."

"It's one thing to travel across lands where there are berries and fruits, but here?" Ishmael swept his hand about. "There's nothing to eat but dirt, sand, and rock."

I realized Kira had slipped closer to us to listen. I shut my mouth and turned toward her. "Do you have something to add?" I asked.

"We won't starve right away. If you help us with your vittle, we can scavenge. It won't be comfortable," Kira said. "But we'll live. I don't know how well we'll fare with the archangel chasing us. It'll be hard to take the time to hunt down what we can off the land. It can be done. But—"

"What?" I asked. I expected the worst, and steeled myself.

Kira swallowed. She didn't like the words she held on her tongue. She sighed slightly with defeat. "We need to go to Nudasi. We won't survive the return to Ninetha without good traveling food. Not with that . . . thing chasing us."

"You want to go back there? To Nudasi?"

Kira folded her arms to hug herself lightly and squinted, with a pained look. "I've been turning it over in my head since I walked around the corner and saw the cornucopia."

"Kira," I said. "They'll murder us."

"There's no other choice that I can see," Kira replied. "Unless either of you has a plan that you haven't told me. I'm willing to hear anything you say."

Ishmael looked across the brown wastes and shook his head. "We're dead either way. Priscilla sent us here to die."

"This is insane," I muttered.

Far down at the end of the street, Zulian waved a strip of

cloth on the tip of his spear to catch our attention. "The archangel has caught up to us," he shouted.

Guardians filtered in from the streets leading out from the cornucopia.

"We found nothing," Inanna reported to Kira. "After the cornucopia failed, they picked everything clean."

"They starved and didn't even try to leave for Nudasi," I marveled.

"They waited too long . . . and then it was too late," Ishmael said.

"They would have waited for their gods to have mercy, for it to start working again," Kira said. "They would have believed it would turn back on at any moment, all the way to their last, dying chant of a prayer in that temple."

"How do you know that?" I asked.

Her words came out heavily: "It's what I would have done."

"This . . ." I hunted for the right words. When I found them, I aimed them straight ahead at Kira. "You sound shaken."

"I met the parents of someone I executed. Fought a broken archangel that killed my guardians. Now, I stand before a dead cornucopia, which was the fulfillment of the covenant between us and the gods if we chose to turn our ways from literacy. What does this mean? Do you know, Librarian?"

"Maybe Tamarlane did something heinous enough for the gods to take it away from them," Ishmael suggested.

"I saw no books," Kira said.

"Or maybe the same thing that shattered the rim of the world and changed the lands around us infected the one city closest to the Cleft. The cornucopia cannot produce sustenance, the land won't take the dead, and the lands are scarred. This part of the world is broken."

"We should leave; we don't have time to waste," Kira said.

"You're not going to tie us up and leave us for the archangel?" I asked.

"We barely have the strength to get to Nudasi. I'm not going to risk any more lives trying to attack you two. He's rested, well fed, and strong. You have the musket." Kira leaned against her spear and pointed at me with her other hand. "I can see the worry in your eyes. I swear to you, Lilith, I'm praying we make it to Nudasi and figure out how to get enough food so that we can part ways and never see each other again."

I stared at her face, full of weariness and honesty. A dangerous woman with her guardians and her spear, but one who ran straight at her goal with no subterfuge.

"We need to slow the archangel down." I shrugged my travel pack off. "I'm going to go do that."

I unslung the musket, then patted my bag of cartridges and the other pouch full of musket balls to make sure they were still tied to my hips.

"I don't think that will do any better than our spears," Kira said. "It's an archangel."

"I have only one way to find out. It's an experiment to test a theory." I handed Ishmael my pack and smiled at him. "You start walking. Without all this on my back, I can catch up by running."

"I'll stand back with you," Kira said.

"No. You need the head start," I said. "All of you do. So, go. Now!"

After inspecting me for a moment, Kira nodded and wordlessly waved the guardians into motion. The green robes headed out into the wastes, parallel to the rim, walking toward Nudasi over the horizon.

Ishmael stood near me, uncertain. I grabbed his shoulder and squeezed. "I'll catch up. I promise."

"Then, I'll see you soon," Ishmael said.

"You're the only friend I have in this world," I told him. "I'm sticking to you like a burr to fur."

Ishmael gave me a forgery of a smile, and then he pulled himself away to catch up with the guardians.

Once I couldn't see him anymore, I dropped my shoulders.

I had no faith that this would work, and the thing I'd seen in Ishmael's spyglass terrified every single one of the hells out of me.

A cold wind rebounded off the rim and swept its way across the dirt toward Tamarlane. A dust devil skipped and bounced over the tumble of rocks outside the city's edge.

I lay on the far slope of one of the roofs and propped the musket on the peak to steady it.

Nothing stirred as I waited.

Just like hunting sand rabbits: I needed patience and stillness.

When the sun glanced off silver and caught my eye, I squinted. The archangel stepped out from the rocks that had hidden it from me and limped its way across the dirt toward Tamarlane. And me.

I'd paced out distances. A hundred steady steps, then I'd dragged a boot to make a line. Another hundred, a second line. A hundred more, and the third.

At three hundred paces, I would strike a target one out of three times with my old musket, Alice. This musket that I hadn't even named was one I hadn't practiced with, so I wasn't sure how temperamental it was.

Better to let the archangel get closer. A hundred steps. If I stayed steady and calm.

Deep, deep breaths, I told myself. Watch the marks. Ignore the discomfort of lying flat on my stomach and chest on a hot roof.

The archangel lurched ever closer.

It stopped at the three hundred mark.

I did not move.

"Come on." I wanted to slide farther back down the roof to hide, but I looked through the sighting notch at the archangel's splotchy metallic statue of a face.

"Come to me," I whispered.

It looked down at the lines I'd scratched into the ground, then twisted to face right at me.

My stomach dropped. "Oh, shit."

I lost my nerve. I could see silver near the top of my sighting notch. This would likely hit the chest, so I fired. A loud clang rang out. A hit! I coughed smoke out of my lungs and stood up just in time to see the archangel topple backward into the dirt.

"I got you!" There was no one to see me scream and hold the musket in the air like a sprint winner holding a trophy up.

I eagerly jumped down from the lower edge onto the soft sand of the street.

"Say my family are heretics," I shouted in glee. "It may be true, but the power of our powder cannot be—"

The archangel stirred.

I slid to a stop and almost fell over.

It sat up, and we stared at each other for a still moment. The expressionless face did not move.

Then, the archangel smoothly stood and dragged its leg

toward me. I started walking backward. I wanted to keep no more than a hundred steps away from it, and I reloaded the musket as we walked.

I took another shot right at its chest. Sparks flew, and a clang filled the air again. The archangel—Arbet—staggered back and onto a knee. It struggled to stand and face me.

"Stop." The archangel's voice crackled, with bird whistles around it. It sounded like more than one voice spoke at the same time, and as though something whispered just after it let the word go.

I reloaded, hitting the musket two or three times into the dirt to tamp the ball. I didn't see a mark anywhere on the archangel. Now, I let it get closer to me as I aimed the musket. Fifty paces. Forty. Thirty. Twenty. My legs shook. I wanted to close my eyes and never again stare at that otherworldly, unyielding silver face.

I aimed for its head and pulled the trigger. The explosion of powder filled the air between us, and smoke swirled around us both. I saw the shot strike the archangel's face. Its head rocked back, and then bowed forward again.

Only a faint pockmark showed on its forehead.

"Tell me all you know about Ishmael of New Alexandria," the haunting voice demanded. "Tell me, but do not lie. I can see your lies; I see all lies. I see you, Lilith of Ninetha."

The wind took the smell of powder completely away as I stared at the archangel. Those jagged shoulder blades shifted as it moved, and the air around them rippled with heat.

Lightning danced from the archangel's broken knee. "Tell me, Lilith, tell me. Lilith, tell me. Unburden your soul, Lilith. Free yourself and tell me about Ishmael of New Alexandria. Tell me everything."

"What are you?" I shouted at it.

I tripped from walking backward. Arbet surged forward and snapped at me with razored fingers. I caught myself, and I jumped back away. The archangel moved like a rattlesnake when it had to.

"Thou shall not suffer a librarian to live," it calmly said to me, and yet it said it with such force, my ears hurt. "There are few rules to the compact. If you will not do what is necessary, I am charged with enforcement. I am charged. I am charged. I am charged."

Arbet's words trailed off.

Shooting it again would do nothing. Kira had been right. I turned and ran.

"Humanity drips with transgression," Arbet called after me. "Your obstinance threatens balance, the ecosystem will fail. Why will you not remain within simple parameters?"

I left Tamarlane behind, panting as I fled the unstoppable machine and desperate to rejoin other humans after the encounter.

"I see you, Lilith of Ninetha! I have marked you! You thwart our will, and you are noticed." The words warped and twisted around the buildings as I ran. How did it know my name and where I came from?

Stupid question. It was an archangel, with the ear of the gods, and I had fired a musket into its unyielding silver face.

"You will tell me where Ishmael of New Alexandria is," the messenger of the gods shouted after me. "You will all repent. The preserve of humanity will have balance."

I ran for a whole day before the glint of the sun off the archangel disappeared in the distance. Then, I slowed to clamber over boulders and rocks to make it nearly impossible for it to follow me. That accomplished, I ran long zig-zagging patterns through withered bushes and sand until I found fresh footprints.

"Arbet is well behind us," I told Ishmael when I caught up to him.

"For now," the librarian said, looking past my shoulder.

Four days later, as we approached Nudasi in the dark early morning hours, near starving and exhausted, Dumuzi hallucinated that the rocks spoke to him. We had to tie his hands and link the rope to On-Ja and Zulian so he didn't run off screaming. By then, none of us had rested for more than a few hours, as we knew the archangel searched for us as we slept. We had lost Arbet in the maze of house-sized rock shards between Tamarlane and Nudasi that had been thrown clear of the rim when the Cleft shattered, but we all knew the archangel hunted us implacably.

"It never tires, never sleeps, and never stops," Ishmael said to Kira at one of our too-short moments of rest, as guardians hacked at a thick cactus for the juice and meat.

"You've lived your whole life looking over your shoulder," I said to him. Now that I had a taste of the archangel, I wished I could spit it out of my life.

We finally stopped and huddled near a boulder outside Nudasi to plan what came next. If my stomach didn't cramp with hunger and my skin ache as I listened, I could have enjoyed the labyrinth of stone all around us. The remains of the rim of the world, scattered around for anyone to clamber over. We stood in a natural hallway of rock. The ceiling was the clouds that rushed toward the Cleft overhead, and the soft carpet of sand below our feet was the floor.

"They know I'm with Lilith. I can't go ahead and ask for food for us all," Ishmael said to Kira. He still hated Kira, I could see. But he wanted to live, and we were all trying to survive together. "All we brought Nudasi was death and destruction. You, and then the archangel. There's no one here who could go there and ask for help."

"If we don't get to the cornucopia, we die," Kira said. "We go in using a spear-wedge formation that drives hard down the road until we get to the cornucopia. They won't try to break through if we hold a formation."

I looked around at the exhausted, hungry guardians who had been scrounging for whatever the land would give us for days, ever since our vittle had ran out. Could these guardians even run?

"And how many people will that kill?" I asked.

"We move quickly," Kira said. "Before they know what's happening, we can be at the cornucopia. Lilith, Ishmael, you will get what we need, and the guardians will form an arc around you both, with spears facing out and the cornucopia to our backs."

"They'll hem us in," I said, imagining it.

"I'll bargain with them," Kira said. "They don't want to waste lives on the ends of our spears."

"What can you give them that lets us leave without fighting our way out?" Ishmael asked.

"The rock witch's murderer," I said. I saw Kira's plan, and I felt a giddy confusion of regret, sorrow, and satisfaction at the delayed justice for my family.

"No," Zulian snapped. "We'll die before we turn over the Lord of Ninetha."

Hearing Kira called that felt like a slap to the face. Even though I knew I wasn't going back to Ninetha, I bristled.

Zulian saw that and looked away from me.

"We can avoid bloodshed," Kira said.

"And what, she returns to Ninetha?" On-Ja asked bitterly.

"It won't matter to me at that point what you do," Kira said, with a glance at me. I couldn't tell what the significance of it was. "I only care that you'll be alive to make those decisions. You decide what comes next after I'm gone."

Zulian looked ready to cry, and Kira softened. She put her hands on his head, and he choked with emotion. "You spoke for the gods," he whispered, his voice wet.

"If that's true, then why is that archangel out there behind us?"

"I don't know," Zulian wept.

"They wouldn't dare to attack us," On-Ja said, and the ten guardians crowded around us muttered agreements. "When we march out, they'll melt away."

"Our back is exposed the moment we move off the cornucopia," Kira said. "Can ten of us keep tight around Lilith and the librarian with enough spear coverage that they can't run the gap?"

"We move quickly," Xiona said.

Emmi agreed.

"And then I die anyway, because I can barely stand without dizziness," Kira said. She let go of Zulian's head and clapped her hands together. That startled the guardians. The old Kira stood up, her back straight, her eyes tight and glinting like the fading stars above us. The boulder rose above her shoulders, and the violet morning sky seeped around the edges behind her. "I have enough for one good run, guardians. We'll force them aside and get to the cornucopia. Then, you'll do as I damn well order, understood?"

The guardians all stood. "Yes, Lord!"

"Leave everything you came here with. Your robe and your spear are all you need."

We started to shuck everything, except Ishmael.

"Librarian," Kira said, exasperated.

"I'll keep up," Ishmael said. He'd dropped half of what he carried, but he'd refolded his pack to include the unmistakable form of his books. The firmness in his voice signaled the finality of his decision. "If I can't keep up, leave me to Nudasi."

"You'll die with your books," Kira said.

"You'll die with your spear in your hand," Ishmael said.

Kira glanced at me again. This time, I could see the sadness as she said, "You win, Musketress. You may yet see Ninetha again."

"No one wins with this plan," I said. I should have liked it, but I felt sick, and it wasn't just the hunger.

"Can you do better?" Kira asked.

Always the teacher and pupil. I shook my head. "I'm not going back."

"You say that now," Kira said.

"Kira." I called on the Lord Musketeer's commanding sureness, and for once I heard it in my voice. "I'll never see Ninetha again. Whatever you started there, I won't be the one to stop it."

Kira looked down at the ground. "Well, Musketress. Maybe I'll live to see that come true."

It didn't sound like she believed that.

"Ready?" I asked Ishmael.

He shifted his pack around. "How ready can anyone be to do something like this?"

My lips had dried, and my heart hammered so hard, I could feel it in the back of my mouth. "I'm scared."

"It would be insane not to be," Kira said. "But focus on getting to the cornucopia. That's all that matters."

We moved on Nudasi at a quick walk, spears out. I went through the steps of readying my musket. Nudasi glittered in the dawn, cornucopia globes switching off as they sensed the rising sun.

"The buildings," Li pointed. A single marble column towered over the ruins of the president's house. Even from here, we saw that the beams of the house had all collapsed inward after fire had chewed through them.

A line of charred homes cut through the heart of Nudasi. It pointed toward the trail up to the rim, which Ishmael and I had climbed to leave the city.

Kira snapped her fingers. Zulian, On-Ja, Alpheus, and Emmi lowered their spears and moved forward into the wedge. The strongest of our sad little group. The rest of us followed as best we could.

Alarmed yelling came from the nearest homes, and windows shut with loud claps. "They see us," Ishkur said, unnecessarily.

More and more senators ran out into the streets and shouted for each other.

"Get ready to run on my call," Kira said.

I swallowed. This was it. I would be in a fight for my life again, only this time I knew I had to fight back. If I didn't, these guardians would die. Ishmael would never get his notes back to New Alexandria. His life's work would die on this sandy street near the end of the world.

I saw knives glint in hands as ten, and then fifteen senators blocked the street. Behind them, the deep black of the cornucopia beckoned, every minute farther out of reach.

"Ready," Kira said, her voice rising.

The next word would launch us.

"Stop!" Priscilla shouted at us over the sandy dirt as she stepped out from a house on the edge of Nudasi. She waved a long stick with a knife roped to the end, a quickly made but effective spear. Two men with similar weapons joined her on either side.

The odds tilted farther away from us.

Kira could see that. She raised a finger to us. Stay.

I quivered with fear and anticipation, my body waiting for me to decide whether to run away or run at them.

"We're the guardians from Ninetha," Kira shouted. "You killed one of my people, Torit."

"I know who you are." Priscilla kept her simple spear pointed at us, as did her two companions. Now, easily fifty senators gathered in the street behind her.

"We could have killed so many of you, but I had us retreat for the rim instead," Kira announced.

Stone-faced, Priscilla said, "You wounded fifteen."

"They live, yes? Torit, you surrounded and stabbed to death. He didn't deserve that. He was almost a child."

"You murdered my daughter." Priscilla shook her spear as her voice broke apart. "*My* child."

Kira stared at the senators, at Priscilla, and at the charred buildings. I counted every one of my breaths.

Kira handed her spear to Inanna. "Hold this."

"Lord—?"

"Just do as I say."

She stepped between Zulian and On-Ja so she could walk out toward Priscilla.

"I see your pain," Kira said softly. She took another step closer to Priscilla. "But you should know that Torit, who you killed in front of me, never lifted a finger against your daughter. He was off chasing dogs and living with his mother at that time."

"Stop there," Priscilla ordered.

Two men stepped in front of Priscilla to protect her. Kira raised her hands to show she had no weapon.

"You slaughtered that poor boy. I know you heard his screams. I heard them. And I saw your hatred as you stabbed him. What did it feel like, Priscilla? Did you expect the knife to puncture skin and hit bone like that? Did you see Torit's confusion and surprise?"

Priscilla shook. From here, I couldn't tell whether it was rage or sadness.

"Did all that anger and hurt go away when you did it?" Kira asked. "Or did you feel horror and sickness for what you did?"

"Stay where you are," Priscilla yelled, and shook her spear again. "And shut up."

"Because I know I felt all those things, when I took life," Kira said, and stopped. "I just want to make you an offer that will stop bloodshed and save lives. Please hear me out."

I aimed my musket. It was a fifty-pace shot.

"Can you hit Priscilla?" Ishkur asked.

"Maybe," I said. "Probably."

"Then do it," he said.

"No," said Dumuzi. I heard the respect in his voice. This was leadership, I saw. That thing Kira could inspire in people. The reason that Priscilla hesitated and kept listening.

Kira stepped right up to the edge of Priscilla's spear. She reached up and gently pushed the knife on the end to her own throat. On-Ja gasped as Kira then left it there and lowered her hands to her sides.

"If you want revenge, if you think another life butchered will set you at peace, then just push. I won't stop you, and they won't attack, if you promise me you will let my guardians go to the cornucopia and get food so they can leave for Ninetha and never come back. Let's put all this into our pasts, and stop the death. I'm tired of the death."

I waited for Priscilla to shove the spear forward. She wanted to. I could see it. I could remember the rage that could possess you after that much grief. But instead, the president lowered her spear and started to cry.

Kira remained in place and lowered her head. "Shackle me, lock me away, just let my people return home."

"It won't fix anything." Priscilla wiped the corners of her eyes. "We were all on alert for anything after you people came through. Patrols around the city. We made weapons. When the archangel arrived, we thought it was a sign, and we gathered around to receive blessings. And then it saw our weapons and attacked."

Priscilla pulled her spear back and drove the butt end down into the ground.

"We were just in its way. It pushed through us. It walked through walls from house to house, shattering cornucopia globes and starting fires. We thought it was an attack, and we all gathered to try to stop it. Slammin' Joe died. Now, I'm alone. Thirty-seven other senators burned to death in their own houses. It's a corrupted, mad thing. A silver demon, a fallen creature."

"Traveler, is that thing coming back?" one of the senators asked.

"Yes," Kira said.

"Why?" several of them asked.

Kira hesitated a moment, and in that fissure I saw a chance to turn our fortunes around.

"Does it matter why?" I shouted. "We all thought archangels were holy, magical beings. But did you see something holy when it burned through Nudasi and killed your people?"

The senators rippled like a nervous flock of birds, as disagreement and confusion bounced around. Kira looked back at me with a growing professional curiosity.

I copied the way she walked out between Zulian and On-Ja. Only I kept my weapon with me.

"Do you want to stop the creature that killed Slammin' Joe?" I asked Priscilla. I knew their creed. I glanced at the burned husks of so many cherry trees. Radical honesty, right?

"Of course," Priscilla said. "But it's an archangel. What can we do against it?"

She leaned against her spear. I could see pain in her eyes at this range. And what I had thought was a wide, white belt across her midriff was actually a bloodied cloth bandage.

"Some of you have seen what this weapon can do." I raised the musket over my head. "But not all of you. Don't be startled; this is just a demonstration. It is loud."

I turned to the side and sighted on a rock. I pulled the trigger.

Senators screamed at the roar. I saw a couple bolt off down the street, shaken by the sound. But most of them stared at the shattered rock.

"I can harness the instant, destructive power of explosions,"

I said. I reached down into my bag of cartridges and pulled one out. I ripped the outer paper apart and set it on the sand, then backed away. "I need fire. And a spear."

Ishkur struck a match for lighting food fires and handed it to me along with his spear. I pushed the match into the spear-point, splitting the wood but securing it to the tip.

I reached out with the spear and touched the flame to the open powder. It went up with a small bright whump, and smoke wafted around me and Priscilla.

"It's an explosion powder," I said. "Ancient knowledge passed down to me by my family. We can use it to destroy the archangel if you help us with your cornucopia. I once saw a barrel of powder blow a hole in the thickest mud-brick and stone wall you can imagine. You can have vengeance for your dead."

Priscilla still regarded me like a bug she wanted to squash under a rock.

"What do you need?" she finally asked.

I had her.

"It'll require blasphemy," I said. "We have to trick the cornucopia."

Kira grabbed me by the hem of my sleeve and yanked me over. I staggered against her.

"Careful," Ishmael said. He'd sidled over as I'd demonstrated the powder's power.

Kira hissed at us, "I can't risk my soul to hinder the archangel. And I know you got the powder recipe from that book."

"Which you burned," I said.

"You copied it, or read it," Kira snapped back. "You dabble in arcane and dangerous old magic."

"The archangel's coming for me," I said bluntly. "I think it's because I helped Ishmael."

"Is that possible?" Kira asked Ishmael.

"I left New Alexandria so it wouldn't hurt the people I loved," Ishmael said. "I've never associated with anyone as long as you, Lilith. Or even you, Kira. It could be true."

"The archangel has likely added you to its list, Kira. It knew my name. It will know yours," I said. And then, because I knew her so well, I dug in at the one thing I knew Kira still believed about herself. "How will you protect Inanna and Dumuzi from that thing? What about—?"

To my surprise, before I could name more guardians, before I could continue pressing Kira, she broke. "Go build your spells, Librarian. Just don't come near me when you're meddling in ink and sin. Let me stand clear and clean."

"Absolutely," I said.

Kira locked her dark eyes on me. "I'll do it for Banda, Sed, and all the guardians who died on the rim of the world. The archangel got close to us near Tamarlane, and I know we can't keep this pace up and live to get to Ninetha. The archangel will catch us. I do it for them, not for you, understand?"

"I understand."

We separated, and Priscilla cautiously approached, suspicion on her face. "What was that?"

"Kira didn't like the plan," I said. A lie, but not quite. Enough of one that Ishmael raised an eyebrow, but Kira didn't contradict me. "But we are in agreement, now."

The four of us stood in a circle. The lord of the guardians, the musketress, the president, and the librarian. We studied each other to see if we could spot deception in each other's eyes.

The president hated the lord guardian for killing her daughter. The lord guardian hated the musketress for what her family did to the cornucopia, and the musketress hated her for betraying and killing her family. The lord guardian wanted to kill the librarian, who hated her for torturing him in the citadel.

We were all bound to each other by ropes of hatred and fear. In a sick way, I felt it pulled us close to each other.

"How do we trick the god-machine?" Priscilla asked.

I looked to Ishmael. "Do you remember the recipe from reading it?"

Getting the papers out to have him read them here in the open would be a disaster, I sensed. No one liked sin right out in the open, so brazen, even if it was a sin that could save lives.

"I remember," Ishmael said.

"Tell them," I said.

Ishmael took the president by her arm. "This recipe will be in parts of three, and the ratio—"

"No!" Kira cut him off. She looked around at the crowd. "You say the recipe out loud, and they'll all know it—they'll all remember it. And then Nudasi marches for Ninetha with muskets. We won't choke under the grasp of a new ruler."

"I have no interest in explosions or Ninetha. It sounds like a dreadful place," Priscilla said.

"They don't lie," I whispered to Kira.

"I have no interest in ancient weapons," Priscilla said. "I swear we will not spread it out around the world."

"Trust her," I insisted.

"It's too risky," Kira said.

"If that happens, just make your own powder, then," I said. "You have barrels of it stored in the citadel anyway. You can be the Lord Musketeer—"

"I don't want that title," Kira snapped. "All your power

came from words, and from the past. It can bring only more ruin to us."

"Kira." I fumbled about as I looked for a way to change her course. But I could only see the truth of it.

"We need a house," Ishmael said to Priscilla. "We can hide the formula from you if you choose people who come to us one at a time. We'll tell them what to ask the cornucopia for, but we will not explain why, or the steps to making powder. Would that work for you, Kira?"

She struggled against her fear of his literary magics before she nodded. "That will work. It'll have to."

Ishmael looked to Priscilla. "And you?"

Priscilla nodded. "I can't trick my people with untruths, but I can tell them you need our help to fight that thing. Anyone who lost family to it will help gladly."

"You'll also need spotters to climb your buildings to warn us when the archangel approaches," Kira said.

"And we need some help to dig a trench," I added.

"Some of us will have to skip the people's line at the cornucopia tomorrow," Priscilla said. "They'll go hungry. But I think they'll agree to the sacrifice."

"Throw them out, or she'll see us all returned to the earth!" one of the senators shouted.

"Shut up, Thomas-David," Priscilla shouted over her shoulder. She muttered, "They'll hold that all against me. There are no rulers in Nudasi. Some of them will listen to you, but many won't. I can't say how many will help."

"Or you could pack all the food you can and run for Ninetha," Kira said.

"No," Priscilla snapped. "I've heard enough about Ninetha's poverty. And you can't promise to protect us even if we made it. The archangel could cross into Ninetha as easily as it did here."

"Ninetha has strong walls," Kira said.

"I will help you. For Slammin' Joe. But I will never walk with you to Ninetha. I'll die before then," Priscilla said.

"We can only make the best choices we can in the moment and pray we chose well." I moved myself between the two of them as I sensed Priscilla's rekindled hatred. I needed to dump water on those embers quickly.

"Well said," Kira murmured.

"Fuck you," I snapped. I would never have dreamed I could spit that at Kira, but I no longer looked up to her. Just across.

Priscilla smiled, a dark and satisfied thing that chilled me even in the day's heat.

"I'll ask my people," she said. "Wait here."

Priscilla left to talk to her senators, and we all watched the huddled conversation. We could hear the hurt and anger in their tones, but we couldn't make out words. I saw a familiar face lean against the wall of a house and regard me. Darcus.

I still had his knife strapped to my pack.

"I think they'll try to kill us the moment we kill the archangel," I said.

"If we kill it," Ishmael said. "I doubt we can."

"Then what are we doing?" Kira asked.

"Well, we need the supplies when it comes time to run." Ishmael grinned at the Cleft, in the direction the archangel would come from. "I won't just be getting the ingredients for powder from Nudasi. I'll be asking them for essentials. In addition to what we really need, I will strangely have found out, and declare, that powder also needs to have vittle and drinkable water added to it."

"Enough for all of us," Kira said.

"Of course. You should scout for a place we can lure the archangel into," Ishmael said.

Kira didn't want to leave the two of us alone. She didn't stir.

"We're not going to run away to leave you to die now," I said to her. "Ishmael and I could have left you anytime between Tamarlane and here."

Kira let go of the suspicion that held her in place and tapped her heart to indicate graciousness, something she'd never done for me.

As Kira walked back to her guardians, Priscilla shouted at the senators around her, and they cursed back at her.

"That's going well," I said with a grimace.

"I'm sorry," Ishmael said.

"For what?" I asked.

"All that pain and confusion in you whenever you look at Kira," Ishmael said.

I didn't deny it. We stood in the city of truth, and I liked that about this place.

"I thought the world seemed orderly and clear just weeks ago," I told Ishmael. "Now, I'm trying to kill an archangel to save your life."

"And yours."

"Obviously."

The crowd of senators finished their conference and walked toward us. Priscilla, her shoulders slumped, headed the other way.

"Where is she going?" I called out. Something must have gone wrong. I stepped back and picked the musket up.

"To give Slammin' Joe back to the land," they said. "Before the archangel arrives."

"Do you really think that we can stop Arbet?" Ishmael asked.

"You've never seen the full power of powder," I told him. "And after all the horrible things it's done in Ninetha, I'd like to use it for good. Just once. Maybe the gods will forgive us. Maybe they'll favor us with luck against the archangel."

"If powder is evil, then what will happen from using so much of it against the archangel?" Ishmael asked.

I didn't know.

We stumbled toward a strange and uncertain future. And the silvered archangel limped inexorably through the shadows toward us.

The senators grudgingly came to offer us a house, and once we set up in it, a steady stream of people came to the door to leave ingredients from the cornucopia that Ishmael had asked for.

"Quit standing around with that knife out," Ishmael hissed. "Be useful. It will not matter whether Darcus tries to kill you by walking in here, or somewhere else. Be attacked while helping out."

"You act like you don't care," I said. "But I know you do."

"Don't forget that Darcus wants to live as much as he wants to kill you. I'll bet you he's also going to wait until we kill the archangel before he tries to kill you."

I set about harassing strangers to help me find five empty water barrels that I could roll into place in a row behind the house. I filled them with round rocks, metal balls, marbles, and a few other things that I thought should work to grind the ingredients together, based on what I'd seen in the powder room at the citadel. Ishmael helped me fill them from a crude scale that he used to follow the formula on my copied papers.

Before the hour passed, the amount of ash and caustic

powder in the air made us cough and retch as we moved about. Ishmael opened his pack to find the mask the cornucopia had made for our trip to the Cleft. I saw the genius of that and did the same.

"Usually we had servants stand and spin the barrels on tumblers, and then they would filter out the debris," I told Ishmael when we finished. Hours of work in the fogged-up mask had left me sticky with sweat and aching.

I called a senator over. "We need strong people in teams to spin the prayer barrels."

"For how long?" she asked.

"Until the archangel is spotted. Hopefully at least two hours," I said. "They will have to spin the barrel four times per line of the prayer they sing. If the prayer is true, the gods will turn the ingredients into powder."

And then we would have five barrels to blow up underneath the archangel.

"Tell everyone: no flames or anything that can create sparks," I continued. I didn't want to come this far just to fail by getting blasted into pieces. "They must be careful to not jostle the barrels, and they should turn them smoothly."

The senator rushed off to find people.

"Will that be enough powder?" Ishmael asked.

"I have no idea," I said. We stopped and turned our heads as we heard shouts from the far edge of Nudasi.

"They've spotted the archangel," I guessed.

Ishmael nodded. "It'll keep sniffing for its target, like a dog on the scent. Can the powder work as is?"

"No. It needs the tumbling and blessing before it grinds together. My father insisted on the time, the prayer, and the speed of the barrel's spin."

Kira used to punish us for being late by putting us on the cranks, muttering the prayer of explosive transubstantiation, and spinning the barrel until our arms burned.

"The archangel is on the horizon just below Suki's Rock," a senator stepped into the door to say. "A forty-minute walk."

I didn't even need to look. I held up two fingers to Ishmael. "We can't rush it. It's still two hours. The transubstantiation will not hurry itself for us mortals."

"A little over an hour's gap," Ishmael said. He leaned to whisper in my ear. "We'll have to flee with what we can grab. We should tell them to run as well. We don't know what Arbet will do to them, or to the city."

Six senators pushed in. One of them coughed at the fumes in the air. "Hello? You need people to help spin drums?"

"Don't leave," I whispered to Ishmael. I squeezed his left arm. "Don't give up on this just yet."

I waved my new acolytes over and led them out back.

"I'm going to teach you a prayer," I told them.

It felt strange to sing the three lines of the transubstantiation prayer outside of the citadel and far from Ninetha. I made them all repeat it, and then made them repeat it again, until I felt that the cadence was burned in their memories.

"I'm a griot," said the oldest assistant with the long, dreadlocked beard and balding head. His eyes twinkled like stars. "I can hold the words in my head. I can hear them now for your prayer. I'll lead them."

"Thank you," I smiled. I didn't go back inside, but I watched them start spinning the barrels.

The griot began the prayer, and I stood and listened for a long moment. I wiped the moisture from my eyes and eased back into the little home.

The moment the door closed, Ishmael squatted next to his traveler's pack. "We have to run, now."

"No." I folded my arms. "I'm going to see this through. I'll go out there and lead it on a chase that will delay it."

"It will kill you," Ishmael said with frustration. "I've lived with Arbet. I know this. You should run away from me, because if Arbet has to choose, it will come for me. Don't waste your life, Lilith. You're the first person in so long that I've gotten to know. I don't want to carry your death on my conscience."

"That's not your call to make," I told him.

"There's no great stand you can take here," Ishmael said forcefully. "We're not ancient heroes in an epic, or even a book. Arbet will rip through spears, toss aside barricades, and shrug off falling boulders. It will strip the skin from our bones, or tear us apart, or do something else just as horrible."

The senators had created a mound of supplies for us. Vittle, thick bread, and jerky. Ishmael shoved as much as he could into his pack, and his fingers trembled as he tied the pack's cover in place.

"If you don't come with me," Ishmael said, "you'll live. You must head in another direction."

"Ishmael, please don't leave me. I don't want to be alone," I said. "I'm scared of it. I can't go with Kira. I can't stay here. Darcus will kill me for who I am, and now I even understand why he hates me so much."

"You can choose loneliness or your death," Ishmael said sharply.

"You are truly the only friend I have in the entire world," I told him. "Kick me away like a stray dog, but I still am going to beg you to stay. It must be a hell to travel with people only for a moment, but eventually they fall away."

"New friends appear." Ishmael pulled his pack on with a grunt.

"Temporary friends," I said. "But every night you will fall asleep and wonder if that night will be the one when the angel catches up and kills you as you dream."

Ishmael grunted as if I'd punched him. "It's true. But our time is also at an end. Accept it."

"Well then, run," I said bitterly. "I'll try to do what I can to it. But you deserve a place you love to live in. New Alexandria, doesn't it call you home?"

"In some ways. New Alexandria is where I go to drop off my notes and any books I've collected for the great library. But there is another place . . ." Ishmael trailed off.

"Leave me your spyglass? To remember you, and so I can see the archangel?"

"I need it for when I run, to keep ahead of Arbet, to make sure I know where it is."

I came over and hugged him. "I wish you good favor and a steady step, then."

He kissed the top of my dusty hair. "Luck and fortune to you as well."

I picked up a spade and wouldn't look him in the eye. "I have to go. Some of us have work to do."

I left him in the house, attaching water canteens to his pack.

"Lilith!" Kira stood on the roof of a house at the edge of Nudasi. I walked until I found the ladder up and joined her. "We need to hurry."

"Where is it?" I wanted to focus on something other than the torn feeling in the center of my chest. I imagined Ishmael walking out of the other side of Nudasi, his canteens clanking against the pack, his back slightly stooped forward against the weight of all the ridiculous books under the more useful food.

The librarian lived for knowledge. Maybe that was more important to him than friendships, battles, or his own life. He wanted to return the stories he'd written down from griots, the observations of cities he'd reached, and, most importantly, what we saw up at the Cleft.

I understood it, now that I knew him. But I also hated it.

"There." Kira pointed to a glint in the distance.

We stared at it together.

"The trench?" I asked.

Kira pointed to a natural gateway formed by three boulders lying against each other. Three guardians dug madly away at the hard dirt.

"The powder?" Kira asked.

"I need to lead the archangel out into the rock field," I told her. "We need more time."

But would it even fall for the trick? It had paused at the outermost line I'd drawn in the sand outside Tamarlane so I could better target it.

It had looked right up at me.

"It might not work," I said.

"I know," Kira said easily. "But you gave us options, and you gave me a second life. We will adjust to what comes next."

She looked healthier, I realized. Something from the cornucopia, no doubt. The other guardians around the bottom of the ladder had looked better as well, with vittle and fresh water in them.

I had to be careful. They might decide to bind me and drag me back to Ninetha yet, if they'd set aside enough supplies.

I shivered, even in the heat. I might see Ninetha again,

before my own execution, if that was what they decided. Kira noticed. "You're scared I will try to capture you still. You think I don't believe you."

"I understand why you came to hate them. My brothers and sisters hid in the shadows." A thunderstorm poured itself angrily into the Cleft in the great bulk of the world's rim that dominated the view behind Nudasi. I tore myself away from the wonder of it. "The people they smuggled back into our rooms, and their attempt to manipulate you into killing our father so they could take his power. I understand why you wouldn't trust me now."

Kira approached me. "You knew they did those things? Do you know why?"

"They hated him." I tried not to think about the moment back in our rooms. The screams in the corridors, and the secrets told to me that I wished I'd never heard. Secrets that had ripped my life apart.

Kira crossed her arms behind her back. "I rage about people's sins, but I knew about the things your father did. I hid them from the citadel. From you. From Ninetha. I thought it protected the city."

"And look at us now," I said.

Kira uncrossed her arms and pulled at her collar. She couldn't find any words, though, and an awkward silence fell between us.

With a chattering heart, I stood up. "I guess it's time."

Kira took a step forward, as if to clasp my hand, and then she changed her mind.

"Keep them saying the prayer," I told Kira. "And don't let them stop turning the barrels."

I clambered down the ladder and walked along the walls in

the shade until I stepped away from Nudasi. It felt like walking toward my own execution.

The guardians digging another trench out in the open nodded to me as I passed. Nichael, Xiona, and Ishkur, I thought. I picked up my musket from the shadow of the boulder where the guardians had left their packs. Mine sat among theirs.

"Fortune," Ishkur wished me as I walked to the trench. I wrinkled my nose at the smell of oil. The archangel dragged its leg faster and faster as it saw me.

On-Ja walked up from behind us all and tossed a torch into the trench they'd spent hours on.

I looked down at the timepiece we'd asked a senator for. Fresh and warm off the cornucopia. After I baited the archangel into the rubble to my left, I would have to keep it chasing me for at least an hour. Back at the rock gate, they would bury the barrels in a stone-lined pit that they had to make in a hurry.

After that, it was my job to lead the archangel to walk over it, and Dumuzi would touch a torch to a trail of powder that led from where he hid back to the barrels.

This was going to fail, wasn't it?

The clank of canteens behind me made me turn around.

"Ishmael? But we said our goodbyes!"

Ishmael sighed. He dropped his pack next to the circle of guardians' equipment. "I realized after a short moment that I'd forgotten that running alone is a weary job. I feel scraped down to the bone, Lilith. I'm numb. And tired. I kept thinking, maybe you found something that could work. Maybe I could finally sleep without listening for metal footsteps. I knew I would always wonder if I didn't try."

I hugged him. "We're going to blow up an angel," I said.

"Or something far worse."

The archangel crawled through the ditch of fire. The flames flickered against its silvered skin, and that mirrored face turned to look at the city for a moment, when it paused at the lip. Then, it turned to us.

"Lilith of Ninetha," it said. "I see you. Librarian—"

I walked forward and shot it in the face again. The archangel Arbet fell back into the oil and flames, limbs twitching as it disappeared back into the heat.

Reload.

"See me all you want."

Ishmael and I hurried toward the fields of boulders as the instrument of the gods crawled inexorably back out of the searing pit of fire and moved toward us.

We ran. It was the best tool we had for evading the archangel's murderous march. For an hour, we no longer walked aimlessly around the natural maze but worked to build distance from the archangel—although not so much that it would lose our track for days. We just needed hours.

When we finally stopped our mad zig-zagging through the stone remains of the rim to catch our breath, I waited until we had both stopped panting and asked Ishmael, "Back by the powder, you said New Alexandria isn't the city you would love to settle in."

"Yes," Ishmael said.

I leaned against one of the squared boulders that people from Nudasi had carved steps into so they could clamber up onto a wide stone shelf with a sharp wall of rock behind it.

On either side of Nudasi, thick ribs of rock rose from the sand and ran toward the rim's foothills, like the world's tendons. I could hear the slight bounce of echoes off the tall towers of natural stone as I asked, "Where would you go?"

"Langston," Ishmael said, without hesitation.

Langston, the rocks above the shelf whispered back to us. The kid in me wanted to clap and yell at them for the echoes. But we didn't want to make it too obvious to the archangel where we were. That broken leg slowed it, but it remained deadly.

"What calls to you in Langston?" I asked. We peered around the edge of the steps. No glint of silver.

"The most beautiful poems I've ever heard." Ishmael closed his eyes. "I didn't write any down at first. I just listened to the griots when they spoke of dreams deferred, and I could feel it reach all the way across the deep time of the exodus, from that world to this one. I found my first book there, an ancient collection of his poems, kept in a glass box to protect it against time."

"His poems? I thought you said it was a city?"

"Langston." Ishmael opened his eyes. "Our cities are all named from pieces of literature from the old world. That's how important words were to the people. They might have agreed to the compact and burned their books by the millions. The sky may have turned black with ink. But the first thing they did here, in defiance of the gods, was to make sure the griots memorized those stories."

"Wait," I said. I checked the timepiece. We'd meandered all around this maze of sand and rocky ruin, to leave clear footprints for the archangel. Even with the broken leg, Arbet kept catching up quicker than I liked.

And whenever we saw the glint of silver, we took off again. "Which cities did they name after books?" I asked.

"Ninetha is from sacred old texts, and the story of Gilgamesh, the oldest adventure in the ancient world. Tamarlane, that name is from the god-poet Poe, who also is mentioned as a demigod in the war against the stars."

A shadow shifted, and we both tensed.

"Did you hear that?" I asked.

"I felt it."

But I could hear nothing now. And nothing turned the corner. I lowered my musket.

"And Nudasi?" I asked, my voice falsely cheerful.

"The words are *new* and the ancient symbols that make *DC*, although the pronunciation drifted. They named it after a city in the old world associated with the god Washtun. You can see the words carved into the tops of every house here. I think when they made the homes, they copied the words in as decoration, but they forgot what they really meant, and they've been recopied as decoration all over Nudasi ever since."

"Priscilla would have a stroke if she realized they'd covered the city in actual words all this time." I laughed a little, and smiled when I heard it reflected back to me from the stone walls above the ledge. "Kira, too."

I pointed at the unmoving shadow as we chatted. Ishmael nodded. Twice, Arbet had gotten too close. The archangel kept anticipating our twists and turns, as if it could see us from above. That scared me, because it made me wonder if the gods did favor the archangel after all, and that would mean our mistakes could damn us.

Ishmael made a *keep talking* gesture.

"I swear it," he continued as he inched forward. "When you

come with me, you'll see all these pieces of that old world that are still alive—in the words of storytellers and hiding in our landscapes."

"Langston." I tested the word out. "Where is Langston?"

"Downriver from New Alexandria."

Ishmael quickly glanced down the corridor of rock.

I twisted around, suspicious at the long period since we'd last seen the archangel. But it didn't attack us from the other side of the rocky passage.

"It should have approached by now," Ishmael said quietly, the lightness in his voice taut with worry.

Another thud made the ground under me tremble. It sounded like a god's footsteps.

"Ishmael?" My voice cracked.

We could hear a thunderstorm of rocks tumbling down into the canyon behind us. A cloud of dust rushed around the bend and filled the air. I coughed and jammed my face against the crook of my arm.

We carefully glanced around the bend.

A wall of rock filled the way out. Ishmael swore.

"It's trying to trap us," I said.

"I know." Ishmael pointed back down the other way. If it had figured out where we were, there was only one other way to get to us now. "Run."

I slung the strap of the musket over my back and dug my feet in to try to keep up with Ishmael. He loped ahead of me, panting as he got farther and farther ahead, until he slid to a stop.

"It has us," he said, shocked.

The archangel dragged itself toward us. We couldn't get around it. I could reach out and touch the rocky walls with either hand at the same time.

Arbet would kill us both the moment we tried to rush past.

My stomach squeezed the bottom of my throat, and panic fluttered around inside of me, with nowhere to escape to.

Arbet pointed at us.

"Ishmael," it said. The word boomed off the rock all around us and lifted over our heads. Pebbles trickled down to smack the dirt between us. "I've found you at last. Stop running. Let me ease your burdens."

Just to the left behind was a right-hand turn. At any point after five minutes from now, Ishmael and I had planned to enter the long, triangular tunnel formed from boulders that leaned against each other, and barrels of powder would be waiting at the exit.

If the guardians had followed our directions, that is.

We'd come so close to the plan working. It hurt me to do it, but I turned around and wordlessly ran back the way we'd come from, knowing we were trapped.

Back at the rockslide, I flitted about to try to find a gap in the large boulders. There had to be a way through. I got on my hands and knees.

"We have to go over," Ishmael said. "There's no way through. I can't see any light coming through."

I crawled back out from under two rocks that were twice our size. "Can we climb this without ropes?"

"There are handholds in the face," Ishmael said. He pointed at several divots leading up the biggest chunks of rock.

"No. We should run back toward Arbet. Right after I shoot him in the face, we can run past on either side," I suggested.

Ishmael linked his hands together to make a step and moved closer to the giant rockslide.

I shook my head. "There has to be another way."

"There isn't, so hurry," Ishmael said.

"Dammit!" I put a foot in his hands and he easily lifted me up into the air over his shoulders. I pushed against the rock and tried to find a handhold, but pieces crumbled off in my hands and cracked to brittle pieces around Ishmael.

"Push me higher," I said.

I balanced against the rock as Ishmael pushed me higher. My leg started wobbling, I felt my balance shift, and I dug my fingernails into the rock. After I steadied myself, I felt around for a better handhold.

I needed all my breath to kick my legs around to find a small foothold, and then I crabbed my way onto one of the lower boulders of the entire mess.

For a moment, I could only just pant.

"Okay, now you," I called down. I wrapped the strap of the musket around my foot, and then hugged the rock. I dangled my feet down as far as I could.

I grunted as Ishmael grabbed onto the musket and pulled.

For a small eternity, he swayed and twisted about. I heard rocks break away. They clacked and bounced down the boulder's face, and Ishmael swore as he struggled to climb. Every time he shifted, my fingers slipped, but I found a deep crack I could get my fingers wedged into and held on. Ishmael moved up to my foot and pushed off the rock again. The strap on the musket broke, and I felt weightless for a second.

"Ishmael!"

I heard him bounce off the rock with a cry and then thud into the dirt below. I pulled myself up so I could turn and look down. He lay on his back, and his left arm flopped on his stomach. It was bent in the wrong direction.

Ishmael shook himself, took a deep breath, and sat up. We both stared at the broken arm.

He picked the musket up with one hand. "I don't think it got harmed."

"I'm not worried about the musket," I shouted.

He probably didn't think I could hear it, but Ishmael gasped as he used the musket to help himself stand. "Go see if there's a way through up there," he called up to me.

I turned and squinted through a gap in the jumble of rocks ahead of me. The steep roofs of Nudasi glimmered in the sun on the other side. I could just slip through. If I held my breath.

"Can you see a way through?" Ishmael asked.

"No," I lied.

"You have to find a way through and use it," Ishmael said.

"No."

Kame had died helping me escape. Torit had died because I'd tried to hurt Kira. How many people had died to pry my family away from the city's cornucopia? I didn't want Ishmael's death to be my fault also.

I turned back and rolled onto my stomach, careful to avoid hurting my chest, and I eased my way down the side of the rock.

"Lilith! Get back up. I can face the end of my time with dignity. I've always known that Arbet would finally get to me, somewhere, somehow. Don't—"

I slid down farther, scraping my palms to slow myself, bunching my robes up over my thighs, and fell to the ground. I rolled and coughed. Ishmael ran over.

"Dammit. You could have kept trying. There would have been a way out if you'd kept looking," he said.

"It looks like it from here," I told him. "But there's no way back in this direction to Nudasi. Now, hand me the musket."

I pulled out a cartridge and bit it to start the loading process. I spit out paper.

"Even if I'd found a way back, would the guardians take me in? A few nights into the journey home, Kira would slit my throat." Kira and I were allies for now, but it was a convenience. I couldn't bet my life on some fantasy of reconciliation. I would never see Ninetha again, one way or another.

"Lilith—"

"We're going to get out of here," I snapped. "You'll take your books to New Alexandria. We'll blow the archangel up, because when we figure out how to get out of here, the guardians will have rolled the barrels into place and filled in the trench. We're almost there, Ishmael. Everything's going to be different after this."

It couldn't be like this forever.

I pulled Darcus's knife from my belt and sliced cloth off my robes to make a quick sling.

"You are the only friend I have in this world," I said. "Who else can show me the way to Eufra and the other cities? And without Arbet chasing you, we can dally at any of the places you told me about and truly explore them for your books."

"You need to get back up there." Ishmael grabbed me and used his one good arm to push me back toward the rock pile, but I shoved him right back, and he gasped as his broken arm shifted about.

"I am not going to do something just because you order it, Ishmael."

"You shouldn't have jumped down," he said. "Even if you can't climb over, go hide and wait up there until Arbet leaves."

"It's too late," I said. "You can't push me back up. We need to rush the archangel in the wide sand by the rock steps."

I smacked the butt of the musket against the hard ground and started forward.

"It will catch one of us," Ishmael predicted.

"Librarian, shut up and run," I yelled. "Think of all the stories you have yet to read. Think of the *Count of Many Crickets*."

"*Monte Cristo*," Ishmael corrected me, exasperation in his voice. As I'd hoped.

"So, run!"

We slipped around the corner and found the archangel waiting on the other side of the rocks for us, where the canyon narrowed. The sun dazzled my eyes as it slid over the archangel's silver body.

"Ishmael, there is nowhere to go," Arbet announced. It sounded like a sandstorm blew in between the archangel's words now, and I froze as it dropped to its hands and knees like a runner.

"A librarian in this world is a disruption that risks undoing lifetimes of work," it said. "We can come to an agreement, Ishmael. I can give you almost anything you have ever wanted to fix your error."

Ishmael grabbed my arm and pushed me toward the carved stone stairs on the boulder as the archangel loped toward us like a three-legged animal.

Jumping off the steps and out onto the big stone slab, I turned around and had my aim ready just as the archangel raised its head over the stairs.

The musket kicked, black smoke filled the air, and the archangel walked through the powder smoke, a silver clockwork tiger with shredded metal wings.

"That cannot harm me," Arbet said matter-of-factly, as it turned its head toward me. "Leave Ishmael to me. You are not a librarian; you cannot read, so you are only an irritant, not a threat."

It lurched forward to grab me, and I jumped back.

Like a calm shepherd's dog, Arbet corralled us up to the stone walls. I reloaded the musket from memory and feel, and kept my eyes locked on Arbet as we tried to circle around it.

I danced forward. The archangel lunged, and I sprinted to the side. Arbet expected it and rolled over its shoulder to move out in front of me. For the briefest second, I thought I'd skipped by. But a cold, hard hand grabbed my ankle and squeezed. The unyielding metallic hand cracked bone. My ankle collapsed beneath Arbet's grip, and I tasted my tears.

When my back hit the stone as I twisted and fell over, I kept my wits about me. I pulled the musket out and aimed it back between my knees.

Arbet knocked the barrel aside right as I fired.

"I'm tired of this toy," it said emotionlessly, and then grabbed it. For a moment, the grip on my ankle let go, and I thought it would be okay.

The archangel bent the musket's barrel, wrenched it away from my hands, and threw it aside with a clatter.

"Why it so hard for your kind to follow instructions you have agreed to?" Arbet dragged me closer as I flailed about.

I kicked, punched, and spat at Arbet.

"It is not death; it is transformation," the archangel explained, and a long spike of black god-machine oil slid out of its finger. "A nanosecond of complete change."

It reached out for me. I took a deep breath as I stopped fighting and stared at the oily black stuff.

The black spike aimed at my eye became the largest and most important thing in my entire universe.

Ishmael hurtled into the archangel and knocked it clean off its two arms and single working leg. They tumbled around on the rock.

"Go!" Ishmael screamed, and then he coughed and choked on a knot of black oil that rose from Arbet's shoulders to shove itself down his throat. Oil boiled up out of the stone itself and snaked up Arbet's legs. But Ishmael wasn't dead, so why was the ground reclaiming him?

"Ishmael!" I couldn't just leave him here, but I knew if I moved any closer, Arbet may turn its attention to me. The archangel seemed to be able to control the oil inside of it, and just under its feet.

Ishmael pleaded with just his eyes now. The oil ran up his nose, down through his mouth into his throat, and even leaked from his eardrums.

Then, Ishmael smiled, a new satisfied, peaceful expression that settled across his face as the black oil dripped from his pores and wrapped his body until a midnight-black statue of Ishmael stood at the center of the long slab of rock.

Black oil slowly seeped back into the ground that sustained it.

I struggled to my feet and screamed with rage, hurt, and fear. The archangel had murdered my guide to a world that I knew so little about.

I hopped awkwardly over to the musket. It wouldn't fire again, but with another strip of cloth wrapped around my ankle to stabilize it and the musket, I had a crutch.

I wobbled my way down the stairs and away from Arbet, who hunched over Ishmael's body.

Arbet rose and stared at me. "Where are you going, Lilith?"

I didn't answer this time. I had no hiss left in me, no claws left. I clutched the barrel of the musket and limped my way along the dirt path through the rocks.

"Lilith! Where are you going?" the archangel asked. It followed, dragging its own leg in the dirt.

I lurched past pools of fetid water.

"We must destroy that forbidden weapon," Arbet said. "I have work to do in Ninetha if you're all tricking the cornucopia again."

I grunted as I turned left. I could just imagine the "work" Arbet would do to the city I had once thought belonged to my family. I might never see Ninetha again, but I forced myself to ignore the pain so I could move faster.

Ishmael!

I didn't look back. I couldn't. I couldn't save him. I couldn't even sing his death song as the land took instructions from the archangel and killed his still-living body.

I was alone in the world. Utterly alone, with no one to help me even stand.

"Lilith!" Dumuzi ran and pulled my arm over his shoulder. He looked at the archangel with wide, horrified eyes. "Where's the librarian?"

"Move," I ordered him. "Move, damn you, move."

The pain was making me sweat. It stung my eyes as Dumuzi half-dragged me down the triangular tunnel of rock. My ankle bounced off the ground and hit pebbles, and I spit my pain through gritted teeth.

We passed over dirt and sand that had been a trench just hours ago.

"How many barrels could you fit?" I asked Dumuzi.

"All of it. We hurried when we heard your screams."

"Let go of me." I shoved Dumuzi away. I hopped to the side, so that Arbet could see me from the tunnel of rock. "Go get ready to fire the powder trail!"

Arbet stopped several lengths short of the tunnel's threshold as Dumuzi ran back to where a torch of cloth strips and a wooden stake burned off to the side.

"Dumuzi! Now!"

"It's not at the threshold!"

Arbet looked toward the stone walls in the direction of where Dumuzi now crouched near a trail of gunpowder that led to the packed trench.

"Come and fucking get me!" I screamed at Arbet. "Come on!"

All this death had to mean something. It had to end for a reason. My friend couldn't die for nothing.

The archangel took a tentative step backward.

"It has to be on top of the barrels," Dumuzi shouted. "Kira said that."

The archangel had created a rock wall to trap us. I might not kill it, but I could trap it as well. Then, I could make more gunpowder. I remembered the recipe. Or I could, if I sat down in the quiet for a while and thought.

I threw myself forward as best I could, with the musket to support me, as Arbet turned around. I snatched the torch from Dumuzi before he could say anything.

"Run!" I yelled, and threw the torch at the trail of gunpowder.

It fizzled, smoke puffed as the fire raced toward the trench, and I flailed my way toward Dumuzi.

The blast knocked me down to my face. Dirt whirled all

around me as the tunnel collapsed on itself. I rolled over just in time to see the largest boulder, like a keystone at the top of an arch, fall and crush the archangel under it.

Arbet's severed head rolled away from its body.

No one wanted to go forward to see if the collapsed tunnel had really killed the archangel, so I crawled under the rearranged debris and pulled the head free.

"Lilith of Ninetha," it said clearly in the archangel's strong voice.

I screamed and dropped it.

"Dumuzi, we need to make more powder," I said. He hovered several lengths away, ready to run.

"Don't do that," Arbet said, looking up at me from the ground. "My brain case is surrounded by a hyperdense dyrillium sheath. There is nothing you can imagine or make that will pierce it. But you are safe from me. I will not regain the mobility adaptations of a bipedal body. I am preparing for a reincarnation."

I didn't like the sound of that.

My voice wavered as I thought about a lifetime of running. "And then you'll come for me?"

"I'm returning to the stars, Lilith. After all these years, I can go back out into the empty gulf between suns. It is quiet and soft there. The passage rewards contemplation. The next time I return, Lilith of Ninetha, you will have long since become just a memory."

"That's not my name anymore." I leaned on the musket and tried to look past the rock. I could feel waves of pain crashing against me. But I wasn't done. "Why did you have to kill Ishmael?"

"In that second before he died, he lived a thousand lives.

Every question he ever had was answered, all the things he wished to do were done. Go back to him and look at the satisfaction in his expression."

"You lie."

"If you want proof, just rest your eye against mine, and you can get the answer to anything you've ever wondered in your life."

"I'm not interested in your tricks," I said. The archangel, the land, and the cornucopias were all connected. I had no wish to die like Ishmael had.

The guardians surrounded us in a large semicircle, with senators arriving behind them.

"Too bad," the archangel's head said. "Make sure the land takes you within an hour of your death, and you'll know everything he did. They might be like gods to you, the ones who made this place, but they love you. You can preserve your consciousness and join with something greater and larger than you can imagine."

"Some of the gods don't like us." I pointed toward the Cleft, changing the conversation, as I didn't understand the archangel fully. Many tales and beliefs spoke about afterlives, and the archangel had suggested that it wasn't just our bodies that returned to the land but our souls, or our minds. I wondered what Ishmael would make of that.

He would probably write it all down for others to read about.

"The gods didn't do that. Nor a demon. Your people did. Beings you can barely comprehend made your people a paradise, and they couldn't accept it. Imagine putting an animal in a garden and giving it anything it wants, letting it roam where it pleases. Thus satisfied, it will ask no questions. But a human will ask, why do I get this reward? Must I have done something to deserve this? Does that other human deserve this, or have they been punished? You create stories, you investigate, you can't help yourselves. Meaning has to be created, even when it doesn't exist in this vast, random universe. Humans did that, in trying to break our supervisions."

"What are you?" I asked. So many questions whirled around us.

"Synchronization and upload almost complete. May you find satisfaction and peace," the archangel's head whispered.

"Answer me!"

But the head fell quiet.

I threw the archangel's head under Ishmael's body when we burned it. We chipped the god-stuff off the librarian's feet so we could move him, and even though the ground refused to take him, we surrounded him and sang the song of endings anyway.

He would have liked that.

He wouldn't have liked what I did next. I gently let the papers with the recipe for powder flutter out of my fingers into the flames as the song finished. I watched them burn in the fire as Kira stared at me. The guardians around her stepped away from the inky smoke that rose from the pyre.

This isn't the end, I said to myself. Ishmael came to Ninetha and changed my world. I shook my head. He changed what I *understood* about the world. By learning more about it, asking questions, seeking information.

What lay over the horizon? I'd wondered that so often as a child.

Ishmael didn't stop at wondering. He, and his people, sought information. By page, or by travel, he wanted to understand the world as it truly was.

He'd changed me. And Kira's softening face, her quiet triumph at seeing those apostate pieces of paper shrivel into ash, didn't understand me.

Was I a bookist now?

Not as I'd thought about it. It wasn't about the paper; it was about the things on the paper. Just like language, we could use words to denounce, to harm, or to build. It was the same with paper. These weren't arcane spells, or evil; writing was just communication. Words frozen in the real world, not left as memories in the hearer's mind.

It may never come to Ninetha, but there was a place in the world where I could learn more about it. Where I could finish what Ishmael had started.

New Alexandria.

When the funeral ended, Kira sat next to me at a long table to eat round, ripe fruit from the cornucopia.

"You burned your father's papers."

"You'll be happy," I said bitterly. "No more blasphemy."

"There's still an entire bag of books," Kira responded. She'd looked for them. I'd hidden them in a bag I had asked the cornucopia for, and then placed it inside a water tank.

"True."

The wooden bench creaked as Kira moved about to face me. She had braided her hair, and the tight plaits ran in careful lines to the back of her neck. "Will you burn them?"

I pushed a thumb under the rind of an orange and inhaled the burst of freshness. I hadn't had one since Ninetha. What a miracle to eat sweet fruit from the cornucopia. I had never really thought about it before. I'd taken these things for granted.

I'd looked down at the world our ancestors had come from, as round as the orange, and about as large.

"Those books do not belong to me," I said to Kira after I stopped peeling the orange. "It might be a sin, but I'm going to finish a dead man's mission, because he saved my life. I'm going to return those books to his people."

I wanted to make it clear to her that I owed a debt to Ishmael. The sort of debt that meant picking up what had once been carried by another. He deserved that much.

"I've been thinking on that, all the way up the rim, and on the way back." Kira picked up an apple. "The gods forgive many sins. Maybe they'll forgive yours. Or mine. Spilling blood is a sin as much as reading, I think."

"The gods say that vengeance is their right, not ours," I said softly.

"The archangels enforce this," Kira nodded. "It will be dangerous for you to walk this path still."

I didn't tell Kira that few, if any, archangels still walked among us, according to Ishmael. They'd all been pulled back into the earth's tar, he'd said on the way to Nudasi. After the edge of the world, after Nudasi and then Ninetha, I would come to Eufra. I could take the river toward the other towns I knew were out there. Places I could reach with less danger than traveling the scarred land out here near the edge of it all. I'd been trained to survive out here, so this would be a far easier journey than everything I'd already come through. Albeit a lonely one.

"To judge others is to claim godhood yourself," I said.

Kira grabbed my shoulder and squeezed it in a friendly grip. "A wise saying. I'll respond with this: despite that, you cannot come back to Ninetha. But you can travel with us until we get to the boundary marker. Then, go your own way, and I will never see you again."

My ankle, carefully bound and wrapped in a cast from the cornucopia, had mostly healed.

But I didn't want to walk the wastes alone.

"We can part at the boundary stones," I agreed. But I knew I would sleep by myself, and lightly, with one hand on a knife. This new peace between us felt important, a change in the road. A return to the way things had once been. "I'm not going back to Ninetha, but to the other places beyond it."

I wanted Kira's warmth to be real, so much so it hurt the very pit of my stomach. Because I had no one left from my old life now that Ishmael was gone. No one but Kira. I grabbed Kira's hand and squeezed it back.

"We leave in two days, after we recover and finish packing for the trip," Kira announced as I treasured the moment of contact. She'd been like a mother to me once.

On the fourth night, out of sight of Nudasi and as the guardians piled together to stay warm, Kira came to kill me.

I stood up and let the overcape Priscilla had gifted me fall from my shoulders so that Kira could see the musket, even in the dim starlight.

"You can't fire it. The archangel bent it," Kira said.

"I worked with a pipe man to straighten it. It'll either kill you or blow up in my face if we made a mistake. I am ready to find out. I have nothing more to lose in this world, Kira. You and the archangel have taken everything away from me."

I did not say that with any bitterness, though. From this fire, I'd come out a different material. I wasn't sure what it was, but I certainly did not feel a tremor as I aimed the barrel at her.

I'd faced an archangel with my musket; Kira was just a person.

"How did you know I was coming for you?"

"Because I know you, Kira. I wanted to believe we would walk together and leave each other, but I know you're still worried about Ninetha." I smiled wistfully. "You love it more than before, even. I know that because so do I."

"And now you'll have it," Kira said sadly, resigned to her fate. She let the dagger in her hand fall to the ground. "Just, please be fair with the cornucopia. The Bountiful People, they're greedy."

"It should belong to all the people," I agreed.

"Instead of a Lord Musketeer, they will have a Lord Musketress."

I carefully kept the musket aimed at Kira as I pulled the heavy bag of books, water, and kibble over my shoulder. She frowned.

"I told you, outside Nudasi, that I knew I wouldn't see Ninetha ever again."

I switched the musket over to my other hand and pulled the other strap on.

"You're really going to go to that den of sinners in New Alexandria?" Kira asked.

"Goodbye, Kira," I said. Maybe one day, reading would

reach Ninetha. Some librarian from New Alexandria, or maybe somewhere else. But they would know how to find Ninetha, and Nudasi. Because I would bring that new knowledge. If they were anything like Ishmael, the new knowledge would be precious to them. "Be gentle to Ninetha. And if you can bring yourself to do it, tell them a story or two about me, when you feel the city is ready."

I backed away from her and into the darkness. A few minutes later, and I turned a corner by a small hill.

I was alone, but I had a bag full of books. Ishmael had taught me the sounds of the letters. He told me that a world of heroes and dead poets waited to talk to me in their pages. I couldn't read, but I would try.

I was once Lilith of Ninetha, a musketress, but now I was a librarian with my musket strapped across my back, off to find the libraries of New Alexandria to tell them the end of Ishmael's story, so that they could write it down and never forget him. Because I would not let the wonders he found die with just him. The revelations about our world, the old world we circled, and the Cleft could be lost in the scattered wind of just my sole voice. I would, I decided, learn how to memorialize the librarian forever, in print.

Somewhere on this new journey, I would unlock the magic he knew, and those ancient voices hidden away in the black marks on paper would speak to me as well.

Maybe someone else would learn my story and hear my thoughts as I reached them across the gulf of minds, time, and space.

Maybe this time, the gods would leave our stories alone.

AFTERWORD

At the end of Ray Bradbury's novel *Fahrenheit 451*, all
the rebels gather in camps to memorize chosen pieces of
great literature so that the book burners can't stamp it all out.
The idea of losing printed literature to oral tradition scared
me at the time because a teacher once had us pass a message
from person to person down a row of desks in a game called
"telephone." The end result? A garbled and unrecognizable
phrase. Without Ray's chilling end, the idea of losing all our
literature wouldn't have lived rent-free in my brain for decades.

But it was another Ray who inspired me to reinterpret
that ending: Dr. Ray Person is a professor of Deuteronomic
literature and oral history. He specializes in conversation
analysis, a way to examine oral tradition, as well as the way
community serves as a reservoir of oral history, and how stories
get passed down through the generations. One of the striking
things I learned in conversation with this other Ray was
that oral tradition features a form of error correction: when
storytellers tell a community a story, they will interact with
the performance if the story goes awry. It's for this reason that
Indigenous Australians can still tell stories about volcanoes

that erupted almost ten thousand years ago, or describe bays that had different water levels from thousands of years past.

That tension between stories passed down, and the supposed impermanence of paper, led me to start imagining a world in which stories ruled, and paper had been lost to time. The opening phrase of this book sat in my head for years as a result, and I have both Rays to thank for that.

I have to thank my family, as always: my wife, Emily, and my daughters, Thalia and Calliope. Having a writer around means having a spacey housemate. They get to listen to these ideas in nascent forms, before they're fully cooked. They're very patient people.

My thanks also to the publishing teams who made this book happen. Hannah Bowman, my agent, who worked with Steve Feldberg at Audible to build a deal that allowed me to sequester myself and work on this book as the pandemic crashed down around us. My thanks to Audible for the amazing Janina Edwards, who was one of my dream picks to have as a reader on the audiobook. She was an amazing voice for this book.

My thanks to the great, and patient, Tachyon Publications team, for pulling this edition together. Jaymee Goh, the editor, worked hard with me on the changes they wanted for the print edition. And, although this is a book about spoken stories, it's also about a love of print, so seeing this story become ink is a whole moment of actual magic for me.

Lastly, thanks to you reading this. I don't get to do more of these without your support, and I'm now in my third decade of getting to share my strange dreams and thoughts with you all. I am, as ever, so appreciative. It's been amazing, and more amazing for having you along for the journey.

Called "violent, poetic and compulsively readable" by *Maclean's*, science fiction author Tobias S. Buckell is a *New York Times* bestselling writer and World Fantasy Award winner born in the Caribbean. He grew up in Grenada and spent time in the British and U.S. Virgin Islands, and the islands he lived on influence much of his work.

His Xenowealth series begins with *Crystal Rain*. Along with other standalone novels and his almost one hundred stories, his works have been translated into twenty different languages. He has been nominated for such awards as the Hugo, Nebula, and World Fantasy, plus the Astounding Award for Best New Science Fiction Author. His latest novel is *A Stranger in the Citadel*, an Audible Original free to anyone with an Audible account.

He currently lives in Bluffton, Ohio, with his wife and two daughters, where he teaches creative writing at Bluffton University. He's online at http://www.TobiasBuckell.com and is also an instructor at the Stonecoast MFA in Creative Writing program.